When Light Breaks Through

ALSO BY BRENDA MURPHY

Fiction

After the Voyage: An Irish American Story

Becoming Carlotta: A Biographical Novel

Non-fiction

The Theatre of Tennessee Williams

Eugene O'Neill Remembered (with George Monteiro)

The Cambridge Companion to American Women Playwrights

Understanding David Mamet

Tennessee Williams and Elia Kazan: A Collaboration in the Theatre

Congressional Theatre: Dramatizing McCarthyism on Stage, Film, and Television

The Provincetown Players and the Culture of Modernity

American Realism and American Drama

When Light Breaks Through

A Salem Witch Trials Story

by

Brenda Murphy

2023

This book is a work of fiction. References to historical events, real people, or real locales are used fictionally. Other names, characters, places, and incidents portrayed herein either are the product of the author's imagination or are used fictionally.

Library of Congress Control Number: 2023907710

ISBN: 978-0-9973669-9-0 (hardcover)
ISBN: 978-0-9973669-7-6 (paperback)
ISBN: 978-0-9973669-8-3 (ebook)

Cover design by M. H. Pasindu Lakshan

To George

and

Aunt Edna

In loving memory

Contents

Preface

In 1626, Roger Conant left Plymouth with a small group of settlers and eventually landed at a place called Naumkeag ("fishing place"). True to its name, it had a fine harbor and a generous network of rivers and streams. Its population had been depleted severely in recent years by tribal conflict and an epidemic, probably smallpox carried by Europeans, that wiped out many native inhabitants of the coastal regions that came to be known as Massachusetts Bay. Conant served as leader of the group of English immigrants until the Massachusetts Bay Company sent their own governor, John Endecott, to the colony it was funding. The people became farmers, fishermen, traders, and eventually merchants and shipbuilders.

Central to the lives of these people, both public and private, was their official religion, a version of Calvinist Protestantism called Congregationalism. The original settlers of the colony, often given the pejorative label "Puritans" by Catholics and less fervid protestants, had fled from the official dominance of the Church of England to live their lives in a place where they were free to practice their religion as they saw fit. Their governance structure reflected the centrality of their own official religion, mixing the organization of the church with the political organization of the colony and its settlements.

The place, now called Salem ("peace"), soon became the most prosperous town in the colony along the Atlantic coast in what is now Maine, New Hampshire, Massachusetts, and Connecticut. Within just a few decades, some of its citizens accumulated great wealth from maritime enterprises and trade. The population of the narrow strip of land around the harbor grew so fast that the town could no longer provide adequate farmland to feed itself. To yield more food and fuel, Salem began granting large tracts of interior land to people who agreed to farm them.

In 1672, a separate church was established by the farmers, essentially creating a new entity known as Salem Village. In 1689, this name was made official when its minister, Samuel Parris, was ordained, making it a fully recognized church where the sacraments could be administered.

Three generations removed from Salem's founding, in the 1690s, Salem Village was suffering from overcrowding of its own. The originally large farms had been divided among sons and grandsons who quarreled with each other and their neighbors over rights to the land and deeply resented upstart newcomers who began as renters and gradually built larger and larger farms as they bought up the land from the original owners. The families who had been prosperous landowners thirty years earlier now looked with envy at the wealthier merchants and shipbuilders of the town. And unlike the town, whose interests were global and cosmopolitan, the farmers were intensely local. Many were consumed by quarrels with their neighbors, their fellow church members, and Salem Town.

It was here that the events of 1692 unfolded.

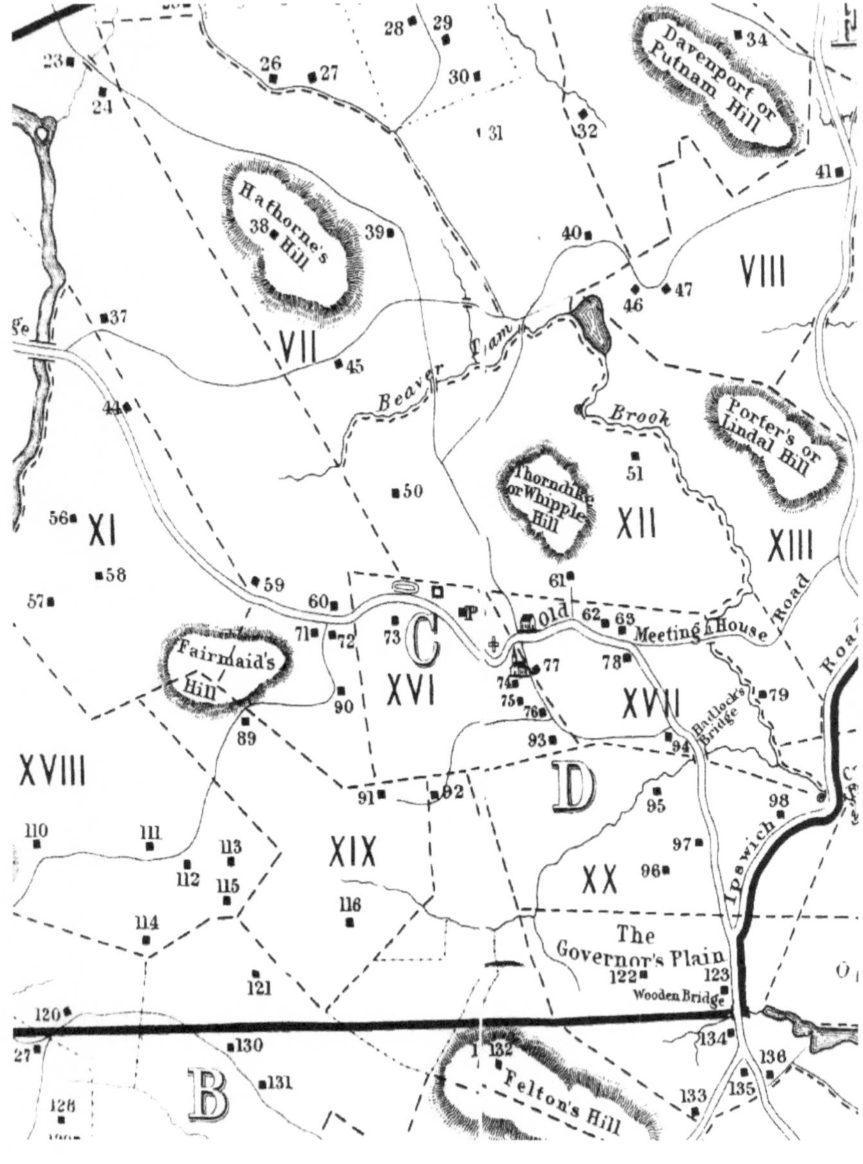

Davenport or Putnam Hill
Hathorne's Hill
Beaver Dam
Brook
Porter's or Lindal Hill
Thorndike or Whipple Hill
Fairmaid's Hill
Old Meeting House Road
Hadlock's Bridge
Ipswich Road
The Governor's Plain
Wooden Bridge
Felton's Hill
VII
VIII
XI
XII
XIII
XVI
XVII
XVIII
XIX
XX
C
D
B

Index to Salem Village Map

+ Nathaniel Ingersoll
P Rev. Samuel Parris/ Rev. Joseph Green
▢ Captain Jonathan Walcott
23. Edward Putnam
24. Thomas Putnam (Ann Senior and Jr.)
26. Ezekial Cheever
32. Joseph Putnam
39. Mary, widow of Thomas Putnam Senior
41. Jonathan Putnam
47. Captain John Putnam
50. John Hutchinson
57. John Buxton
62. Rev. James Bayley
71. Samuel Sibley
79. Nathaniel Putnam
95. Francis Nurse (Rebecca)
96. Samuel Nurse
97. John Tarbell
128. Giles Corey (Martha)

Map by W. P. Upham, 1866

Part One

Ann Putnam

1692

Chapter 1

1692

Ann Putnam emerged from the dusky meetinghouse into the open air in an unusually cheerful mood. She turned with a smile when Abby tapped her on the shoulder and whispered, "Meet me in the clearing after dinner. I have something to tell you." Then Abby went off toward the ministry house, her cousin Betty in her wake as always.

Ann was as quick as she could be about helping to fetch the family's meal from the wagon and serve it in the meetinghouse. After helping to put things away, she asked her mother if she could visit Abby for a few minutes before the afternoon sermon.

Distracted by baby Timothy's fussing, her mother only said, "Make sure you are here in good time. Mercy will want your help with the children."

Once she was out of sight, Ann ran all the way to the hidden clearing in the woods where she and Abby had been meeting for two years now, since she was ten and Abby nine and they were first sent on errands without supervision. Abby was her dearest friend. They shared secrets she would never tell her sisters or cousin. When she got to the oak tree, she saw Abby and her cousin Betty, two years younger, sitting on the big log and waiting impatiently. Abby jumped up and ran to her. "I must tell you about our plans," she said. "We are in for some great sport."

Ann could not help but catch her excitement. "What is it, Abby?" she asked. "Tell me."

Abby responded eagerly. “Do you know about the Goodwin children?”

Ann shook her head.

“They are bewitched. It is all in a book by Reverend Cotton Mather. I heard my uncle talking about it with Reverend Noyes. They are much impressed with these children. They run about the house as if they were flying and talk in gibberish and get into cupboards and will not come out, and they fall on the floor with their arms and legs all askew. The adults are most careful of them all through the day, and then at night they get better and eat and sleep like anyone else.”

Ann was mystified. “But why are they allowed to behave in such a way? I think my father would chastise such children severely.”

With a knowing smile, Abby answered. “Because they are bewitched. The doctors and the ministers have said so. It is a fearful thing, and they are most concerned with punishing the witch, not the children. They believe they cannot help themselves.”

“It must be a sight to see.”

Abby smiled. “Yes, and it is a sight I am going to make here.”

Ann began to feel anxious. “What do you mean, Abby?”

In seconds, Abby’s eagerness changed to resentment. “You know that I have had more and more of the house’s work fall on my shoulders in the last weeks. Aunt Betty has not recovered well from Susanna’s birth, and often she leaves Tituba in charge of the housekeeping.” Her green eyes seemed to darken. “She gives me the worst of the work to do, as if I were a servant below her, and she were not a slave. I bore it for a while, but one morning when she sent me to empty the chamber pots, I refused, and I told her it was not my place to do such tasks, but hers. We argued so sharply that it drew my Uncle Parris from his study. ‘Stop that shouting and come here, Abigail,’ he said.

“I had to go to his study and stand in front of him while he discoursed sharply with me.” She drew herself up straight and imitated her uncle's severest tones. "'Abigail,' he said, 'you are not a little child anymore. You are nearly twelve years old. You are my wife's niece, and I am your guardian, but you are not a daughter of this house. You will have to earn your own bread in life, and it is time you began. Up until now, we have indulged you too much. You must contribute to this household, and you must have the proper training so you can be placed as a maid if you are not needed in our house. That means you do the work you are given, and you thank the Lord that you have a roof over your head and food and clothing. If your aunt tells you to do what Tituba bids you, that is what you will do.' He said more about being modest and quiet and so on, but that is the important thing."

"I cannot think of you leaving here," said Ann. "That would be terrible."

"Yes, but I will not give in to it."

"But Abby, what can you do?"

Abby smiled. "I might become bewitched. And Betty too."

"How? We know no witches. And why would anyone bewitch you? Abby, you must be practical."

She laughed, her green eyes dancing. "Oh, Ann. You are such an honest girl. Not really bewitched, but feigning it, for sport. We have been practicing, have we not, Betty? Let us show our friend what bewitching looks like."

Betty jumped up and ran around the little clearing with glee, flapping her arms and crying, "Whish, whish! I am flying." Then she threw herself on the ground and rolled around, crying out as if in a fever fit. Suddenly, she sat up and stared ahead of her, calling out a lot of nonsense words.

"Show her your arms, Betty," she said. Betty's arms were suddenly twisted behind her and up so that it seemed impossible they were not broken. She let out a shriek, as if in great pain, and then immediately relaxed them again.

"You see, it is not hard," said Abby. "You need only show people things they are not used to seeing and make them believe you are in pain. It is so long since adults were young that they do not remember when their own limbs were as loose as Betty's. She is better at it than I am." Betty beamed under Abby's praise.

Abby suddenly jerked her head far to the right so that she almost faced backwards, a strange grimace distorting her features and her left arm jerking up as if someone was twisting it so that it was almost out of joint. So wildly did she scream with pain that Ann thought she must really have hurt herself and ran to her, but Abby jumped to her feet with a laugh.

Ann looked at her. "And you will just try these tricks and see if they think you are bewitched?" she said.

Abby shook her head. "Not so crudely," she said. "I will follow the lead of the Goodwin children. Little things first, like being distracted for a few minutes, and then when they notice that, speaking some gibberish, and then crawling about and hiding under furniture and in cupboards. If they rise to it, then we will try some fits."

A troubled expression crossed Ann's face as she shook her head. "I think you are risking a beating, Abby. That is what my father would do to rouse you from your distraction."

"Perhaps, but I think I know my uncle. He is fascinated with this witchcraft. I think the hint of it under his own roof would set him off to study it. And then if Dr. Griggs comes and cannot name it anything else, he will seize on witchcraft if my uncle suggests it. And my uncle never beats Betty. Her mother will not allow it because she is delicate. Are you not, Betty?"

Betty giggled. "They do say so," she said.

Ann grew more insistent. "But he does not think *you* delicate, Abby. There is nothing to stop him beating you."

"No, but it is a risk I will take. I have suffered worse things in my life than Uncle Parris's beatings."

Since they had stayed longer than they should have, they all ran back until they were in sight of the meetinghouse, and then they became modest young girls who walked demurely up to join their families. Ann helped her cousin, Mary Walcott, and the servant, Mercy Lewis, to shepherd the younger children up to the gallery to listen to the afternoon sermon.

On the very next Sunday, Abby reported with great satisfaction. "My aunt and uncle are much bewildered," she said. "Betty and I run about the house as we will, or sit still and stare ahead, pretending to be in a trance and that we hear nothing when they talk to us. Sometimes we call out senseless things, and they listen closely and try to decipher them. It is great sport."

They continued this for the next few weeks as the short, cold days of January kept everyone virtually trapped in their houses. Abby reported regularly to Ann, exulting that she had avoided wash day by pretending to be in a trance or that Tituba had had to feed the chickens and gather the eggs on a particularly cold and snowy day while she and Betty sat under the benches by the fire in the keeping room. She laughed about her uncle carefully writing down their gibberish.

On a cold day toward the end of January, Ann's mother was much vexed as she prepared meat pies to go into the oven.

"The last of the sage will not stretch," she kept saying. At last, she told Ann to find Tom. He would have to go to Aunt Mary and get the dried sage she had promised to see them through the rest of the winter.

Ann responded brightly, "The boys are working in the barn, Mother. I can go to Aunt Mary."

Her mother hesitated a moment, and then said, "Well then, Ann. You go. But do not let Aunt Mary delay you overlong with gossip. You will be all morning if she gets started, and we need some of these pies for our dinner."

"Yes, Mother, I will be quick about it," she answered, already drawing her thick shawl around her shoulders.

"It is cold," said her mother. "Put on my cloak and wrap your head up well."

Ann was gone before her mother had time for second thoughts, and she made her way to the house up the road as quickly as she could, running part of the way. She answered Aunt

Mary's questions about the family as she warmed herself quickly by the big fire in the keeping room, but managed to get away after just a few minutes, explaining that they needed the sage for their dinner. About halfway home, she stopped and looked around her. It was a deserted place, where she knew there was a little clearing behind the line of fir trees beside the road. They often stopped to rest there on the way to Uncle Edward's house during hot summer days.

She slipped into the woods and took off her mother's cloak, folding it and laying it carefully on the ground. Then she ran back and forth across the clearing, flapping her arms and crying "Whish, whish!" as she had seen Betty do. The feeling was strange. She had not done anything so silly in years. She felt foolish, but she also felt like laughing. There was something very cheering in it. She stood in the middle of the clearing and twirled around until she was dizzy, feeling her head spin. It was lovely. She let herself collapse onto the frozen ground.

After a while, she remembered her purpose, and deliberately called to mind the sharp pain the last time her mother had pinched her arm and twisted, her special discipline. Remembering, she grabbed her arm and shrieked, no thought of laughter this time. She summoned up the griping pain when she had been so sick with the bellyache in December and grabbed at her middle, her body hunched over as if in great pain.

And then, with determination, she thought of her father's last beating. Feeling the blows on her back and legs, she writhed around on the ground and let out the screams she had forced herself to stifle at the time. Once she had opened herself to it, there was a feeling of freedom about the wild screaming and violent movement of her body that was strangely comforting. After a few minutes, she sat up and wrapped her arms around her knees until the wild feeling had passed. Then she tried twisting her limbs about as Betty had done. It did not come easily to her, but she could see how her limbs could be stretched awkwardly with practice.

Finally, Ann lay on the ground, her shawl wrapped around her, and looked straight above her to the sky. Lying perfectly still like someone in a trance, she let a daydream come into her head as she often did. When she was younger, she had been punished for sitting idly and dreaming. She had learned to choose her times, but she still found great comfort in her imaginings.

Now it was the story of Delilah that entered her mind and would not leave her, the woman who had cut off Samson's hair and taken away his strength. Ann had always been drawn to this story. She knew that Delilah was a bad woman, but she secretly loved her. The idea that a woman could take away a man's power by just cutting off his hair made her breathless when she really thought about it. She kept her eyes turned to the sky and let the story run in her mind. With the image of Samson pulling down the temple pillars in revenge, she suddenly came to herself and looked around. Realizing that time had passed, she jumped to her feet and, pulling on her mother's cloak, ran back to the road and most of the way home.

When she met Abby and Betty the next Sabbath, Ann admitted that she had gone out to the woods alone and tried her hand at the tricks they had shown her. "Do you think I could get them to believe it?" she asked.

"Let me see." Abby watched critically as Ann showed her versions of the tricks.

"Your fits are wonderful," she said. "When you sit staring, with your pale face and those pale blue eyes, it frightens me, and I know you are dissembling. And you scream like someone who knows what pain is. Do not try running about or twisting your limbs until you practice some more. It does not come naturally to you, I think. Try falling to the ground and act like you are sore in pain from pinches and gripings."

"Do you think I should try it?"

"Wait until I tell you but keep practicing. My uncle talks about calling in Dr. Griggs, and I think we must bring out our bigger tricks now. Before long, Dr. Griggs will have spread the word about what is happening in our house, and then your people will be more ready to see what the Parrises see."

All this time, Reverend Parris had kept silent publicly about the events in his house, but when the girls began to throw themselves on the floor and roll around, screaming in pain, his wife insisted that Dr. Griggs be called in. After witnessing their fits, the doctor examined the girls and found no clear physical cause. "It was as I predicted," Abby told Ann. "My uncle asked him if he thought it could be witchcraft. 'It is much like the Goodwin children in Boston,' he said. Griggs, the old fool, was only too glad to have a way out. 'I am sorry to say it seems much like witchcraft, Mr. Parris,' he says, as if he knew anything about it. 'I think, as minister and doctor, we must look into this together.' So Betty and me have been giving them a show, twisting our limbs about and acting like we are being pinched and pricked.

"The doctor has been coming to our house every time we stir it up, and they sit discoursing about it long after it is over. We are great persons there, are we not, Betty? Our doings are of great importance. And my uncle has made no more speeches to me about emptying chamber pots. You must join us soon, Ann. It is the best sport in the world. Elizabeth Hubbard, the doctor's niece, has questioned me about the fits. I have told her nothing of the truth yet, but I think she is eager to join in."

Abby was right that word would get around the village quickly after Dr. Griggs was involved. The next Wednesday, when the elder Parrises had gone to Reverend Noyes's lecture at the Salem church, Mary Sibley, a church member, visited the ministry house. As they sat at the table in the keeping room, she asked Abby what had been happening to her and Betty. She nodded knowingly as Abby spun her tale of spirits pinching and hurting her, and said, "I know a recipe that will kill a witch's specter. 'Tis from a book my mother had."

Tituba looked up from the pot she had simmering on the hearth, her quick glance at Goody Sibley showing that she had taken it all in and chosen to participate. Tituba was very weary of life in Reverend Parris's household. She disliked the dreary religion of Massachusetts almost as much as the weather and she resented having to listen to her master every day at family prayers and twice a week in the meetinghouse, droning on about it. Here was a little excitement that reminded her of things she had seen back in Barbados. "I have seen such a thing," she said, "but the minister would never hear of it in his house."

"He would not need to hear of it," said Mary, "if it was just between ourselves." She explained the recipe, which required mixing some of the girls' urine into a corncake and baking it in the fire and then feeding it to a dog in order to draw the witch's spirit out of the girls and into the animal.

"It is like what I have seen in my own country," said Tituba. "We will try it. No need to tell the master and mistress, but they will be as glad as me not to have these girls running about and rolling on the floor, shrieking." Tituba and her husband John mixed the witch cake, baked it, and fed it to the dog. It had no effect on Abby and Betty, or on the dog, but word did get around the village of the attempted remedy.

On the same day, Ann Putnam began falling into trances and seeing spirits and having fits in which she seemed to endure a great deal of pain from their pinching and pricking her. Having heard the rumors about the bewitchment at the ministry house, Thomas Putnam went to see Reverend Parris. When confronted directly, Parris told Thomas what had been happening and that Dr. Griggs had confirmed that the symptoms most probably came from bewitchment. "We are trying to get to the bottom of this," he said. "We need to have the children tell us who is afflicting them, but they have so far said only that it is spirits, and they cannot identify them."

Thomas cast him a determined look. "We must search them out," he said. "We must find out who afflicts our children. I think both of us must question the girls closely to get them to identify the specters. Surely, they can tell us about their features and clothing if they do not know their names. We can identify people who might wish them harm."

Mr. Parris was taken aback. "What have these young girls done to make enemies?"

Thomas spoke with great intensity. "It is not only them who are being attacked. It is us and our families. Anyone who wishes harm to you or me or our wives might afflict our children. We must search them out before this becomes much worse."

On the last Saturday in February, both men questioned their girls at length, dwelling on the physical details and clothing of the specters. Abby, having prepared herself for this, gradually revealed through various clues that one of the specters was Tituba and the other was Sarah Good. She was angry at Tituba for ordering her about and for trying to put an end to their sport, and she thought being named a witch would take her down a peg. Besides, people would be more likely to believe that an Indian from Barbados was practicing witchcraft than anyone else. Sarah Good, a woman of very bad reputation in the village, was always begging food from the ministry house and others in the village. She was never grateful for what she received, and she often turned away from the door muttering what many believed to be curses. Many already called this spiteful woman a witch.

Ann was at first reluctant to name anyone until she had conferred with Abby, but when she saw her father losing patience as he bore down on her with more and more questions, she began to give out details that pointed in a certain direction. Thomas Putnam concluded that she was being afflicted by Sarah Osborne, the widow of his kinsman, Robert Prince, who had fought with him over Prince's estate. Ann had often heard him railing against her and what a greedy and covetous person she was. Ann thought such a person might well want to harm Thomas's daughter, and she knew he would be eager to believe she was a witch.

On the Sabbath, Thomas Putnam and Samuel Parris met with the church deacons, Ann's uncle, Edward Putnam, and the village's tavern keeper, Nathaniel Ingersoll, and concluded that the time had come to take legal action. Witchcraft was a capital crime, after all, and the perpetrators must be brought to justice. Thomas and Edward volunteered to go to Salem to make a formal complaint and Edward found two church members not immediately concerned in the matter who agreed to join them after they had heard the story. On Monday, the four men rode to Salem Town and swore out a complaint against Tituba, Sarah Good and Sarah Osborne before the magistrates, John Hathorne and Jonathan Corwin.

When Thomas Putnam arrived at home, he found the house in turmoil. He had asked a neighbor, Lieutenant Fuller, to keep an eye on things while he was gone. Fuller and several other neighbors were there observing Ann, who was in a strange state, sitting on the bench in the keeping room and staring at the hearth. They said she had been out of her wits for at least an hour, sometimes falling to the floor and screaming that she was being beaten and pinched, pleading with her afflicters to stop. As her father watched, she suddenly stood up and shrieked, "Stop! Put down that knife!" She backed away several steps, put her hands to her neck, and struggled, as if she were trying to pull something away from her, but someone or something very strong was holding it there. "No, I will not cut my neck!" she cried. "Take the knife away! Begone! Begone!"

At last, she gave one frenzied push at the empty air and fell to the floor, where she went limp and her eyes stared at the ceiling, without seeming to see anything. She seemed to hear nothing anyone said to her. Thomas picked her up and laid her on the bed in the parlor. "Leave her be," he said. "She will come out of this." An hour later, Ann's mother was directing her niece, Mary, and the maid, Mercy, as they put supper on the table for the guests. Ann appeared in the keeping room, looking like herself.

"Are you well, Ann?" asked her mother.

"Yes, Mother," she said.

"Do you remember what happened?" her father asked.

"Yes," she said. "Goody Osborne and Sarah Good and Tituba came and hurt me. They hurt me terribly. Then Tituba pulled out a knife. She said I must cut my own throat with it, but I refused. She held the knife against my throat, but I fought her and would not do it, and then they went away."

Thomas turned to the others. "This is serious business," he said. "We shall hear more of it tomorrow when Mr. Hathorne and Mr. Corwin come to examine these women to see if they should be accused of the crime of witchcraft."

There was a somber mood in the house as the neighbors sat down to supper with Thomas and his wife. When Ann went to help Mary and Mercy put the meal on, as she usually did when guests were present, Mrs. Fuller spoke up. "The child must be tired and hungry after that ordeal," she said, "could she not sit down with us and take something?"

Ann Senior glanced at her husband, and seeing no response, said, "Yes, Ann. Sit here with us. Mary and Mercy can serve the meal."

Ann saw a look pass between the two older girls, who were used to giving her jobs to do, not serving her supper. She really was exhausted and hungry, and she sank into the place at the end of the bench where Mrs. Fuller had made room for her. The elderly lady laid a comforting hand on her arm. As the adults spoke soberly of witchcraft and the danger it presented to the children and the community, Ann attended to her supper, not looking up unless she was addressed directly, but she took it all in. She had done what Abby had told her to do, but she could tell that this had become something bigger than Abby's game. Something adult. She did not know where it would lead, and it frightened her a good deal.

The next day was the public examination of Tituba, Sarah Good and Sarah Osborne by the magistrates to determine whether they should be accused of witchcraft before the Grand Jury. Ann had almost no time to confer with Abby. They spoke in hurried whispers as they sat together on a bench in the front of the meetinghouse before the court proceeding began. Abby told her to follow her lead. They had to stop talking when the magistrates came in and sat at the table directly in front of them. Sarah Good was led in to be examined first. Ann sat covertly watching the magistrates and the prisoner. Having been well schooled to keep her feelings in check, she appeared impassive, a pale little figure with eyes modestly downcast, but she was aware of everything that happened, and deeply anxious about her role in the proceedings.

When Judge Hathorne examined them, Sarah Good and Sarah Osborne at first staunchly denied hurting the girls or having any involvement with witchcraft or the Devil. But under questioning, Sarah Good accused Sarah Osborne. Sarah Osborne said that she did not know if the Devil went about in her likeness to hurt anyone, but insisted she knew nothing about it if he did. Then Judge Hathorne directed the girls to stand up and look directly at the accused. At his direction, they identified the women as the ones who had tormented them and identified Sarah Osborne's clothes as the ones habitually worn by her specter. Following Abby, the girls fell to the floor, seemingly in agony, when the accused denied the charges.

Tituba's examination also began with denials that sent the girls into fits, but she eventually said that the Devil had come to her and bid her serve him, and that it was Goody Osborne and Sarah Good who had hurt the girls, along with two women and a tall man from Boston she did not know. Under Hathorne's questioning, Tituba confessed that she too had hurt the girls because Good and Osborne told her that she must hurt the children or they would do worse to her. Again following Abby's lead, the girls had begun to subside with the confession. Finally, they all sat listening as Tituba said the Devil had appeared to her as a black dog and told her to kill the children, and that the others had forced her on the previous night to ride to the Putnam house on a stick and to attack Ann Putnam with a knife, saying they threatened to cut her head off if she refused.

When she was asked to describe the clothes of the Boston people she did not know, Tituba said the man wore black clothes and had white hair and the woman wore a black hood with a white silk hood inside it and topknots, marking them as wealthy Bostonians. She also said she saw Sarah Good suckling a yellow bird, and that she had seen a creature with Sarah Osborne the previous day, a hairy thing with a long nose, two or three feet tall, that walked on two legs like a man.

Tituba's testimony made Ann very anxious. Up to this point, the girls had been in control of the story. They decided who would be accused and what they would be accused of, but Tituba was weaving her own story, and Abby had no control over her. When Ann glanced at Abby, though, she did not see uneasiness. Abby's green eyes were shining. Ann could tell that she was exerting a great effort to keep herself from smiling. After the hearing, they managed to have a whispered conversation as they lagged behind the adults on the walk from Ingersoll's tavern to the ministry house.

"Tituba worries me with her talk of people from Boston and fantastical creatures," said Ann. "We know not what she might say next."

Abby smiled. "Do not worry. It is all familiar to me. Those creatures come from pictures in one of my uncle's books. She used to scare us with them to make us mind. The people from Boston are people of wealth who visit my uncle sometimes. I do not know why she is out for them, but we may want to use this ourselves."

"Be careful, Abby," said Ann. "This thing grows apace. I feel it is already beyond us."

Abby shook her head. "Courage, Ann," she said. "Tituba has helped us today. Did you see the faces of the magistrates? There is no question in their minds now that we are bewitched. They will take whatever we do as proof of that, just like my uncle. What we must do now is stay two steps ahead of them." She smiled. "I do not think it will be so hard. Tituba has given us much that we can make use of. You will see."

Ann soon saw evidence of the effect that Tituba's testimony had on the village. The people had been hearing the rumors of bewitchment swirling around the ministry house and the Putnam house for weeks, and it made sense to them that the perpetrator was an Indian slave from Barbados. Although most had accounted Goody Osborne a sickly and harmless woman, many had stories of Sarah Good that confirmed her character as spiteful and wicked. It was not hard to believe that she was a witch.

Over the next few days, Ann heard her father, who, as Village Clerk, was helping to record things for the magistrates, say much more. Once Tituba had been imprisoned in the watch house, she had elaborated on the basic facts she had given during her first examination. She told the magistrates that the Devil had told her he was a god and promised that he would give her many fine things if she would bind herself over to serve him for six years, as was common for a bondservant. She also said that the Devil had brought her a book to sign in blood and that there were nine other signature marks in the book, including those of Sarah Good and Sarah Osborne, although she did not know who the other seven marks stood for. Questioned closely about them, she said the Devil would not tell her who they were, but some lived in Salem and some in Boston. She said that it was the tall man from Boston who had made her pinch Betty and Abigail, and claimed that she would not have hurt Betty without being forced, for she loved the little girl.

Chapter 2

1692

During the first week of March, the news of the three witchcraft examinations had spread quickly through the congregation and the village. It seemed that everyone had an old grievance or a suspicious anecdote to share about one of the women, and by the end of the week, there appeared to be overwhelming evidence of their guilt. But there were some who spoke out their doubts, a thing that angered Abby and frightened Ann.

The loudest of the skeptics was Martha Corey, a church member who was known for her stubbornness and her bluntly stated opinions. Goody Corey freely expressed her view that the girls were more likely distracted in their minds than afflicted by witchcraft. She dismissed their claims as outlandish and it got back to the girls that she had said she half hoped they would charge her because they could not stand up to the truth told by a Gospel woman like herself. She told more than one neighbor that the eyes of the ministers and the magistrates had been blinded by the tricks of these distracted girls, and that she would soon open them if they questioned her.

On the next Sabbath, Ann and Abby managed to take a short walk outside the meetinghouse together. Arm in arm, they looked like two young girls consoling each other for the misfortune that had befallen them. What they were talking about was how to deal with the skeptics, especially Martha Corey. Abby was insistent about a swift retaliation.

"We must make people see that it is dangerous to question us," she said. "There must be no space for doubters."

Ann volunteered to call out her name. Martha Corey had been a villain in Thomas Putnam's house as long as she could remember. Her father was given to vehement denunciations of the whole Corey clan, who, he declared, were out to destroy his family. His attacks on Martha's husband, Giles, were especially passionate, full of accusations that Corey had tried to steal his land.

Ann's mother, always susceptible to her husband's turbulent emotions, began to grow more anxious with each day. She listened intently to Thomas's rants and agreed with him, dredging up all the offenses the Coreys had committed against them over the last dozen years. Sensing imminent explosion in the house, Ann began to fall into fits in which she seemed in great pain and pleaded with Goody Corey to stop hurting her. Her cousin, Mary, and the maid, Mercy, were riveted by Ann's actions. Soon, they began to have fits as well, and the screaming of the girls filled the house.

Ann's younger brothers, Tom and Eben, went outside and kept themselves at work as long as they could every day. The little ones were terrified. Baby Timothy wailed constantly, and the little girls, Betty and Deliverance, cowered silently in corners observing their big sister and their cousin, nearly grown figures they held in awe, as they rolled on the floor, writhing and screaming. Several times, Uncle Edward was summoned from his farm down the road to witness the fits.

Just as the pale early light was making its way into the house one rainy morning, Ann was jerked awake by a piercing scream. She sat up and listened in disbelief until it came again, the unmistakable sound of her mother's voice, but as she had never heard it before, even in childbirth. She was screaming in agony, in terror. Betty and Deliverance also woke. They lay where they were in the bed and looked at her with staring, fearful eyes. Across the room, Mary and Mercy sat up and looked across at Ann. "Someone should go down," said Mary, rising from her sleeping pallet.

“I will go with you,” said Ann. They slipped into their shoes, pulled their shawls from the hooks on the wall, and made their way downstairs in the dim light. When they got to the keeping room, they found Tom already there.

“You go in, Ann,” said Tom. “That will vex them least.”

Ann nodded, and knocked lightly on the parlor door, saying softly, “Mother?”

“Come in, Ann,” her father’s voice called, in a tone she had seldom heard, quiet and shaky.

Ann’s mother lay on the bed, her body rigid as if her insides were in great pain, her blue eyes staring upward. Her husband kneeled next to the bed in his nightshirt, holding her hand and trying to get her attention. Next to him, Timothy lay in his cradle wailing and ignored. Then Ann watched in horror as her mother seemed to mimic the very behaviors she and Abby had invented, writhing in pain and screaming at Martha Corey to let her be. After what seemed like a very long time, she lay on the bed in a trance, screaming from time to time as though she had taken a sharp blow. Ann did not know what to make of it. Was her mother feigning this? Had she herself somehow done it to her with her lies? She heard her father speak soothingly to his wife, as if to a horse that was spooked or a cow that was calving. He did not speak so to his daughter.

At last, the fit seemed to pass. Ann’s mother looked at her husband and daughter with recognition and asked Ann to bring her some cider to drink. In the keeping room, Eben and Mercy and the two little girls had come down and were there with Tom and Mary, sitting around the table. They all looked at her expectantly. “Mother had a fit,” she said, “but she is all right now. I am getting her some cider.” Behind the parlor door, the baby had stopped crying. They could hear the insistent sound of Thomas Putnam’s voice and the murmuring responses of his wife. Bringing the cider, Ann found her mother sitting up in the bed and nursing Timothy, her husband sitting on the bed next to her. Thomas glanced at Ann.

"Get the others up and get the breakfast," he said, "your mother is better."

In the keeping room, Ann told the others that all was well and they could get dressed and have their breakfast. After a few bewildered moments, everyone set about their usual morning tasks, and the routine of the household took over, but beneath it was a deeply unsettled feeling, especially in the younger children. It was bad enough for their big sister, Ann, to succumb to this strange thing that seemed to have her in pain and distracted in her mind from time to time, but to have it happen to their mother was another thing. In their different ways, all the members of the household were deeply afraid. Ann felt that this thing she and Abby had unleashed from their own minds might be having a real effect on the person her family's daily lives most depended on. The younger children felt the loss of their mother as they knew her. All of them feared the loss of Ann Senior's influence in the house. It was she who kept them from the worst of Thomas Putnam's rages. She alone could sometimes tame her husband's wildest moods.

Ann had no appetite for the fits now. She did her work and waited anxiously as her mother slowly quieted and her father came out of the room and went straight to the door. On his way out, he turned to Ann and Mary and Mercy, all looking intently at him. "I am going to see my brother, Edward," he said. "Bring your mistress something to break her fast and feed everyone dinner if I do not return in time."

Over the next few days, Thomas Putnam was often away, consulting with his brother and Reverend Parris and others. At ten o'clock on the morning of March twelfth, Edward Putnam came to their house with his neighbor, Chief Constable Ezekiel Cheever. Edward told his brother that he was coming in his capacity as deacon to query Ann Junior about Martha Corey officially. He told Ann to take notice of Goody Corey's clothes when she saw her specter that day. They would return in the afternoon to ask her about them before they went to the Corey house. Then they would compare Ann's description with what they saw so they could tell whether she might be mistaken in the identity of her tormentor.

When they returned, Ann was sitting on the hearth bench in the keeping room. Edward picked up a stool and placed it in front of her. He sat down and looked into her eyes, asking quietly, "Ann, can you tell us what clothes Goody Corey wears today?"

"Uncle," she said, "I am sorry, I cannot see that today. After you came this morning, the specter of a woman came here and blinded me so that I could not see the spirit world. She said her name was Corey. She said I should see her no more until nightfall, so that I could not tell you what clothes she has on, but that she would return then and pay me off if I spoke against her." Ann cast her eyes down. She was worried. It was a thin story, the kind of lie her uncle had often caught her in as a child and chastised her sharply for, but she was so nervous that she could not make up a better one. She sorely wished that she had been able to talk to Abby. Then, to her surprise, her uncle simply took her hands and told her to be easy, that he would return that evening.

When Deacon Putnam and Constable Cheever arrived at the Corey farm, Martha was alone in the empty house, waiting for them. "Come and sit," she said cordially. "I know what you have come for. You come from the church to discourse with me about being a witch. I can only tell you that I am not a witch, and I cannot help people talking about me."

"We do not come on the basis of idle gossip," said Deacon Putnam. "We come because an afflicted person has made a complaint against you."

Martha smiled. "Does she tell you what clothes I am wearing?" she asked.

When the men made no response, she asked. "Does she tell you what clothes I have on?"

Deacon Putnam responded. "No, she does not, but she told us that you had blinded her so she could not tell us."

Martha smiled, but said nothing, and they went on with their interview. After a while, she told them she did not think there were witches in Salem.

Deacon Putnam replied, “We are satisfied, as are the magistrates, that the three persons who have been accused are guilty.”

“If so,” said Martha bluntly, “I do not blame the Devil for making witches of them, for they are idle slothful persons, and they mind nothing that is good. How can you think I am one of them when I, like you, have made a profession of Christ and rejoice to go and hear the word of God? If the magistrates call me, I shall open their eyes to the truth.”

Edward warned her that an outward profession of faith was not enough to shield her from prosecution, for evil persons had crept into the church under the cloak of such professions before, but she insisted that she had nothing to worry about because she was telling the truth. When he stopped at his brother’s house on the way home, Edward found that what Ann had told him in the morning was true, for she had not been troubled by Goody Corey all day. The next day, however, Thomas came and told him that Ann had been much afflicted at night.

“We must try a direct encounter,” said Edward. “We shall only get to the bottom of this if we see Martha Corey together with the child.”

Only too eager to confront her accusers directly, Martha agreed to appear at Thomas Putnam’s house the very next day. No sooner did she enter the house than Ann fell to the floor, clawing at her throat and gasping that Goody Corey was choking her. She called out that she was blinded, and then suddenly her hands and feet were so twisted that she screamed at Martha to stop wrenching them. Then her tongue was drawn out of her mouth and her teeth clamped down on it so that she screamed again. At last, she was quiet, lying on the floor, her eyes closed. After a few minutes, her uncle gently raised her, helping her to the bench by the hearth, where she slumped against the wall. Looking at

Martha, she said, "Goody Corey, why do you do this to me? What have I done to you that you should afflict me so?"

Martha stood where she was, just inside the door, and said, "I do nothing to you." Edward and Thomas Putnam watched intently, looking for physical signs that Martha was practicing witchcraft on Ann at that very moment.

Ann said, "I see a yellow bird suckling between your forefinger and your middle finger." When Martha instinctively rubbed between the fingers, Ann said she could not see the bird anymore. Then she got up from the bench and approached Martha, but fell to the floor before she could reach her. Pointing from where she sat on the floor, she said she saw a man on a spit on the big hearth of the keeping room fireplace, and that Martha's specter was turning it. Mercy Lewis picked up a stick and struck at the place where Ann was pointing. The vision went away and then returned. Ann told Mercy not to strike it again if she wanted to save herself from Martha's wrath, and Mercy screamed that there was pain in her arm. Ann cried out that Goody Corey was striking Mercy with an iron rod. At that point, Deacon Putnam had seen enough and told Martha to leave, but Mercy's torment continued for some time after she was gone.

Before this encounter, Ann had been worried that Abby would not be there, and she might not be able to think fast enough to make the adults believe her, but she found that they were all too eager to believe her, and after she had done her physical tricks, she just let her mind wander freely and described whatever pictures came to her. Seeing the effect her words had on her uncle and father made her feel something she had never felt before, a sense of power. These men whose word was law were suddenly hanging on every one of hers. She had been tempted to more outlandish claims just to astonish them.

A week later, Martha Corey was arrested and brought before the magistrates for an examination to determine whether she should be accused of witchcraft before the Grand Jury. During the week, the accusers of Martha Corey had swelled to ten. Besides

Ann and her mother and Mercy, Abby and Betty and Dr. Griggs's niece Elizabeth Hubbard had accused her, as well as Ann's cousin, Mary, and three more married women. All of them accused her of sending out her specter to torment them in some way. The girls had been summoned to the examination and were seated on the front benches of the meetinghouse. Ann was surprised to see that Betty Parris was not there. The building was full to bursting with spectators. The people could hardly be contained in the main room and the two small galleries projecting above it at either end.

Ann was nervous about all the adults who had joined 'the afflicted.' This was a new and unwelcome element that they could not control. She and Elizabeth had had only a few minutes to confer with Abby in the last few days, and they agreed to follow Abby's lead in reacting to the testimony, which had been a successful strategy in the first court session.

Abby had thought up a new strategy for their behavior in court, which would be sure to convince the judges that they were being tortured then and there. They would bite themselves on the arm, hard enough to make a mark that would be well hidden by their clothes. They would claim in court that Martha was sending out her spirit to torture them and display the bite mark for all to see. They could also hide pins in their clothes and then stick them into their skin and pretend that Martha had done it. It could be very dramatic in the court, but they would have to time it just right. Ann had passed the plan on to Mercy and Mary, but they would all have to trust Abby's wits and her own in the courtroom.

When Martha Corey was called to stand before the magistrates, she came forward with a confident step. She looked around at her neighbors with a smile, stood behind the chair provided for the accused in front of the magistrates, and waited to tell her story.

Judge Hathorne was obviously not pleased with her attitude. He straightened himself in his chair and looked down at her sternly from his raised platform. "You are now in the hands of authority," he said. "Tell me why you hurt these persons."

Martha answered loudly and clearly, "I did not," and asked the court to give her leave to pray. Judge Corwin looked at Judge Hathorne, whose irritation with this witness was clearly growing by the minute. Corwin shook his head and Hathorne nodded slightly.

In a curt dismissal of her request, he said, "We do not send for you to go to prayer, but tell me why you hurt these persons."

Martha answered with confidence. "I am an innocent person. I have never had anything to do with witchcraft since I was born. I am a Gospel woman."

Hathorne tried again to exert control over this headstrong woman. "Do you not see these complain of you?" he demanded, making a sweeping gesture toward the girls and women in the courtroom.

Martha turned her head and ran her eyes down the line of accusers on the benches beside her. "The Lord open the eyes of the magistrates and ministers. The Lord show his power to discover the guilty," she prayed.

After a few more accusations and denials, Hathorne changed tactics. He had before him Edward Putnam's deposition about his visit to Martha Corey. After the magistrates called on Putnam to read his account, Hathorne asked Martha who told her that they were going to ask her about her clothes. Martha could not remember and was flustered by the question. She answered that she knew they had asked about clothing in the previous examinations, that her husband had been to the court and must have told her. Hathorne turned to Giles Corey, her elderly husband, who was sitting in the meetinghouse among the spectators, and asked whether he had told his wife that the others had been asked about clothing. Corey denied it.

Hathorne kept insisting that Martha answer the question of who told her about the clothes until he was interrupted by a shout from Abby. "There is a man whispering in her ear!" she cried. A collective gasp rose from the crowd of spectators.

Hathorne turned immediately on Martha. "What did he say to you?" he demanded.

Martha was beginning to lose her confidence. "We must not believe all that these distracted children say," she said.

Hathorne ignored this. "Cannot you tell what that man whispered?"

"I saw nobody."

"But did you not hear?"

"No."

Abby pitched forward onto the floor and clutched at her stomach, screaming. Ann and the other girls immediately followed, and the adult accusers erupted in screams as well. For fifteen minutes, the dusky little meetinghouse was a bedlam of sound and motion, with the girls and women screaming Martha Corey's name, writhing and rolling around the floor, their families and friends and the officials trying to calm them. Then, as Abby slowly got to her feet, the others did likewise. They collapsed on the benches, seemingly exhausted by their torments.

Hathorne demanded that order be restored and waited until the marshal had corralled the crowd before returning to his interrogation. He called on Martha to confess, saying, "Do you not see how these afflicted do charge you?"

Martha now seemed angry at the turn the events had taken. She was defiant. "We must not believe distracted persons," she said, suggesting that these girls and women had lost their wits, or worse, were possessed by the Devil.

Hathorne turned to her reported expressions of doubt about the legal process. "Did you not say our eyes were blinded and you would open them?"

She did not back down. "Yes, if you accuse the innocent."

When Hathorne called upon Martha's son-in-law to give evidence, he quoted her saying that the girl, Ann, could not stand before her. "What did you mean by that?" Hathorne asked her.

"I saw them fall down," Martha said.

“It seems to be an insulting speech, as if they could not stand before you,” he said.

“They cannot stand before others,” she replied.

Looking through the depositions in front of him, Hathorne changed tactics and asked her what she was turning on the spit at the Putnams’ house.

“You believe the children that are distracted. I saw no spit,” she said.

After Hathorne referred to the testimony of several more witnesses, Martha said, “What can I do? Many rise up against me.”

“Why, confess,” he said.

“So I would if I were guilty,” she said.

He demanded again, “Now tell me the truth, will you? Why did you say that the magistrates’ and ministers’ eyes were blinded, and you would open them?”

Apparently, the question struck her as ridiculous. A little laugh escaped her, which angered Hathorne more. He put the question again. Finally, she answered. “If you say I am a witch.”

The magistrates were out of patience and Martha was clearly weakening. The time had come for the girls to execute their plan to bring her down. Abby nudged Mercy, who was sitting next to her. When Martha bit her lip, Mercy cried out. “She bites me!” Pulling up her sleeve, she rushed up to the magistrates’ table and showed them teeth marks on her arm.

Martha gripped the back of the chair she stood behind. “Oh, she pinches!” cried Elizabeth. Soon, several more were showing teeth marks and other red marks. Tired from the grilling, Martha leaned against the chair. To Ann’s surprise, suddenly, the genteel Mrs. Pope shrieked and grabbed her belly, screaming that Martha Corey was trying to press her bowels out. She threw her muff at Martha, and when that missed, took off her shoe and hit her on the head with it. The magistrates did nothing.

Then came Ann’s turn. She said she saw the yellow bird suckling between Martha’s fingers. Hathorne ordered Martha to come up to the table so the magistrates could see if there was any mark there. Thinking fast, Ann cried, “It is too late! The bird is gone. Then she shrieked and grabbed her head. “She has taken a pin and stuck it in my head!” When the marshal examined her, he pulled a large pin from her hair and held it up for all to see.

Hathorne turned to Reverend Nicholas Noyes of Salem, who was considered something of an authority on witchcraft, and asked for his opinion. The minister said, “I believe it is apparent that she practices witchcraft in the congregation.”

Hathorne turned to Martha Corey and said, “What do you say to all these things that are apparent?”

Martha’s faith that her Lord would make her innocence plain to all seemed at last to be exhausted. “If you all would have me hang, how can I help it?” she replied.

The magistrates committed Martha Corey to the Salem jail to await trial.

Chapter 3

1692

Abby was elated after the Martha Corey examination. She drew Ann aside as Reverend Parris, who had served as recorder for the examination, stood outside the meetinghouse deeply engaged in conversation with Ann's father. Making their way through the crowd, the girls slipped around to the back of the building. As soon as they were out of sight, Abby threw her arms in the air and sang out, "We have done it!"

"Done what?" asked Ann, laughing. Abby could break her most solemn mood when she was like this.

"Do you not see?" said Abby, with her broadest smile, green eyes glowing. "We have taken down Martha Corey." She tossed her head. "Foolish woman. She said we could not stand before her, but it was she who could not stand before us. And now she is in the jail for her sins."

Ann nodded. "I think we are safe from Goody Corey. She will not try to stand before us now."

"Oh, do you not see, Ann?" cried Abby. "It is so much bigger than that. There are none who will try to stand before us now. We can call out the name of any person in the village and the magistrates will bring them to be examined. And all who are there will believe what we say is true, whatever we choose to show them. It is we who control Salem Village now."

"I am not so certain of that," said Ann, shaking her head slowly. "I know I do not control my father's house." She looked closely at Abby. “Where is Betty today?” she asked. “I would have thought she had to come, as she is one of the afflicted.”

Abby shrugged and looked away. “It seems my aunt and uncle prevailed on the magistrates to allow her to be absent because she is so young and is somewhat undone by the proceedings. They took her to Salem to stay with our kinsman, Stephen Sewall, to get her away from it. I hope the Sewalls can calm her. She has come to believe in her fits. She really thinks the Devil is a big fearsome man coming to take her to Hell.”

Fear struck in the pit of Ann’s stomach. “Will she give us away?” she asked.

Abby did not seem bothered. She answered carelessly. “No, I think not. She is too afraid of what might happen to all of us. And if she should suggest that we are dissembling, I think the magistrates will believe our denials. They are getting as far into this as we are. See how they answered Goody Corey? They would not hear of it that we are distracted persons.”

Seeing that the crowd had dispersed, Ann hurried to join her parents for the ride home. It was true that she did not feel powerful in the house of Thomas Putnam. It was her mother everyone was looking to now. Just the week before, everyone had attended to Ann as she led the others—Mercy, Mary, and her mother too—in calling out Goody Corey, but her father had not been satisfied with this. On the Sabbath, the day after the incident with the clothing, she had heard him talking intensely with her mother in the parlor as she rested from the fits of the morning.

“Corey is not our greatest threat,” he said. “Do you not think the Towne family would attack us first? Those three sisters, posing as such devoted church women. They wish us evil from the bottom of their foul hearts. Do not forget, their mother was accused as a witch. It was only the influence old Towne had in Ipswich that kept her from the court.”

“’Tis true,” said his wife. “I know it is Rebecca who put out that horrid rumor about our little Sarah, and her posing as such a loving neighbor all the time. I cringe when she comes to our meeting and sits in mother's old seat in the meetinghouse. I can feel the evil coming from her."

Mulling this over, Ann had seen a way of quelling the uncomfortable wave of jealousy and resentment against her mother that had risen in her. The witchcraft doings had been hers and Abby's. Now they were slipping away. Here was a way to get them back and please her father, too. Later in the day, as the household joined in prayer along with her Uncle Edward and several neighbors who had come to join them, Ann fell to the floor and called out that Martha Corey and another woman were tormenting her. After she calmed down a little, her father stood her up, grasped her shoulders and said, "Who is it, child? Who is with her?"

She stared at a corner of the room. "I cannot tell," she said. "It is a cloudy specter. I do not recognize the face."

"Is it a church member?" asked Deacon Edward.

"I think it is a woman who sits in my grandmother's seat in the meetinghouse sometimes."

"Is it Rebecca Nurse?" her mother asked eagerly. "She is a member of the Salem church, but she often sits in my mother's old seat when she comes to our meeting."

"I think so," said Ann. In a moment, she grabbed her stomach and screamed, "Stop! Stop! I know it is you!" She fell to the floor again, rolling around and grabbing her arms. "She hits me with a stick! Stop! Stop!" she cried, and then went limp, as if in a trance. Her father picked her up, put her on the bed in the parlor, and returned to the keeping room.

"This is a serious development," said Edward. "Rebecca Nurse is a woman of great reputation for goodness and piety in the village. I can hardly credence such a thing of her."

"We must investigate," said Thomas. "God will reveal the truth eventually. Time will tell." He had gone to the ministry house the next day to discuss the new development with Reverend Parris. Hovering outside the minster's study, Abby had heard enough of the conversation to know what her next move should be.

On Tuesday, Abby had cried out Rebecca Nurse's name for the first time. On Saturday, when the village's former pastor, Deodat Lawson, was sitting with the Parris family, she had unleashed her arsenal. Staring straight ahead as if called, she had suddenly jumped up and begun running back and forth in the keeping room, despite the attempts of Deacon Ingersoll and his wife to hold her back. She had run back and forth for a while, flapping her arms and crying, "Whish, whish!" Then she had stood stock still and said, "There is Goodwife Nurse! Do you not see her?" She had struggled as if pushing something away, and said, "I will not, I will not, I will not take it. I do not know what book it is. I am sure it is none of God's book. It is the Devil's book for aught I know." Then she had run straight into the big fireplace, picking up firebrands and throwing them into the room, presumably at Goody Nurse. The adults had been hard put to keep the room from catching on fire and Abby from climbing up the chimney.

On the same day, Ann's mother had had a terrible fit that went on for hours. In lucid intervals, she had said that both Martha Corey and Rebecca Nurse were torturing her because she would not yield to their hellish temptations to sign the Devil's book. She had said that if she had not been upheld by an Almighty arm, she would not have survived the night. Ann had seen the campaign against Rebecca Nurse proceeding with a vengeance.

When her father had called her to him after family prayers, Ann had been unnerved, but also gratified to be the center of his attention once more. "Daughter," he had said, putting his hands on her shoulders and turning his dark, intense eyes on her, "you see that it is not just Martha Corey who attacks your mother, but Rebecca Nurse as well. I know her specter has hurt you, too. We must be certain that the magistrates know of her foul doings. Do not fail to tell them in the court when next you go there."

Ann had looked up and returned his gaze, replying, "I will, Father," and he had nodded as if she pleased him.

During Martha Corey's examination, Ann had quietly put Rebecca's name into play in the court. She had said that one day when Lieutenant Fuller had come to her father's house to pray with her, she had seen the specters of Goodwife Corey and another woman, who she thought was Goodwife Nurse, praying to the Devil at the same time. She knew it was only a matter of time before Rebecca Nurse would be brought in to be examined.

On the day after the Martha Corey examination, Ann's mother suffered a fit like no other. At the break of dawn, she began writhing in her bed and awakened the household with her screams, calling out to Rebecca Nurse to stop tormenting her. Ann went to the parlor to help, while Mary and Mercy saw to the younger children. She did what she could to soothe her mother, but she could tell she was far gone in her fit.

Ann Senior seemed to argue with Goody Nurse, insisting that she would not sign her red book. "I will not yield to your hellish temptations!" she cried. "It is blasphemous to deny the power of the blessed God and my Lord Jesus Christ to save my soul." Then she began reciting Bible verses, as though she would convince the specter. "Comfort ye, comfort ye my people, will your God say. 'Speak comfortably to Jerusalem, and cry unto her, that her warfare is accomplished, that her iniquity is pardoned, for she hath received of the Lord's hand double for all her sins.'"

"Isaiah 40," said Thomas. "She often asks me to read it."

"Thomas, read 50," she cried out, and he read verse 7. "'For the Lord God will help me, therefore shall I not be confounded; therefore have I set my face like a flint, and I know that I shall not be ashamed.'" As he read more of the Bible verses, Ann's mother seemed to relax, and she gradually returned to herself. After she had rested, she told them that Rebecca Nurse had appeared to her in her shift, as if she had just risen from bed, and, trying to get her to sign the Devil's book, had tempted her to despair over her own salvation. "I strove with her," she said. "I strove mightily using God's word, and I have triumphed. She is gone."

The next day, Reverend Lawson, their former pastor, came with Jonathan Putnam to visit Ann's mother and found her lying on the bed, recovering from a fit. He began to pray with them. As he prayed, her eyes were closed as though she were asleep, but her body went rigid. Thomas picked her up off the bed and tried to set her on his knees. At first, she was so rigid that he could not bend her legs, but then she sat and, as he held her around the waist, she began to fling her arms and legs around as if fending off an attack. After a while, she began to argue with Rebecca Nurse, shouting at her to be gone. "I know what you would have, but it is out of your reach; it is clothed with the white robes of Christ's righteousness."

Ann assumed she meant her soul and watched her strive mightily not to succumb. She started talking about a biblical verse and cried, "I am sure you cannot stand before that text. I will tell, I will tell it." Her body went rigid again, and she seemed to struggle against someone. At last, she seemed to break loose, and cried, "It is the third chapter of the Revelation."

Thomas asked Reverend Lawson to read the text, but he was hesitant, for it seemed to him like folk magic or 'white witchcraft,' as they called it, using a charm against the Devil. At Thomas's insistent urging, he decided that it would be all right to do it once, for an experiment, and began to read. At the end of the first verse, Goody Putnam's eyes opened, and her rigid body seemed to relax. She was fully aware and herself by the time he got to verse 5, "'He that overcometh, shall be clothed in white array, and I will not put out his Name out of the book of life, but I will confess his name before my Father, and before his angels.'" Then she was able to talk quietly with Reverend Lawson about her struggle against the evil threatened by Rebecca Nurse.

After her fit, Edward Putnam and their cousin, Jonathan, swore out a complaint against Rebecca Nurse. She was brought to Salem Village to be examined the next day. Goodwife Nurse was far different from the brash and confident Martha Corey. A stout, elderly woman with many children and grandchildren, she had been sick in bed for the previous week. She did not hear well and entered the packed and noisy little meetinghouse with an arthritic limp and a bewildered air. She did not argue with the magistrates, but answered that she was innocent of the charges they made against her.

From the moment the elderly woman appeared, Abby was writhing and screaming, accusing her of attacking her and saying she saw the Devil whispering in her ear and a yellow bird that was her familiar spirit. When Hathorne charged her with this, she said, "It is all false. I am clear." When he asked whether or not she thought the girls suffered against their wills, she replied, "I do not think these suffer against their wills."

The rest of the girls and women, including Ann's mother, began to writhe and cry out that Goody Nurse was tormenting them at that very moment. They screamed that they were being bitten and pinched. Several of the girls showed the marks on their wrists and arms. When Rebecca slumped forward against the chair she stood behind, Mercy screamed that her breast was being pressed with a great weight. When she straightened up, Mary was drawn backwards until it looked like her back would break. When Rebecca cocked her head toward Hathorne so she could hear his questions in the din, Elizabeth Hubbard's neck was grotesquely twisted, and she screamed in what seemed like great pain until Abby told the marshal to hold up Goody Nurse's head.

The meetinghouse was chaos. Amid the screams and the bodies rolling on the floor, the officers of the court joined the friends and relatives of the girls and women, trying to calm them. Some of the spectators left the room, but most remained, riveted by the scene and adding to the din.

Finally, the girls were exhausted. Following Abby's lead, they gradually relaxed and grew silent. Then, with the help of those around them, they got up from the floor and went back to the bench. But so extreme were Ann's mother's fits that she lay on the meetinghouse floor, apparently unable to move. After getting permission from the magistrates, Thomas picked her up and carried her outside into the quiet, sunny day, where she soon began to recover. Having finally succeeded at restoring order and quiet to the meetinghouse, the magistrates committed Rebecca Nurse to the Salem jail on the basis of what they had seen in front of them as well as the charges of previous abuse by her specter.

Reverend Lawson preached to the Salem Village congregation that Sunday. He suggested that the defection of church members to the Devil might be part of a plot on Satan's part to divide the churches internally and overthrow God's people in New England. He warned against the dangers of what seemed to be comparatively innocent practices like the kind of counter-magic Goody Sibley had suggested with the witch cake and various common conjuring tricks to foretell the future. All was divination, he warned, and could open the door to Satan's wiles.

Ann was not so lucky as her mother. She and Abby had succeeded in taking back the witchcraft doings from her, but at a great cost. On the day after the Nurse examination, her Uncle Edward visited their house. Her father met him at the door and told him that Rebecca Nurse's specter had come back to torment his niece. As he entered the keeping room, Edward found Ann sitting on the hearth bench, leaning back against the wall, her eyes closed and her face as pale as death. As her uncle and her father watched, she began to struggle. She bent over as if to shield her head and cried, "Stop! Please stop!" She screamed and jumped up, screaming again and crying out to stop beating her. When she came to herself again, she sank back down on the bench and murmured that Rebecca Nurse had beaten her with a chain in retaliation for the testimony against her at the examination.

"You are a witness," said Thomas to Edward. "Please to examine her." Looking at his niece's heavily bruised arms and back, Edward saw the marks of chain links repeated at least six times. Ann could sense that Edward's tender heart was fairly broken at this brutality to his niece. "Who would do such a thing?" he whispered to his brother as Ann's mother helped her to do up her clothing. "It tries my faith to think the Lord would allow it to happen."

Ann shuddered at her father's reply. "We must trust in God as always," said Thomas, his dark eyes fixed on his brother's. "We must believe it is a providence in the service of God's greater plan for us. It is a privilege for my daughter to serve in the fight against the forces of the Devil."

Chapter 4

1692

Everyone had supped. The table was cleared, and the plates and cutlery had been washed. Ann relaxed into the momentary peace that had fallen over the family on a day when there were no visitors and no fits, her father away at the ministry house, and everyone drawn to the warm red glow of the fire in the keeping room. But soon, the outside door was flung open, letting in a chilling blast of April rain and wind, and Thomas Putnam stepped into the room. Tom and Eben threw on their hats and coats and charged out into the storm to see to their father's horse. Ann jumped up to help Mercy as she hurried to remove her master's soaking-wet hat and cloak and hang them next to the fire to dry. Betty and Deliverance drew closer to their mother, who was sitting on the hearth bench with the baby, Timothy. Ann's mother looked up at her husband. "'Tis a foul night, Thomas," she said. "Come closer to the fire. It is late. You must be very hungry."

Thomas ignored this. He stood looking at his family with dark eyes that expressed his fervor. "I have learned much of import at the ministry house," he said. "Abigail has seen a great meeting of the witches in the ministry pasture. She says there were forty or more gathered there. It is evidence of what Mr. Parris and I have been thinking for some time. This evil thing that has risen among us is much bigger than a few women practicing witchcraft in the village. Salem Village has become the battleground for Satan's plot against God's people in New England. We have sought to build the

Kingdom of God here these sixty years, and now the Devil would overturn it with the help of his servants who live among us and set up his own diabolical kingdom with himself as its lord and master. We know that our own family has been victimized in many ways by those who do the work of the Devil. It seems we have been chosen to be at the center of this battle. And if the Devil has chosen us, then God has chosen us too, for in his infinite power, he must grant Satan leave for everything he does."

When he had stopped talking and stood silently staring at the fire, Ann thought he might have exhausted himself. "You must be very tired and hungry, Father," she said. "Shall I serve you? We have kept your supper for you."

Thomas's body jerked suddenly as if he had been struck, and he moved toward her, his eyes like two dark, smoldering coals in a face ashen with anger. "No, I do not want supper!" he shouted. "I want to be listened to in my own house!" Ann's mother instinctively drew Timothy closer to her and watched her husband carefully under half-closed eyelids. The other children sought invisibility, shrinking back against the wall with their eyes on the floor. "This thing we are facing is momentous," he cried. "It is no longer a thing of women and children, with biting and pinching and sticking people with pins. This has become a thing of men, a battle between Satan and Jesus Christ for this land. It is life and death, and more than that, eternal life. We must all fight in this battle."

Tim was whimpering, despite his mother's attempts to quiet him. The rest of the room was silent. Thomas looked directly at each member of his family. "Now," he said, "this militia of forty witches must have a captain, and we must identify him. Abigail said there was someone dressed like a minister who was presiding over this meeting, but she did not recognize him. I have an idea of who this minister is, one who has been an enemy to our own family and who harbors heretical teachings in his heart. My wife, do you know who I speak of?"

Ann Senior looked up at him. "It must be that man they set up in place of my sister Mary's husband James Bayley, who was the first and rightful minister of our congregation. I believe that started all the trouble in our village. It was not long before everyone could see that George Burroughs harbored heretical beliefs, refusing to baptize his children or to participate in the Lord's Supper. A bad minister indeed. Everyone thought so. He was all but run out of the village when he went to Maine before Mr. Lawson came."

Thomas nodded. "Yes, Burroughs. And he went up to Casco Bay and became the minister at Wells and plagued the people there. You were a maid in his house, Mercy Lewis, were you not?"

Mercy began quietly with her eyes cast down, but she grew bolder with each word. "Aye, sir. I worked there for two years after the Indians killed my mother and father. Burroughs was a hard and exacting master to us servants, and he did not spare his children or his wives either. There are those who say he worked his first two wives to death. I was very glad to get out of that house when I got the chance to come here to Salem to work."

"What do the people there think of him as a minister?"

She looked up. "The people there are glad to have any minister. They are so lonely and cut off from the big places around the Bay. But he is not counted much as a man of God. Besides being a hard master, he is very vain and boastful, always bragging of his knowledge and his feats of strength."

Thomas turned to her. "He brags of feats of strength?"

"Yes, sir. No one ever seems to see them, but everyone knows the stories of how he held a seven-foot musket out straight with one hand, and how he lifted a barrel of molasses in his arms and carried it from a canoe to the shore. Such things as that. I do not know if there is any truth to them."

Thomas nodded. He was beginning to relax from his fit of anger. "There could be," he said. "Inhuman feats of strength are a sign of a covenant with the Devil. They are admissible as court evidence. We must look into this question of Burroughs and see whether there is evidence that he is doing harm among us. I would not be at all surprised if he was the leader of this witches' coven."

As the children and maids went to their beds after family prayers that evening, Thomas told Ann to stay with him. He laid his hands on her shoulders and looked into her eyes, speaking in low tones. "I have something important to say to you, Daughter. You must look out carefully for this minister, Burroughs, when the specters come to you. He could well be the vessel the Devil is using to attack our family and the whole colony of New England. If you can spy him out, you could do much to help rid us of our enemies and restore peace to this land. I suspect he is guilty of more capital crimes than witchcraft." Then he said a short prayer and sent her to bed.

A few minutes later, Ann made sure Betty and Deliverance were asleep in the bed next to her and then slipped out from under the covers and moved noiselessly across the room to where Mercy and Mary Walcott had fixed their pallets by the fireplace. "What shall we do?" she whispered. "My father is set on Burroughs as the leader of the witches. He wants me to call out on him."

Mercy snorted. "It is all well with me," she said. "With the beatings I have had from that man, I would happily send him to the gallows. He does have a very strong arm, though he looks a puny little man. He is even worse than—" With a glance at Ann, she broke off and turned to Mary. "What do you think?"

"If you both have fits," said Mary quickly, "you can call out different things. Two witnesses will be better than one."

"Once it gets abroad that Burroughs is accused, there will be many witnesses, believe me," said Mercy. "He is a man with many enemies in Maine, and here too, I think. I can accuse him of bringing me the book to sign. There was a heap of books in his study in Maine. I have seen them many times."

"Father wants a weighty crime to charge him with."

"He abused his wives something dreadful."

"Is it true that people think he killed them?"

"I know not whether they would go that far, but he was a cruel husband."

"Perhaps their specters could speak for themselves."

Mercy laughed. "You are a wonder, Ann. Always a little ahead of the rest. The specters can speak to you, then."

"We should be gradual about it," said Ann. "The way we were with Rebecca Nurse. There are many in Salem who would be loath to hear a minister named as a witch, no matter what his character."

A few days later, on the twentieth of April, Ann had a tremendous fit while her Uncle Edward was visiting and identified Burroughs as one of the specters who came to torture her. The next day, her father wrote a letter to the magistrates warning of 'high and dreadful' things—of 'a wheel within a wheel, at which our ears do tingle.'

Thomas knew that the two magistrates would immediately recognize the reference to Jeremiah 19:3, 'Thus sayeth the Lord of hosts, the God of Israel, behold, I will bring a plague upon this place, the which whosoever heareth, his ears shall tingle.' He trusted that his readers would immediately connect this chapter of Jeremiah, about God's punishment for the idol-worship afforded to Ba'al, with the Satan worship in God's new kingdom in New England. It was a coded message to watch for a central development in the witchcraft outbreak, the 'wheel within a wheel' that gave all the hitherto seemingly isolated and somewhat trivial incidents of witchcraft their significance.

A week later, an arrest warrant was issued for George Burroughs, by particular order of Governor Phips and the Governor's Council, and he was apprehended by the field marshal at his home in Maine and taken by ship to Salem. His formal examination on May ninth was conducted not only by the regular magistrates, Hathorne and Corwin, but by Lieutenant Governor William Stoughton and Samuel Sewall, who was a judge and member of the province's Council. Thomas Putnam saw to it that both Ann and Mercy gave depositions about Burroughs, which were witnessed and signed by him and his brother, Edward, before the examination.

In her deposition, Mercy accused Burroughs of trying to get her to sign the book that would put her in a covenant with the Devil. She said he also told her that he had several books in his study in Maine with which he could raise the Devil. In keeping with Thomas Putnam's views on Burroughs, Mercy raised the stakes by saying he claimed that 'the Devil was his servant,' suggesting he was a more dangerous man than the witches they had been dealing with up to this point. Then she dropped a hint of what was to come: "He told me I should not see his two wives if he could help it because I should not witness against him."

The next day, Ann had a fit in the presence of her Uncle Edward. After it was over, her father told her to describe what she had seen as he recorded her story and her uncle witnessed it. The result was the deposition that was read aloud at Burroughs's examination. Ann testified that she had been tortured by George Burroughs and urged to sign his book. Then Burroughs had told her that his first two wives would appear to her soon and tell a great many lies, but she should not believe them. Immediately, two women had appeared in their shrouds, which had frightened Ann greatly. They had turned red and angry faces to Burroughs and told him that he had been a cruel man to them, and that their blood cried out for vengeance against him. They had said they would be clothed with white robes in heaven while he was cast into hell.

Then Burroughs had vanished and the two women had turned to Ann, looking as pale as a white wall, and told her they were Burroughs's wives and he had murdered them. His first wife said he had stabbed her under the left arm and put a piece of sealing wax on the wound, and that it had happened in the ministry house. His second wife said that Burroughs and the woman he was now married to had killed her in the ship when she was going to visit some friends. Ann said the women had ordered her to tell these things to the magistrates in front of Burroughs, and said that, if he did not admit them, they might come and appear in the court. Then Ann said that Reverend Deodat Lawson's wife and daughter and Goodman Fuller's first wife had appeared to her and told her that Burroughs had murdered them as well.

The depositions were read at Burroughs's examination, and Mercy proved right in saying there would be no dearth of witnesses against him once the opportunity presented itself. Several of the girls fell into fits in the courtroom, but it really was not necessary because important citizens like Captain John Putnam and several other prominent members of the militia joined many of his former neighbors in testifying. Reverend Burroughs denied all the charges and was sent to the Salem jail awaiting the Grand Jury of August third.

Chapter 5

1692

While the Burroughs activity was taking place, the Putnam family was also occupied with someone closer to home. John Willard, who had always been a friend and loyal ally of Thomas Putnam's, was at first eager and helpful in the pursuit of accused witches. He was in the Putnam house to help during several of Ann's fits and willingly arrested a number of suspects in his role as deputy constable. But as the spring went on, he began to have doubts. Backing away from his original belief that all the accused witches should be 'hanged forthwith,' he began to doubt that so many respected members of the church and the community could be guilty of witchcraft. Pondering the subject, he had such a change of heart that he refused to arrest any more suspects and resigned as deputy constable. Thomas Putnam felt this as a deep personal betrayal.

On the morning of April twenty-fourth, Thomas called Ann into the parlor, where her mother was waiting. "Willard is not what we thought him," said Thomas. "He falters in this business and bends to evil. I would not be surprised if he were a witch himself."

Ann's mother was quick to agree. "He pretends to such holiness," she said, "when everyone knows he has beaten his wife unmercifully, and his beasts as well."

"You must look out for him, Daughter," said Thomas. "I would not be surprised if he began to torment our family now that he is no longer our friend."

Ann dropped her eyes. "I will, Father," she said softly.

Ann had a great liking for John Willard. He had been kind to her and her brothers and sisters. When she was a little girl and he lived in the Putnam house, working for her father, he was the adult figure who would listen to her talk about the serious matters in her tiny world. He had been there during many of the important family events, even after he left them. On the morning in 1689 when little Sarah died, he had happened to come to the house and had remained to help her father bury the baby and pray with them for her soul. Ann had no desire to call out his name, but Thomas Putnam willed that she should. Twice that day, in the afternoon and evening, he called her to him and bid her look into his eyes, saying, "Daughter, do you look out for our enemy, John Willard?" She said yes but had trouble meeting his gaze.

Early the next morning, Saturday, Thomas told Ann to come with him to the barn. Planting his boots firmly on the ground, he told her to stand before him and looked sternly down at her. "Daughter, why do you not call out John Willard?" he demanded. "I have told you of the evil he would do to us. I am certain you can see him tempting you to commit the grave sin of disobedience to your father."

She steeled herself against the sudden grip of fear. She was determined to resist this thing if she could. "I do not see it, Father," she said softly. "I can see only his goodness to us."

Her father's eyes blazed, his face drained of color, and his hand shot out and gripped her arm hard. He dragged her to the wall where the harnesses hung. Yanking a bridle off its hook, he said, "You will learn to see what I tell you to see." In a swift, compact motion, he threw her down and hit her with six quick, hard strokes on the back and legs.

"Now," he said, "you will end this disobedience and do as I say." He hung the bridle carefully, turned, and left the barn without looking at her. Ann lay on the ground, crying and shaking. It had taken all of her strength not to cry out, which would have angered him more, she knew. Gradually, the sobs subsided. She moved her legs gingerly, turned over, and sat up. She wiped her face with the hem of her petticoat and sat hugging her knees while the pain came in waves up and down her back and legs. She looked at the welts on her legs and saw there was no broken skin. There would be only marks and bruises this time. She did not see how to keep from hurting John Willard. She knew this beating was only a warning, a reminder that her father was capable of much worse. She laid her head on her knees and cried—for herself, for John Willard, for her family. She did not see a way out of this.

Later in the day, when her uncle was in the house, Ann had a fit in which the pain and wretchedness she was feeling finally found its expression. She did not writhe or roll on the floor but sat on the hearth bench, hugging herself tightly, alternately staring into space and wailing, sometimes jerking her body as if dodging a blow. "I will not!" she cried over and over again. "Leave me be! Why do you torment me?" When the fit was over, she said flatly that Willard had tormented her greatly by pinching and beating her, trying to get her to sign his book, but she had refused. The next day, the scene was repeated before a group of neighbors gathered in the Putnam house after the Sunday service.

After the fit had passed and the visitors had left the house, her father carried Ann into the parlor and laid her on the bed. When her mother came in to look at her, Thomas drew himself up and announced, "I have something to say to you, my wife and daughter. I have seen some truth today that weighs much in this Willard business. He is clearly not what we once thought him. He serves the Devil. I have been much drawn to think today of the day our little Sarah died." His wife, who had her head bowed, but had been watching him carefully out of the corner of her eye, let out a little involuntary cry, but did not respond. Ann lay on the bed, physically exhausted and looking at him under veiled lids with dread in her eyes. He did not look at either of them but stared into the fireplace ash.

"This is what I believe," he said. "There was evil in our house that day. The Devil was afoot in our home. I believe our baby was bewitched to death. You will remember that there were three outsiders who came to our house: Rebecca Nurse and her son Samuel and John Willard. Nurse has attacked us with her talk of colic and such nonsense that has led to mutterings about the child's death in the village, but I do not believe she harmed her. John Willard came just in time to bury the child, and quite eager he was to dig the grave too. He has always been jealous of our family. He has oft remarked that God has blessed us with many healthy and able children. I believe his specter carried out the Devil's bidding to attack our family and destroy our child, and all this time he has been a little smiling hypocrite in our company, the Devil's snake in our home. He must be rooted out of our lives, kept from doing more evil in the world." He looked at his wife and his daughter, who remained silent. "We must do what we can," he said, and left the room.

Ann looked at her mother, who looked away. "Mother," she asked, "do you believe it?"

Her mother took her hand, a rare comforting gesture. "Your father has spoken, Daughter," she said. "We are both bound to obey him. It does not matter what we think. But I will tell you, there was something evil that took over our house that day. Something evil that ended with Sarah's death. I do not know whence it came. It could have been from Willard as well as anything else. I will not speak more of it. You must put your mind at ease. Obey your father and do what he tells you is right. That is all the Lord asks of us."

After her mother left the room, Ann lay on the bed thinking about the day her baby sister Sarah had died. She remembered that cold December day when she was ten years old as vividly as if it were yesterday. This scene had run so often in her head that its details never varied. On that morning, she had awoken with a start from a deep dream of warm summer sunlight and Abby laughing and swinging her basket of blackberries as they walked hand in hand down the middle of the meetinghouse road. Then the awareness of the cold, dark room, of the little boy's warm body asleep next to her, of the piercing baby screams from somewhere below, had stolen upon her. And then she had been truly awake. It was Sarah's screaming that had awakened her. Ann had thought her baby sister must be having a fearful attack of the colic.

After looking at Tom, wrapped up to his ears in his comforter, and deciding he was not going to wake up, she had slid her legs over the side of the bed, letting her feet find her shoes, and then grabbed the heavy shawl from its peg on the wall and wrapped it around her. The meager fire banked in the bedchamber's fireplace did little to warm the cold night air, but it and the moonlight through the window helped Ann make her way to the stairs in the dark. Once she was at the head, the glow from the big fireplace below had guided her down. She had hesitated in the comparative warmth of the keeping room before she knocked lightly on the parlor door where her parents and baby Sarah had been.

"Mother," she said softly, "do you need me to help?"

Her mother's voice responded. "Come in, child." She lifted the latch and opened the door just enough for her slight frame to slip between it and the jamb.

In the moonlight, she could see her parents both sitting up in the bed, her mother's hand out rocking the cradle next to the wall, Betty and Eben lying in the trundle bed on the other side. Her sister and brother lay still and quiet, but she could tell they were awake.

"Shall I take her in the other room and walk her?" she asked.

Her father peered at her in the dimness, his dark eyes glinting in his lean, white face. "No," he said curtly. "You take these two upstairs with you. We will deal with the baby."

Betty and Eben slithered quickly out of the bed and into their shoes. She led them through the other room and up the stairs. She then woke Tom just enough to get him to move over and helped them to slide in next to him. She lay down on the edge of the bed, curving herself around Betty's little body, pulling her comforter over all of them. The little ones had fallen asleep immediately, but Ann lay awake, listening to Sarah's screams. She wondered at her mother. Sarah would not calm herself unless someone walked her up and down, patted her back, perhaps put a warm stone on her belly, which Ann knew must be rock hard with the colic for her to be screaming that loudly for that long. But the screams went on and on, and finally, Ann had drifted into sleep. Later that night, she had awoken again, from what she had not known. The house had been quiet and dark. The moon had set. Perhaps all slept.

When the dim light of a cloudy dawn had woken Ann again, she had taken her clothes from the peg and brought them down to the keeping room to dress by the hearth. She was surprised that her mother was not stirring. There was no sound from the sleeping parlor. She had raked away the ashes, built up a cooking fire in the fireplace, and poured some water into the cooking pot. Then it was clearly day, and still everything was quiet. She went to the parlor door and listened. Then she knocked softly.

"Mother?" she had murmured. "Are you sick?" There was no response, so she opened the door and looked around it. Her father had gone. Her mother sat on the edge of the bed, looking like a girl, still in her shift, her light blonde hair coming loose from its braid. She had her hand on the cradle, but she did not rock it. Ann thought that Sarah must have fallen asleep at last after a very long night.

"Mother?" she asked again. "Are you all right? Is Sarah asleep?"

When her mother turned her head, her pale face looked like death. She said, "Come and see."

Ann crept up to the cradle and looked inside. There was the bundle that was baby Sarah, tightly wrapped as usual against the winter night. Then she noticed that her face was covered too.

"Mother," she had said, "what happened to Sarah?"

Her mother's face had no expression. She looked away from her, down at the bundle. "She died in the night. Your father is outside digging a grave for her."

"But Mother," she said, "what happened? Surely, she was only suffering with the colic."

"Do not question, child," her mother said in a low, flat voice. She did not move or look at Ann. "God has seen fit to take her. It is not for us to know."

Ann nearly burst into tears. Her baby sister, such a dear little thing when she was not taken with the colic, just gone. Looking at her impassive mother, she knew she must not give way, so she busied herself with bringing her mother's clothing and helping her to dress. She had heard Tom clambering down the stairs to dress by the fire and went in to warn him to be quiet. "Mother is not well, Tom," she said. He looked at her and then, without being told, he finished dressing and went about filling the woodbox. When Betty and Eben came down, she fetched their clothes from the parlor and told them to dress quickly and be quiet, for Mother was not well. She combed and plaited Betty's hair and set her cap on and did her best to tame Eben's unruly curls and straighten his clothes as though it were the Sabbath. When Tom had come in with his last load of kindling, she gave him some warm water and bid him wash carefully and comb his hair.

"Why are we taking such care on a Saturday?" asked Tom. "Is the doctor coming?"

"No, Tom," she said. "But Mother and Father have something to tell us."

She fed them all a small breakfast of bread and butter and cider, and brought some into her mother, who still sat there on the bed without moving, her hand on the cradle. Ann set about putting the keeping room to rights, giving little tasks to Betty. Then they heard a horse outside and Tom ran out to see who it was.

"Is your father about, Tom?"

Ann had recognized the voice as that of their neighbor, John Willard, who used to live with them and help her father on the farm. She stepped outside the door. “He is out in the back, John,” she said. “Perhaps you can tell him I have breakfast for him when he is ready.”

“All right, then, Ann,” he said, a warm smile lighting his handsome face. “I just wanted to talk to him about two sheep before I offer them to my father-in-law.”

It was some time before she saw them coming back to the house, both with bowed heads and not talking. Her father stepped into the room and glanced around at the children with the stern look on his face that was their warning to drop their eyes and stay out of his way. “Where is your mother?” he asked.

“She is with Sarah,” said Ann.

“And what do you know of Sarah?” he demanded sharply.

Ann lowered her eyes and said, “I know little, and my brothers and sister nothing, but perhaps you will tell us.”

Her father said, “Come here and look at me, children. I have something to say to you.”

When they stood six feet in front of him looking up obediently, he had said, “We have lost your sister, Sarah. God has taken her home to him in the night. We must pray for his mercy to her.”

Ann was burning to know what had happened to Sarah. She wanted to ask how she died, but even little Eben knew better than to question their father about such a thing that was told to them so solemnly. He and Tom exchanged a stunned look and said nothing. They all kneeled in their places as if for family prayer, John Willard joining them. Their father prayed and read from the Bible. Then he stood and said, “I must finish the grave.”

“Will you not want to break your fast, Father?” asked Ann. “I have a little bread and butter here.” She lowered her eyes. “And you, John, shall I get you some refreshment?”

“Thank you, Ann,” said Willard. “I have broken my fast. But you must have something, Thomas.”

Her father downed the mug of cider and ate a few mouthfuls of bread. “Let us go, John,” he said. “We will finish this sad task.”

A little later, as she was going about the housekeeping, Ann had heard another horse in the yard and gone out to see a young man helping an old lady dismount. She did not know her name, but she had seen her a few times in the meetinghouse. She was a pleasant and comfortable old lady with a greeting for everyone, the kind of grandmother her own grandmother was not. There were always young mothers coming up to show her their babies and get her wise counsel. She came bustling up to the door, with the young man lagging a bit behind.

"Good morning, child," she said. "Such a lovely, sunny day for December. I have come to see your mother."

Ann had no idea what to do. "My mother is not well," she said.

The old lady's smile drooped, showing wrinkles on her face and deep lines about her mouth. "I am most sorry to hear that," she said. "Perhaps I can help her. I am good at healing. I had come with some remedies for the colic to help your little sister. She was so badly taken when I was there on Sunday that I was moved to do what I could."

As Ann looked up at her, she fought to keep the tears from her eyes. "My sister has died," she said, "and my mother has not moved from her side this morning." Despite her efforts, she burst into sobs.

The old lady reached down and hugged the little girl to her. Ann felt the comfort of her warm hand slowly stroking her back. When she had quieted, the lady wiped her face with a little kerchief she carried and put her hands on her shoulders. "You poor child," she said with a kindly look. "Where is your father?"

"He is in the back with John Willard, digging the grave," she said.

"Has anyone sent for the minister?"

"No."

"Samuel," the old lady said, "you must ride over and fetch Mr. Parris so he can pray with these people. I will see what I can do for Goody Putnam."

Samuel nodded and mounted his horse again.

"Now, my child," said the lady, smiling, "have you and your brothers and sister had anything to eat?"

"Yes," said Ann. "I gave them breakfast."

"Your mother is fortunate to have such a good daughter as you," she said. "Where is she now?"

"In the parlor."

With no further ceremony, the old lady came inside, smiling on the three younger children who stared at her in the keeping room before she knocked on the parlor door and went in. Ann could not hear much of what was being said, just the sounds of the voices. The lady's murmuring, trying to comfort, and her mother's growing more and more shaky until she finally burst into sobs. Stealthily opening the door a crack, Ann could see the lady holding her mother and stroking her hair as though she were a two-year-old who had woken from a terrifying dream. Shocked, she closed the door again, and when Tom asked, "What do they do in there?" she had said that he should tend to his business.

By the time Samuel had returned with Reverend Parris, Ann's mother was in a more fit state. She was able to pray with him and the children and the old lady and Samuel. When her father came back in, he seemed surprised and not pleased to find these people praying with his wife and children. "Mr. Parris," he said, "thank you for coming in our time of need, but I am at a loss to understand what brought you all here."

The old lady spoke up. "It was our doing, Goodman Putnam," she said. "I came with medicine for the baby and my son went for Mr. Parris when we heard the sad news. I had no idea the poor little one was as sick as that, or I would have come sooner. But it seemed to be just a bad case of the colic. In all my years of nursing children, I had never known one to die of the colic. I am most sorry for you all."

Ann saw her father stiffen and turn on the old lady, his face stern and his dark eyes glaring. "It is not for us to question divine will," Thomas Putnam said. "God has taken her home to him. His will be done."

"Amen," said Mr. Parris.

Ann's father turned to the minister and said in his formal public manner, "The grave is prepared, Mr. Parris, if you would help us to bless our poor child as she goes to God."

And so, with Mr. Parris praying over the grave, baby Sarah was laid to rest. Ann slowly counted the mourners. Her mother and father, her sister and brothers, John Willard, the old lady, and her son, Samuel; nine in all, including herself. She hoped their prayers were enough to send Sarah's little soul to God.

Ann woke from the memory as if from a recurring dream. She knew now that the kind old lady was Rebecca Nurse. She did not believe that Goody Nurse had harmed Sarah any more than John Willard had. They had simply been there when something terrible had happened and stayed to help. She did not know why her father was so insistent on attacking them, but she had an inkling, one that she tried to keep from thinking about.

John Willard knew the inevitable progression of events after his name had come into play. He tried to stop it by going directly to the Putnam house and appealing to the family he had thought of as almost his own. As he rode up to the house, he looked around the familiar yard and was struck by how normal it appeared. The large house and barn, the newly planted kitchen garden, the pigpen and the chickens scurrying out of his horse's way, a peaceful and prosperous home of the kind he had always aspired to. Could this family really believe he was a witch who was tormenting them? It was Mercy Lewis who responded to his knock on the door. She stepped back with a startled "You!"

"Yes, it is me, Mercy," he said. "Is your master at home?"

She glanced behind her and said, "I will call the mistress."

Goody Putnam's reaction was as startled as the maid's, but she responded more volubly. "What do you want here, John Willard?" she demanded. "Are you come to torment my daughter more?"

"I have not tormented her at all," he said. "I ask only to speak with her that I might learn what this rumor I hear means. Has she truly called out my name as a specter who torments her?"

"Aye, she has, and more too," she said.

"I beg that you allow me to speak with her, that I may hear with my own ears what she accuses me of."

Ann Senior nearly closed the door on him, but she hesitated, saying, "This decision is not mine to make. Stay there while they fetch my husband." She disappeared into the house and sent Mercy to find the master.

Thomas Putnam was not long in coming, as he had been busy in the barn. "It is a brazen thing to come here after what we know of you now," he said to John. "What do you want?"

"I have heard fearsome and false accusations against me that they say come from your daughter, Ann. I cannot believe that she would so falsely accuse me. I only beg that you allow me to speak with her. It is your duty as a brother in Christ."

Thomas looked at him. "Well, then, you may speak to her, but only before witnesses." He called his wife and daughter and told them to go into the parlor. Then he led Willard through the house where he had always felt so much at home. Now, the younger children shrank from him and the maid stared with hostility. Thomas led him into the parlor and closed the door behind them. Ann sat in the chair. Her mother perched on the bed, rocking Timothy in the cradle next to it. "What have you to say to my daughter?" Thomas demanded.

John took a step toward Ann. The small figure sitting in the chair looked like the little girl he had known nearly all her life. Then she looked up at him out of expressionless pale blue eyes, framed by her wan face and the colorless blonde hair peeking out from her white cap. She frightened him. For a moment, she looked dead. "Ann," he said, "is there truth to these rumors? Could you possibly think I wish you harm?"

She dropped her eyes. "Your apparition has done me much harm," she said. "I have been beaten and pinched and choked and otherwise tormented."

"I know nothing of that," he said. "Truly. How could I hurt you, a little girl I have known your whole life?"

She looked at him again out of those lifeless eyes. "What does that mean?" she asked. "It is well known that you have beaten your own wife so harshly that the sticks have broken on her body."

That old story from Margaret's hateful relatives. "You know it is not true," he said. "It is a vile rumor spread by those who hate me. I would not hurt Margaret, and I would not hurt you. I swear this is true." He faced her frankly and directly.

As she looked at him, a little blush came over her face, and something flickered in her eyes. "I would believe you, John," she said softly. Then she straightened up and seemed to make a decision. "If you do not hurt me more, I will not complain of you to the magistrates."

"That is all I ask, Ann," said Willard, clasping her hands with intense feeling. "You know I would never hurt you."

Thomas Putnam came forward, his eyes blazing. "I do *not* believe you, John Willard," he said, "but I will give you this reprieve if it is what my poor afflicted daughter wishes. She has a much more forgiving nature than I have. Do not hurt my daughter further or you will face the consequences. Leave us now, for the love of God, and call your specter back. You are not welcome here." Willard left the Putnam house in the grip of fear. He had a faint hope that Ann would somehow manage to stay true, but he knew what to expect now.

Ann had expended all her strength in this slight rebellion. Her father beat her again, more severely this time, and there was no sympathy from her mother. She spent three days recovering enough to be able to feign a fit convincingly. On the third night, she performed a fit in front of visiting neighbors, calling out that Willard was tormenting her and trying to get her to sign the Devil's book. She had then gone into a trance, lying absolutely still on the floor for many minutes. When she came out of it, her father asked her what she had seen.

"I saw the apparition of my little sister, Sarah, who died when she was about six weeks old, crying out for vengeance against John Willard," she said flatly. "I also saw the apparition of a woman in a winding sheet, who told me she was John Wilkins's first wife, and that John Willard had a hand in her death." News of this vision spread quickly through the village.

Although they were far from friendly to him, John Willard felt he had no other resource than to seek help from his wife's family. He went to the remote northwest area of Will's Hill to ask his wife's grandfather, Bray Wilkins, an elderly, much revered man, to pray with him in his difficulty. But he got to the farm just as the old man was leaving on some urgent business. Bray promised to pray with him when he returned, but was delayed, so John had to leave without his crucial support.

At a large dinner in Boston a few days later, Bray Wilkins felt that John had given him a strange look, but he did not speak to him. Then Bray was taken with a terrible pain in his bowels and back and had a great deal of trouble urinating. He was examined by a doctor who could find no other cause than bewitchment. The suspicion immediately fell on John Willard. When his wife's cousin, Daniel Wilkins, a young, healthy man, suddenly fell seriously ill, the family felt they had all the evidence they needed.

On May tenth, a warrant was issued for John Willard's arrest. As a former deputy constable himself, he was well prepared for this. Before the constable arrived at his farm, he had seemingly vanished. Two days later, Mercy and Ann visited Bray Wilkins, who was still suffering a good deal of pain, and said they saw John Willard sitting on his belly. On May sixteenth, Daniel Wilkins died. Mercy and Mary were on hand to see the specters of John Willard and another accused witch sitting on his chest as he gasped his last breaths. A jury of men was appointed to examine the body. They concluded that it was 'an unnatural death by some cruel hands of witchcraft or diabolical act.'

On the same day, John was apprehended while he was hoeing a field on some land he owned, miles from Salem Village. The story was told that as soon as John Willard was put in shackles, Bray Wilkins felt great relief from his pain, and his urine began to flow again.

That evening, at Ingersoll's tavern, Mercy and Mary, along with Goodwife Sarah Bibber, had fits and cried out that John Willard was choking them. Since the magistrates saw an imminent danger of further murders in the case, John was quickly examined two days later. As soon as he was led into the meetinghouse, Ann, Mercy and Mary fell into fits. During the reading of the depositions against him, they cried out that he was beating, biting and choking them. John listened in amazement while Ann's deposition, taken down by her father, was read out.

> He did set upon me most dreadfully and beat me and pinched and almost choked me to death, threatening to kill me if I would not write in his book. But I told him I would not write in his book though he did kill me: after this I saw the apparition of my little sister Sarah who died when she was about six weeks old crying out for vengeance against John Willard. I also saw the apparition of a woman in a winding sheet which told me she was John Wilkins's first wife and that John Willard had a hand in her death: also I being carried to Wills Hill on the 15th of May at evening to see the afflicted persons there, I saw there the apparition of John Willard afflicting of his grandfather Wilkins and Daniel Wilkins: and Rebecca Wilkins: & he also told me that he would kill Daniel Wilkins if he could but he had not power enough yet to kill him: but he would go to Mr. Burroughs and get power to kill Daniel Wilkins.

John's hope of ever refuting these charges dwindled to despair as Ann's testimony was reinforced by that of Mercy and

Mary and several others. Then the Wilkins family weighed in with their old stories of horrible beatings that he had supposedly inflicted on his wife and of cruelty to his animals. John called them out as lies and begged that his wife might be called to testify. The magistrates ignored his plea and let the testimony stand as it was. They administered the touch test, ordering him to touch Mary Warren's arm as she sat immobile, staring ahead. Her fit stopped when he touched her. Two of the girls testified that his specter had come from his body to afflict them in court.

John stumbled several times when the judges ordered him to say the Lord's Prayer, another folk test. Three times, he started to say the prayer, but was so nervous about reciting it perfectly that he tripped up. When the magistrates pressed him to confess, he refused desperately. Finally, he simply said, "If it was the last time I was to speak, I am innocent." As he was led off to the Salem jail, John looked back at Ann Putnam. She sat on the bench next to Abigail Williams, her father's hand on her shoulder. She did not lift her eyes to his.

On June second, Thomas Putnam took his wife to the court recorder, Stephen Sewall, to give sworn testimony for the upcoming Grand Jury hearing. Looking at Goody Putnam, her face white and perspiring, her hands gripping each other tightly in front of her, Sewall immediately pointed to the chair next to his table. "Please to sit down, Goody Putnam," he said. "Are you sick?"

She sat down and gripped the arms of the chair. "Not sick, Mr. Sewall," she said, "but I have had a great fright, and it does not help to be with child."

"You need not give this testimony now," he said kindly. "I can take it another day."

Her eyes widened in alarm. "Oh no, Mr. Sewall," she said. "I would speak now. I am well enough."

Her husband laid his hand on her shoulder and briefly squeezed. "I will look after her," he said. "She is most anxious to have her testimony recorded."

Once Goody Putnam had begun to talk, Sewall could hardly keep up with her. She said that the apparitions of Samuel Fuller and Lidia Wilkins had appeared to her in their winding sheets that very morning and told her that if she did not go and tell Mr. Hathorne that John Willard had murdered them, they would tear her to pieces. Then, she said, the specter of John Willard had appeared and told her that he had killed not only these two, but Goody Shaw, Fuller's second wife, Anna Elliott, Isack Nicholls, Aaron Way's child, Benjamin Fuller's child, Phillips Knight's child, and two of Ezekiel Cheevers's children, as well as her own child, Sarah, six weeks old. She said the specters of Fuller and Wilkins had told her they would appear to the magistrates if Mr. Hathorne did not believe her.

Sewall dutifully recorded her testimony. After she had sworn to it and made her mark, she seemed much relieved. She held tightly to her husband's arm as he escorted her outside. Sewall sat at his table, slowly shaking his head. What hell these witchcraft doings had wrought. He offered up yet another brief prayer of thanks to God that the Parrises had sent their little Betty to him and Margaret at the beginning of all this. After several long months, the child was no longer troubled with evil apparitions or nightmares.

Chapter 6

1692

The first official trial of one of the accused, Bridget Bishop, was held on June second. During the brief trial, Ann sat with folded hands and watched as Goodwife Bishop stood before the justices and staunchly denied the accusations that she had bewitched five girls—Ann, Abby, Mercy, Mary, and Elizabeth. Unlike Martha Corey, Bishop was not one to risk matching wits with the judges. She had been through this kind of thing before. Beginning with her examination in April, her strategy had simply been to repeat that she was not a witch, that she had no commerce with the Devil, that she did not hurt the girls and had never laid eyes on them before she saw them in court. Her straightforward strategy was not successful. She was found Guilty of witchcraft and sentenced to death. On June eighth, Justice Stoughton, on behalf of the Court of Oyer and Terminer that had been convened by the governor, issued a warrant for her execution, and on the tenth, she was taken from the Salem jail to what came to be known as Procter's Ledge and hanged, the first of the accused witches to be executed.

Ann and Abby met in their secret clearing on the Sabbath after the hanging. Ann had felt a new disquiet among the people in the meetinghouse that morning. Neighbors who before had clustered around her and her mother, eager to hear what they might say and to help if they fell into fits, were now keeping their distance and turning their eyes away. Ann herself had been deeply unnerved by the events of the hanging. The hideous spectacle of Bridget Bishop's body jerking and twisting at the end of the rope as her tongue was thrust out of her mouth and her face turned purple was enough to give her nightmares, even without the enormous sense of guilt she suddenly felt. Being exhibited at the front of the crowd of spectators as the perpetrator of this grisly sight made her disturbance worse. What had begun a few months earlier as an exciting though dangerous game had spun completely beyond control. She was determined to convince Abby that they had to do something about it, and she wasted no time when they met in the clearing.

"Abby," she said, gripping her friend's shoulders, "the witchcraft doings have got too far beyond us now. It is a horrible thing. We are killing people. *Killing* them. We must find a way to stop this before it gets worse."

Abby regarded her with a look of infinite patience. "Aye, it is terrible," she said, "but that is not a reason to stop. Bridget Bishop deserved to die. She was a witch. Everyone had known it these ten years since she was last accused. We were just the instruments of God's providence in ridding the village—the world—of her, a woman who did the Devil's bidding."

Ann gazed at her in disbelief. "You sound like my father," she said.

"Aye," said Abby, "I have been thinking on your father. I have been thinking that there is truth in what he says. Both my Uncle Parris and Reverend Lawson say that Satan makes war on New England in order to destroy God's kingdom among his people here. It is wicked people who serve the Devil and would destroy us. I think the witchcraft trials are part of God's plan to root out the wicked people and take them from this earth." She lifted Ann's hands from her shoulders and held them. "Ann, why should we not be the chosen instruments of God to search out these people? He must choose someone. Why not us? As your father says, the people we accuse are evil. Us calling them out for witches is just the way God has chosen for them to be punished."

"But this is not putting people in the jail or having them whipped. This is death, Abby." Ann grasped her friend's hands harder and looked into her eyes. "We are sending people to death with lies. It is murder. It is a fearsome thing."

Abby nodded slowly. "Yes, it is a fearsome thing," she said, "but it is not murder if it is done in God's service. Would your father be sending these people to their deaths if he thought it was murder? I cannot think it. He knows it is a righteous thing. He has told you that it is upon us to see it through." She looked into Ann's eyes with an intensity that was like Thomas Putnam's. "I believe him, Ann," she said. "The witchcraft doings are not ours anymore. They are God's. It is a fearsome thing, and we must see it through."

Although these words were very similar to her father's, hearing them from Abby's mouth made them sound different to Ann. Instead of commands to do her father's bidding, she heard a challenge to do God's. She felt a wave of relief at the thought that what they were doing might not be the grave sins of lying and murder, but the work of the Lord after all. "Perhaps you are right, Abby," she said slowly.

"I know I am right," said Abby. "Think of the good we are doing in the fight against Satan. More than any of the men who listen to us and do our bidding, God's bidding. We must keep on, Ann. It is what we have been chosen for."

Ann did not offer any more arguments. She knew she would have many doubts when she was alone, but when she was in Abby's presence, she could never resist her for long. Abby and her father could be right. Why should they not be the chosen instruments as well as anyone else?

At Governor Phips's request, just five days after the execution, the leading ministers of the colony produced a report on the witchcraft proceedings. It warned against several practices of the court that would not pass legal scrutiny. They included the presumption of guilt in the magistrates' method of questioning, the use of the touch test, and above all, the use of spectral evidence, especially the claims of witnesses to be afflicted by the accused person's specter in the court itself. The report, called "The Return of Several Ministers," had no effect on the practices of the court, but, when it was read from pulpits throughout the colony, it undermined the people's trust in the trials, which had already been shaken by the hanging.

In Salem, some events in the courtroom were threatening to undermine the public trust further. At the trial of Sarah Good on June twenty-eighth, Abby was roused suddenly from a trance, screaming that Sarah Good's specter had stabbed her in the breast, breaking the knife in the process. Judge Hathorne ordered her body to be examined by two women sitting among the spectators. They found a cut on the girl's chest and took part of a knife blade from her bodice, holding it up for all to see.

"Bring me the blade," said Hathorne to the marshal. As he examined it, a young man stood up and said that he had broken his knife just the day before, in Abigail's presence, and that he had thrown away the broken blade.

Hathorne regarded the young man grimly. "Do you have the knife?" he asked.

"I have it here," he said, and brought it up to the bench. With the knife in hand, the judges could not help but put it together with the broken piece to see if they matched. They did.

Judge Hathorne looked sternly at the youth. "Young man," he said, "I do not know what tricks you are up to, but I warn you not to play with this court. The child was clearly afflicted. You can see how she suffers even now." Abby leaned forward on her bench, her arms crossed tightly over a makeshift bandage on her chest, a grimace of pain on her face. "What have you to say?"

The youth was flustered. "I do not know," he said. "It happened as I said. I make no attempt to deceive anyone."

"Leave the court now," said Hathorne. "I admonish you solemnly to be truthful if you ever address this court again." The trial went on, but the proceedings, and Abigail Williams, had been undermined in the eyes of the public.

After the Guilty verdict was delivered that afternoon, Chief Justice Stoughton, the lieutenant governor, beckoned to Samuel Parris, who had been sitting with the spectators. "A word, Mr. Parris," he said, then pivoted and walked to a dark corner of the room, Parris following. As the people were filing out of the meetinghouse, Stoughton's voice was low, but his long thin face was red, and the intensity of his anger was unmistakable.

"Mr. Parris. I have heard of the antics your niece has gotten up to in the magistrate's examinations, and I tell you now, I will not have such things here. Such lies undermine the credibility of these proceedings and the dignity of the court. I have passed over it today in the interest of our greater cause. The conviction of these first defendants is paramount if we are to root out the Devil's minions and turn back his assault on God's Kingdom here. But I tell you now I will not tolerate it. If Abigail Williams disrupts these proceedings again, she will be barred from the court."

Parris lowered his head and spoke humbly. "I understand, Mr. Stoughton," he said. "I will do my best to convey this to her, but she is a headstrong and wayward child. It may be necessary to send her away from this place as I did my daughter."

"Do what is necessary," said Stoughton. "We have many other witnesses."

In the ministry house, Parris summoned Abigail to his study and questioned her relentlessly about the incident in court. "Were you lying, Abigail?" he demanded. "If you were, you must confess and face punishment. If you do not confess, your eternal punishment will be far more horrific than anything I can administer to you here."

For the first time, Abby was afraid of her uncle. She had always been able to manipulate him, and for the most part to avoid physical punishment by pretending meek submission to his harangues. But this time, he seemed not only beyond her control, but beyond his own. He was afraid, she realized suddenly, afraid of Mr. Stoughton and the court. He was desperate to govern her.

Abby dropped to her knees and gripped her hands together in supplication. "I am sorry, Uncle," she cried, "I do confess it. It was wrong. It was wrong to lie. I only wanted to make sure that evil witch Sarah Good is taken from this world. I meant to help the court, not to harm it. I truly meant no harm to you, Uncle, you who have taken me in and given me everything I have. I would never hurt you."

Parris was somewhat mollified by what seemed to be heartfelt remorse in the child. "I believe you, Abigail," he said solemnly, "and I forgive you. But you must understand that this can never happen again. And you must never again disrupt the proceedings of the court. Mr. Stoughton is far stricter in his control of the proceedings than the Salem magistrates were. You will be barred if you disrupt them again, and I have told Justice Stoughton that I would send you away if I can no longer answer for your behavior in court."

Abby bowed her head and said humbly, "I understand, Uncle, and will strive to do better." She took her beating for lying, a considerably less severe one than it would have been an hour before, and prayed with her uncle for the Lord's forgiveness.

The next day was the Rebecca Nurse trial, the biggest test of the court's legitimacy that it had yet faced. Unlike Bridget Bishop and Sarah Good, Rebecca Nurse was a church member, a respected member of the community, and the beloved mother of a large and prosperous family. A strong campaign had been mounted in her defense, with petitions, depositions, and testimony by many influential members of the community. There were nine Putnams who had signed petitions for her, and Lieutenant Nathaniel and Captain John Putnam, the family's elders, had testified in her defense.

The jury's verdict was Not Guilty. While it was not unusual for someone to be acquitted in a trial for witchcraft, in the Salem Village proceedings, it was a shock to participants and audience alike. The magistrates had routinely imprisoned those they questioned in the preliminary examinations, including Rebecca

Nurse, and bound them over for trial. The verdicts of the previous trials had never been in question. The justices were as surprised by this outcome as the spectators were.

As soon as the verdict was announced, Abby fell to the floor, clutching her belly and shrieking. In two minutes, all the afflicted girls and women who were in the court began screaming, falling to the floor and rolling around, and setting up a clamor the likes of which not even this meetinghouse had ever heard. Justice Stoughton called a recess, and the justices conferred about what to do next while they waited for the racket to die down. When they reconvened, Justice Stoughton requested that the jury reconsider its verdict, reminding it that Goodwife Nurse had referred to a confessed witch, Goodwife Hobbs, as 'of our company.' The jury retired to discuss the verdict while the crowd remained, loudly discussing and debating the proceedings among themselves.

Amid the din in the meetinghouse, jury foreman Thomas Fisk returned to ask Rebecca what she had meant by the remark 'of our company,' but she stood silently looking down at the floor, apparently refusing to answer. The jury deliberated again, and this time brought back a revised verdict of Guilty. A bewildered Rebecca Nurse was taken back to the jail.

After her family explained to her what had happened, Rebecca appealed to the court and the jury, stating that, 'Upon my saying that Goodwife Hobbs and her daughter were of our company, I intended no otherways than as they were prisoners with us, and therefore did then and yet do judge them not legal evidence against their fellow prisoners.' In the courtroom, she stated, she had not had the opportunity to explain, 'I being something hard of hearing, and full of grief, none informing me how the court took up my words.' The appeal had no effect, but once again the credibility of the court had been undermined when the judges had coerced the jury into issuing the Guilty verdict they wanted.

Moving with the crowd after Rebecca's trial, Abby and Ann slipped behind the meetinghouse for a private talk, which was rare these days. Abby told Ann what had happened at the ministry house. Ann thought her friend was in exceedingly good spirits, considering that she had suffered a beating and was under threat to be sent off somewhere. "Ann," said Abby, her green eyes dancing as they used to, "I have a plan that will help the court and get me back into Stoughton's good graces."

Ann had learned to be skeptical when Abby was in this state. "What is it, Abby?" she asked.

"I have heard my uncle talking to your father about the other ministers. There is a paper written by Reverend Mr. Cotton Mather that many ministers have signed criticizing the court and the judges. I think it is the real reason for the state my uncle is in. 'Tis being read in many churches so the people know about it. It attacks the very idea that the witches send out their specters to come and hurt us and says our evidence should not be used in court."

"This is a fearsome thing," said Ann. "Cotton Mather is a great man."

Abby nodded agreement. "It would be too much for us to attack one of the Mathers, I know, but my uncle says Reverend Willard in Boston has been preaching sermons against us and saying that the Devil may appear in an innocent person's shape, so that seeing someone's specter is not evidence that the person is a witch. I shall call out Reverend Willard. If he is dragged into court and put in jail, it will put the fear of God into the other ministers and likely silence them."

Ann shook her head, warning, "'Tis a great risk, Abby. I would not call out such a minister, especially not now when the people question the court. It is one thing to attack George Burroughs. Many think him a Baptist or another kind of heretic, and he has a bad reputation in other ways, but Reverend Willard is a greatly respected man."

"But do you not see, Ann? This paper shows it is the ministers who make the people question us. They are in every town and village reading it from the pulpits. We must call out the ministers.

They are our enemy now. Our best chance is to make them fear us before it goes any further."

"'Tis a great risk, Abby," Ann insisted. "They have a great deal of power, the ministers. What if the judges fear them and turn on us?"

"The judges are already fighting the ministers. You see how they ignore their complaints and listen to us as before. I think they will welcome the chance to bring them into court."

As they heard the last of the crowd leaving the meetinghouse area, they had to cut their conversation short and join their families. Ann wished she had had more time to try to convince Abby not to attack Reverend Willard, but she knew there really was no use when she was in this state.

The next day, the trial of Elizabeth How had lengthy testimony from witnesses other than the girls, mostly long stories about Goody How bewitching various horses, oxen and cows. In the middle of one of these tales, Abby suddenly jumped up and fell to the floor, screaming and writhing. She called out several times, "I know you hate this court! But you are a minister of God, Samuel Willard! I have done nothing to you! Do not torment me!"

When Abby had subsided, and seemingly fallen into a trance, William Stoughton said to the bailiff, "Take away this child. She is mistaken and probably distracted. We cannot have this disruption of the court." Ann watched dumbfounded as the bailiff unceremoniously picked Abby up off the floor, slung her over his shoulder, and walked out of the room. From the bench, Stoughton looked meaningfully at Parris as he followed them out.

Samuel Parris could move decisively when it suited his purpose. He forbade his niece to leave the ministry house and yard except for church services. He wrote to a kinsman who was bringing up a family of small children in Providence, telling him that Abigail was old enough now and trained to be of use in his household if he wanted her. Assuming the general news of the witchcraft outbreak had gotten to Providence, he wrote that he hoped to get the girl away from the Devil's business that was now plaguing Salem Village, but he did not go into details.

Parris was able to send the letter by way of a church member who was sailing for Providence the next week, and he received a timely reply in which Abby's cousin said his wife was much in need of help, and it being very difficult to find a good maid to live with them, they would welcome Abigail whenever she could come. Parris arranged for Abigail's passage on a ship that was sailing a week later. In a month's time, it was done.

When her father spoke of Parris's plan to send Abigail away, Ann feared that she would not have the chance to really talk with her again. But on the Sabbath before she was to leave, Abby flashed their old signal to meet in the little clearing after the noon meal was finished. Ann saw that Reverend and Mrs. Parris were deeply occupied with church members during this break between services and would not be bothering themselves with Abigail. As soon as her family had eaten their meal and packed up the remains, Ann slipped away without telling anyone, not giving her parents the chance to forbid or delay her. In the clearing, she found Abby sitting on the big log the way she always did. She jumped up and ran toward Ann, and they threw their arms around each other, Ann bursting into tears.

After a few minutes, they sat together on the log, Abby's left hand gripping Ann's right one. Abby looked at Ann's usually pale face, now red and blotchy with weeping, and gave a little smile. "Pray do not cry for me, Ann. It will do neither of us any good. I am leaving this place, and I mean to make the best of it. I hear that Providence is a fine place, and not nearly so strict as it is here. And it will be a relief to be out from under my uncle's thumb and out of the ministry house with its everlasting prayers and church services. I am sick of the witchcraft doings. I look forward to some good fun and sport and laughter where I am going."

"But Abby," said Ann, "I will miss you so. Who will I talk to? How will I manage the witchcraft doings and the court and my father without you?"

"You have never taken advantage of the witch doings," said Abby. "You must make use of them. Yes, your father has taken them over, but that does not mean you can do nothing. I made a mistake going for the minister. You saw that clear. But you have more sense than I do, and you can control this thing. You can have more power than the ministers or the courts if you do the right things. And remember, you can use your power over your father himself if he becomes more than you can bear. The court will believe you. I am sure of it."

"Oh Abby," Ann said, "I could never attack my father and destroy my family. You have not grown up with your family, so you do not have the feeling for it. I think it will be all I have after I lose you."

"'Tis well," said Abby, "suit yourself. What more can we do? I certainly aim to suit myself from this time out."

It was the last conversation the two girls had. They never saw each other again. Since both were illiterate, there was no way for them to communicate. Abby, who had set the wheels in motion, left the witchcraft outbreak behind her, but for Ann and Mary and the others, it was far from over.

Most of those accused in June Ann did not know either by name or by sight. The web of witchcraft suspects had long since spread beyond Salem Village. Many were people from Salem and Boston and neighboring villages whom the men of the Putnam family considered to be of evil intent, having designs on their land or having injured them in the past. Some were public figures who, from the Putnam point of view, sought to deliver the whole colony into the Devil's hands. One observer described the 'afflicted girls' who appeared at John Alden's examination on June second as 'wenches who played their juggling tricks, falling down, crying out, and staring in people's faces,' and complained that one of them pointed to the wrong man until the man standing beside her told her which one was Alden. It was true. Ann could not have identified any of the accused that day if her father had not been there to tell her who was who. The net was cast even wider in the middle of July, after Abby had been barred from the courtroom.

Ann missed her friend terribly. She had lost the one person she could talk freely with and count upon to understand her. She had also lost the guiding hand of the witchcraft doings. With Abby gone, what had begun as exciting play and miraculously tolerated rebellion had turned into yet another grim part of Ann's life that was in her father's iron grip. She felt she had been brought to heel once more. Mercy Lewis was gone as well, sent to work for John Putnam Jr. when she showed too much of an independent streak in her accusations. Ann saw her only when they came to court. Ann's cousin, Mary, was still in the house, but she was so much older that she seemed like another adult. More and more, Mary conferred with her father and uncle rather than with Ann, who was told who to accuse next.

On the fourteenth of July, Ann and Mary were called to nearby Andover to help identify the witches who were apparently afflicting a woman named Elizabeth Bullard. When they entered her house, they observed her in the grip of a fit and identified the specters who were tormenting her, with names Thomas Putnam had supplied. This opened the floodgates in Andover, with accusations, examinations, and confessions coming so fast that even the execution of Rebecca Nurse on July nineteenth did not stay long in the public mind. In Andover, seeing that it was people who refused to confess who were executed, those accused quickly confessed and began naming others. The Andover outbreak became a self-perpetuating machine, with far more people named in August, September and October there than were ever named in Salem Village.

At John Willard's official trial on August fourth, the depositions of Ann and her mother figured greatly, but new ones were also sworn against him. They ranged from accusations that he had beaten his wife to Samuel Wilkins's testimony that he had seen a black hat following him after being knocked off his horse into the river and had later seen Willard in a black hat. At the trial of Reverend George Burroughs the next day, there were four separate indictments for afflicting Ann, Mary, Mercy and Elizabeth. Their testimony accused Burroughs of murdering his first two wives and others, tormenting the girls and tempting them to write in his book, and performing unnatural feats of strength.

On August nineteenth, George Burroughs and John Willard were executed along with John Proctor and two others. Because the execution of a minister for witchcraft was a momentous event, an even larger crowd than usual was present and several ministers, including the renowned Cotton Mather, were there to witness and sanction it. To a person, the condemned protested their innocence. They asked Mather to pray with them, and he complied. They forgave their accusers and refrained from attacking the judges and juries. They prayed earnestly for pardon of their sins and for their ultimate redemption. One spectator wrote that they seemed to be 'very sincere, upright, and sensible of their circumstances on all accounts, especially Proctor and Willard, whose whole management of themselves, from the jail to the gallows, and whilst at the gallows, was very affecting and melting to the hearts of some considerable spectators.'

As he was about to be hanged, Reverend Burroughs said a prayer that moved many in the crowd to tears, pointedly ending it with a flawless recital of the Lord's Prayer, an implied rebuke to the court's use of this folk test to condemn many of the accused, including John Willard, to death. So restive did the crowd become in response to Burroughs's words that Cotton Mather mounted a horse to address them, reminding them that the Devil has often been transformed into an Angel of Light. The crowd calmed down enough for the executions to continue, but powerful seeds of doubt were sown that day.

On September twenty-second, the last eight hangings of accused witches took place, including that of Martha Corey. Martha had been excommunicated by general consent of the Salem Village congregation on September eleventh. Three days later, Reverend Parris, along with the deacons and a witness, went to speak with her in prison. Parris wrote in the church book that they found her 'very obdurate justifying herself' and condemning the witch trials. After a little discourse, 'for her imperiousness would not suffer much,' and prayer, 'which she was willing to decline,' Parris pronounced the sentence of excommunication, her damnation seemingly sealed eternally.

Part Two

Joseph Green

1697–1700

Chapter 7

1697

At noontide on a Saturday, Joseph Green had good reason to offer a little prayer of thanks as he rode out of Roxbury toward the Wenham road. He had dismissed the boys a little early and taken some bread and cheese to eat on the way. It was a glorious October day. The sun shone brightly in an impossibly blue sky and the most beautiful of fall colors—from the pale yellow of the birches to the flaming red orange of the sugar maples—surrounded him. If Eden had anything better to look at, he reflected, he would be surprised.

As he thought of what he had to look forward to in the next two days, a broad smile transformed Joseph's regular features and lit his warm hazel eyes. First, and always, there was Elizabeth. The thought of her laughter, her wit, her radiant goodness vied with the more insistent vision of her, to him, perfect face. "Oh, I am smitten," he said out loud, laughing. "I am love's fool, and what is more, I care not."

Joseph had fallen in love with Elizabeth the first night he met her. His minister had had a small supper for her father, Reverend Gerrish, when he had preached for them at Roxbury, and Joseph had set himself to conversing with the minister's daughter. At first, she had seemed just a demure young maiden. She was not beautiful in the current poetic fashion of golden hair, blue eyes like limpid pools, and cherry lips. She had a pleasant face. Her nose was straight and a little long. Her complexion was not lilies and roses, but a healthy pink with freckles that bespoke hours working in her family's kitchen garden. Her light brown, almost golden eyes were her best feature. Far from limpid pools, they were bright, attentive, and humorous. Her brown hair kept escaping from underneath her cap in pretty little curls that she tucked back in absentmindedly without breaking stride in her conversation.

It was the conversation that had first captured Joseph. Elizabeth had a quicker wit than any young lady he had ever conversed with, and they had laughed together throughout the evening. It was then that her eyes lit up, and her lips, though perhaps more pink than cherry red, parted to reveal pretty white teeth. But she was not a trifling or superficial girl. She was adept at discussing serious subjects. Joseph suspected that, between her reading and listening to her father, she had accumulated more knowledge of the scriptures and their learned commentary than he had in his years of rather haphazard study at Harvard. But when he talked, the warmth of her eyes enveloped him and she listened to him as he felt no one had ever listened before.

By the end of the evening, he had known he was hers. The miracle was that Elizabeth returned his love. A proper and modest young lady she was, both in their all-too-rare meetings and in her letters, but things had passed between them. When they met, and they both took every opportunity to meet, she never failed to give him a special look or a little touch on the arm, and once, by returning his ardent hand clasp, had shown him what she felt.

It was Joseph's most fervent wish that he could ask Elizabeth to marry him. But although Reverend Gerrish encouraged their courtship, he had made it clear that Joseph had to be more settled in his life before he would give him his daughter. Joseph had indeed come far in the last year from the sort of schoolmaster-by-default he had become after taking his Harvard degree. He had done well with the Roxbury Grammar School he had inherited from an ineffectual predecessor. The town credited him with restoring the school's excellent reputation by correcting the lax discipline and creating an eagerness for learning among the boys. He had worked hard, but mainly on instinct. Having been converted from an idle and undisciplined boy himself, by a gifted schoolmaster and a devoted college tutor, he had ideas about what methods worked with boys and what did not. Physical punishment was a last resort. He got much better results with attention, praise, and kindness.

Above all, in the last year, Joseph had found his faith. Although he was even now just twenty-one years of age, he felt that his conversion had been a long time coming. As he rode along, he blushed to think of the disobedience and unruliness of his boyhood and his failure to profit from the advice and prayers of his kind and religious parents. At Harvard, he'd been worse. How stupid he had been not to make better use of that precious time and how thankless for the great gift that he, the eighth son of a tailor, had been given when the friends of his deceased brother, Percy, a far better scholar than he, had gotten up a subscription to pay his tuition.

Joseph knew he did not have a deep or subtle intelligence, but the Lord had gifted him with a knack for Latin, Hebrew, and Greek, and a very good memory that had carried him far. Mathematics had been the one area where he worked diligently. His interest was more in navigation and astronomy than in theology and biblical studies. Although his patrons were paying his tuition to prepare him for the ministry, his secret hope had been to follow his brother, Edward, as a naval officer and become captain of a ship someday. Looking back, Joseph recognized that in his early college years, he had spent more time fowling and fishing, and, he had to admit, dancing, gambling and drinking, than he had spent on his lessons. Beyond the obvious violations of proscriptions against dancing and gambling and drunkenness, it was a sinful waste of time and of the gifts he had been given to neglect his mind that way.

Joseph thanked the Lord for the hundredth time for providing him with William Brattle as a tutor. During his wayward years, Mr. Brattle had been insistent but patient, keeping him up to the mark in his work, encouraging his interest in mathematics.

Then came the darkest event of his young life, the fever that had consumed the entire summer of his seventeenth year. The time of the fever was a blur to him now, a seemingly never-ending cycle of burning up and deathly cold, of terrible pain that wracked his bones and made his head feel like it would burst. His stomach had swollen up, and he had not been able to eat. They told him it had lasted for weeks. If it had not been for the constant care of his mother and his sister, Bethya, he knew he would have died. And when the fever had passed, he'd felt half dead. His strong, muscular frame was gone, and he lay wasted and gaunt, mostly too exhausted to move. It had taken all his mother's skill to bring him back, starting with beef tea and broth, and slowly adding foods until his body was able to digest them again.

His brain never did recover fully. His memory was broken. He had forgotten huge swaths of knowledge that he thought had been committed to memory forever. It had seemed impossible for him to relearn it or to learn anything new. Shaken to the core, he had gone to Mr. Brattle and asked him what to do. After quizzing him on the knowledge he would need to go into the next term, his tutor had realized that the situation was grave. He looked at him frankly.

"I must tell you, Joseph, that you have an enormous task before you. There are great holes in your knowledge. You seem to have forgotten many rules of grammar as well as your Latin and Greek vocabulary, and many mathematical principles as well. I can think of nothing for it but to go back to the beginning with each lesson and see if you can learn again what you do not remember. I hope that your memory can be stimulated in this way and it will come back to you."

Joseph sat before him in disbelief. He was still exhausted and weak. The ten-minute walk from his mother's house to Mr. Brattle's rooms had tired him out. His brain felt like mush. And now he was being asked to learn everything all over again. "I cannot do it," he said. "I shall have to leave the college."

William Brattle put his hand on Joseph's arm and looked at him with sympathy. "I know it seems impossible to you now, Joseph, but your education is not something to abandon lightly. You have come this far, and you have just a few terms to go. Let us try. I promise you that I will do all I can to help you with the work, and there is every hope that your memory will return."

Mr. Brattle had been true to his word. They'd begun that very day. Joseph found he was able to learn things over again with great effort, and during the next few months, much of what he had known slowly came back to him. He cut all the vices and distractions from his life. With his tutor's help, he learned to concentrate all his power on the task before him and keep at it when it did not come quickly or easily. It was the hardest thing he had ever done. Looking back, he counted it as the time when he had grown from a boy to a man. In that sense, the fever had been a providence. He did not know where the path he had been on before would have led him, but he was certain it would have been astray. In the end, he and Mr. Brattle counted it a great accomplishment that he'd earned his degree, even though he had finished twentieth in a class of twenty-two.

Although Joseph had matured immensely in his last two years at Harvard, it was not until he had been teaching for a year that his conversion came. He credited Reverend Walter, his pastor in Roxbury, and Elizabeth's father, Reverend Gerrish, for that. They had spoken seriously to him about the state of his soul and lent him the books that opened his eyes to the grace of God. He would be eternally grateful to Cotton Mather for writing his book upon the Lord's Supper, which made him feel that he was called to share in this community, and to Mr. Walter for urging him forward and reminding him of the Prodigal Son when he doubted his worthiness to become a full church member.

Joseph had been going to church services every Sabbath since he was a small child, but it was these men who had opened to him a world of prayer and of feeling blessed rather than guilt-ridden when he awoke each morning. He had felt inadequate and unworthy when Mr. Walter had first invited him to preach a sermon in Roxbury. Eloquence with words was never his gift. He knew he was no Cotton Mather. But when he had forced himself to do it, he had felt the same kind of connection with the congregation that he felt with his boys in the classroom. These were people in need of someone to explain the scriptures and to help them find their way to God, and he could do that in plain and heartfelt language.

After preaching thirty sermons at Roxbury, Joseph had hopes, even in his humility as a returned prodigal and poor scholar, of someday becoming a minister with his own congregation to shepherd, and of helping them find their way to God as he had. Reverend Gerrish had written that he might be able to assist him. A glorious day indeed.

The light was waning when Joseph reached the ministry house in Wenham. When Elizabeth appeared immediately on the doorstep with her hand raised in greeting, he knew she had been watching for him. “Good day, Mr. Green!” she called as he dismounted. “We have been expecting you. Did you have a good journey?”

“A fine journey,” he called with a little bow and a large smile, “with a perfect end.”

Mr. Gerrish’s servant came and saw to the horse. Elizabeth led Joseph to the parlor where her mother sat sewing. “Mr. Green is here, Mother,” she said quietly.

Anna Gerrish looked at the two young people in front of her, trying so hard to appear modest and decorous but almost bursting with joy in each other. Her daughter stood demurely, her hands clasped in front of her, but her sparkling eyes and irrepressible smile said everything. Joseph Green stood before her with a modest, respectful attitude, a young man of healthy, pleasing appearance and medium height, not remarkable if one did not see the eager warmth in his hazel eyes. He bowed and said, “I am very happy to see you, Mrs. Gerrish.”

She smiled. “And I you, Mr. Green. You must be tired and thirsty after your long ride. Please to sit down, and I will organize some refreshment for you.” Before Elizabeth could offer to do it for her, she was up and out of the room, leaving the two of them together.

Elizabeth offered Joseph a chair, and he turned, smiling into her eyes, as they sat next to each other. “Your mother is kind to give us these minutes to ourselves,” he said.

“Yes, Mother is very kind,” she said, returning his look. “I am very glad to see you.”

They sat enjoying the moment they had both been dreaming of for days and days. “Father has good news, I think,” she said. “He is eager to talk to you.”

He nodded. “Yes, he was most eager to have me come today. Of course, I am overwhelmed by the invitation to preach here tomorrow. I am delighted that he has such confidence in me. But he also said he had something particular to talk about tomorrow.” He spoke softly. “Do you think it concerns our hopes?”

She blushed and dropped her eyes. “I think it may,” she whispered. And then she looked up at him. “I pray that it does.” She flushed redder.

Mrs. Gerrish bustled into the room with a tray holding a mug of cider and a slice of bread and butter. “Here is a little something for you, Mr. Green, until our supper is ready. Mr. Gerrish is meeting with some of the congregation, but he will be here soon. I will leave Elizabeth to entertain you until he comes.”

Although it would look like mere idleness to an observer, Joseph and Elizabeth made the best of the half hour until Mr. Gerrish arrived. They talked more openly of their hopes for the future than they ever had, and he took her hand and held it in his. Whatever else happened, Joseph thought, this trip had been more than worth the effort. After a cheerful supper with the family, he retired with Mr. Gerrish to his study for a brief consultation about the next day’s service before he fell into a comfortable bed in the boys’ bedchamber and enjoyed sweet dreams of his beloved.

Joseph awoke before the light, thinking about the day to come and the first sermon he was to deliver outside of Roxbury. As well prepared as he was, he anxiously went over the points in his mind. It was a sermon he had delivered before, on one of his favorite texts—Isaiah 55:7, 'Let the wicked forsake his ways, and the unrighteous his own imaginations, and return unto the Lord, and he will have mercy upon him, and to our God, for he is very ready to forgive.' Both Reverend Walter and the Roxbury congregation had commended his sermon. Fighting a familiar feeling of unworthiness, he told himself that if the people in Roxbury had found his words useful and inspiring, then there must be some in Wenham who could profit by them, too. For Joseph, the sermon was a message from the heart, inspired by his own experience. He knew the joy that came from forgiveness and the hope that followed.

Joseph rose and washed himself thoroughly to prepare for the Lord's Day, then broke his fast with Reverend and Mrs. Gerrish before the children came clattering down the stairs. Just before he was to leave for the meetinghouse, Elizabeth appeared, looking lovely with her pink cheeks and the little curls escaping from beneath her freshly laundered cap. "I look forward to your sermon, Mr. Green," she said. "I know you will give us something to think about."

As he preached, Joseph tried to engage his listeners as he did his pupils and the now familiar members of the Roxbury congregation, but he knew he looked more often at Elizabeth's encouraging face than at any other in the congregation. Afterward, a number of them came up to thank him and to say that he had given them a great deal to think about. Reverend Gerrish shook his hand, smiling warmly. "A fine sermon, Mr. Green," he said. "You are not one for the fancy words, but you have a genuine connection with your hearers."

"Thank you, Mr. Gerrish," he said. "I am working to improve. I have only recently been able to buy some books with a bequest my brother Edward, the Captain of the *Eagle*, gave me to the purpose."

After the family dinner, a simpler meal than usual between the two Sunday services, Mr. Gerrish invited Joseph into his study. "I would like to talk with you before you set off for home," he said, "if you can spare an hour."

"Of course," said Joseph. "It would be my great pleasure."

When they were settled in the study's two comfortable chairs, Mr. Gerrish got right to the point. "Mr. Green," he said, "I think you know that my wife and I look favorably upon your courtship of our daughter, Elizabeth. You are a young man of virtue, and of great promise, I think."

"I shall strive to be worthy of your good opinion, sir," Joseph said quietly, though his heart leapt.

"Now, what I would like to discuss with you today concerns your prospects. After hearing you in the pulpit today, I think I can join with Mr. Walter and Mr. Brattle and others I know who think you will make a fine minister one day." Joseph was surprised, wondering who these others might be. Could he really be the subject of discussion among New England's clergy?

Mr. Gerrish looked at him appraisingly. "Would you be interested in hearing about a possibility that you might be suited for?"

"Yes, sir. Most certainly."

"I do not know if you are aware that Salem Village has been without a minister for more than a year."

Salem Village. Joseph was stunned. Who did not know of the crazy doings there? The witchcraft trials in 1692, with the pastor's involvement, and then the village's interminable wrangling afterward. "Yes, I have heard of it," said Joseph.

"The congregation has been searching, I think zealously and in good faith, for a minister since Reverend Parris resigned in July last year. I myself have been with them twice to participate in Days of Humiliation to seek God's help in finding a minister, but as yet, they have not been successful."

Joseph nodded. "I have heard that several ministers refused them. Two of them I know from the college, Mr. Pemberton and Mr. Emerson."

"Yes, and others as well, including Reverend Hale's son, Robert, and Simon Bradstreet, and James Bayley, who was the first minister there. He has been preaching there sometimes, and they were hoping to call him again, but he refused."

He spoke frankly to the young man across from him. "I will not suggest that this congregation does not present deep cause for concern. The witchcraft trials in 1692, which you no doubt know about, deepened, and I think sprang from grave divisions in the village and the congregation which have existed for a long time. They are still there. And anyone who takes on the ministry will have to address them if he is to succeed in bringing the people together as a congregation in fellowship with Christ."

He took in Joseph's apprehension and smiled. "Now, there is some good news here as well. I can tell you the people there are getting fairly desperate for a minister, and they are in a conciliatory mood. I think the time is right for a straightforward and plainspoken young man who eschews guile and subterfuge of the kind they have been used to these many years, to come to these people and bring them together with God and with each other. I will not pretend that this is not an enormous challenge, but if you think you can rise to it, I would be pleased to recommend you."

This was not at all what Joseph had expected when Reverend Gerrish had said he had an opportunity for him. He was thinking of a junior ministry, perhaps at Wenham itself, or a lower office in one of the bigger churches. A pulpit of his own was beyond his imagining. "You overwhelm me, Mr. Gerrish," he said. "I am not yet twenty-two years old, and my education is sadly lacking for the ministry, as I had not felt the call until after I took my degree. I am trying to remedy that, but at my best, I will by no means be the kind of scholar that Robert Hale and Ebenezer Pemberton are."

"I understand that," said Gerrish, "and it is why I wanted to hear you preach before I recommended you. After hearing you, I am satisfied that you can do much to bring this congregation back to the path of fellowship. And you have a great deal of energy and a way with you that inspires respect. Mr. Walter has told me what you have done to restore the good order of the Roxbury Grammar School."

"But with respect, sir, there is a great deal of difference between a group of unruly boys and a congregation of adults who are engaged in constant quarrels and contention."

Gerrish smiled at him, his blue eyes bright in his genial, round face. "Not as much as you might think, Joseph," he said. "When you have been at this as long as I, you will see that there is not that much difference between the boy and the man."

Joseph smiled back and nodded. "I take your meaning, sir, but would I not seem just a boy myself to most of them, and hardly fit for the spiritual authority of pastor?"

"That is up to you, I think. If you are ready to become a pastor, you must be ready to serve as shepherd to your flock. That means pointing out to them where their path lies and when they stray from it."

"Of course, you are right, Mr. Gerrish. I am just a bit dazed. It is quite a daunting task you lay before me. Can you tell me any more about these people? I have heard about the enmity that lay beneath the witchcraft outbreak. You know, Mr. Thomas Brattle, who wrote the well-known letter about it, is my Harvard tutor's brother, and one of my own patrons. But I have never understood the local underpinnings of it. Being so close to Salem Village, you must know more of this."

Gerrish sat back in his chair and slowly shook his head. Joseph thought he even rolled his eyes a bit. "I am afraid it would take much longer than the hour we have to tell what I know about contention in Salem Village," he said, "but I will try to give you the salient facts."

He looked down, thought a moment, and then began. "Generally speaking, the most important family in Salem Village, in both church and village affairs, is the Putnams. Edward Putnam is a church deacon and his brother, Thomas, is the village clerk. The Village Committee seems always to be full of Putnams, and any delegation I have seen from the place always has one or two. Thomas Putnam was a close friend and ally to Reverend Parris, and a chief figure in the witchcraft trials. His daughter, Ann, accused many people, and she is generally accounted as a leader of the 'afflicted girls.' Thomas served as recorder for many of the proceedings, as well as taking depositions, many from his wife and daughter, and filing complaints along with other Putnams."

He stopped to think for a moment. "As far as the minister is concerned, I would say that Edward and Thomas Putnam are the most powerful people in the church, but they are not necessarily the most powerful in the village. One of the feuds in the place is within this family itself. They have a half-brother, Joseph, who inherited the largest share of their father's estate, which would traditionally have gone to Thomas, the eldest son. And young Joseph is now one of the wealthiest men in Salem Village. Thomas and Edward were staunch supporters of Parris and, of course, the witchcraft trials. Joseph and his in-laws were opposed. They did much to resist the trials, and they were working to rid the village of Parris until he finally resigned last July."

Joseph had been following this closely. He nodded. "I see, I think. This main Putnam faction was allied with Parris and controlled the church, which supported the witchcraft prosecutions, while Joseph and his allies were opposed."

"In a nutshell, yes."

"Is this the main division in the village, a family feud? Joseph and his brethren?"

Gerrish smiled. "It is *one* of the main divisions. Another important one has to do with the Topsfield land. Salem Village was originally part of Salem Town. As the town grew and became crowded with people, it was felt necessary to open up some more land to farming, so land grants were made to a number of men, Governor Endecott among them, who would agree to clear and farm the land. Topsfield was doing a similar thing. It seems that fifty years ago, when the farmland was being granted by the towns, both Salem and Topsfield gave title to the same lands up north, near the Ipswich River. The farmers who were granted the land were old John Putnam, the patriarch of the clan, and the Towne family. The families are still fighting over it in court, I believe, and there has been violent conflict in the past, with each of them seizing land from the other. Thomas Putnam is central to that fight over the land, which had grave consequences for the witchcraft trials."

"So," said Joseph, "this is where things get complicated."

"That is one word for it," said Gerrish. "The Towne family included three sisters, Mary Esty, Sarah Cloyce, and Rebecca Nurse, all of whom were accused of witchcraft by Thomas's daughter, and two were executed. That profoundly deepened the enmity between these two families. The group who formally dissented within the Salem Village church and eventually succeeded in ousting Samuel Parris was led by Samuel Nurse, the son of Rebecca, John Tarbell, her son-in-law, and Peter Cloyce, the husband of Sarah. They now tend to form an alliance with Joseph Putnam and his in-laws, the Porters, occasionally succeeding in taking over from the Thomas Putnam faction on the Village Committee."

Joseph had listened with growing apprehension. He shook his head. "This seems insurmountable," he said. "How could such people ever meet in loving fellowship at the Lord's Supper?"

Reverend Gerrish gave him a kindly look. "I am painting its starkest outlines so you can see where the divisions come from, but I do not think the situation is hopeless, or I would not suggest that you think about taking it on. These people have had a hellish time these last five years. I meant it when I said they were desperate for a minister. I believe they are coming to realize they must find a way to live and worship together. They are farmers and tied to the land. Many of the families have cleared the land and built up their farms over three generations. Unless they are willing to sell out and start again in Maine or somewhere equally wild, they are not going anywhere."

He leaned forward. "These people started and built up the church. They built the meetinghouse with their own hands, together. What they need is a person of good will and strength of character who will speak to them in plain terms of the covenant they have sworn and their obligation to restore their fellowship in Christ. And it would not hurt if that person was a modest and congenial young man who is skillful in working with people rather than an arrogant prig who thought and behaved as if he were superior to these farmers while he wrung every last shilling that he could out of them for his salary." He glanced at Joseph. "Not that I am referring to anyone in particular, of course."

Joseph laughed. "I get your drift. And I assure you that, as the eighth son of a tailor, I have no pretensions to being superior to yeoman farmers."

Reverend Gerrish nodded his approval. "I am not suggesting that you should make any kind of commitment to these people now," he said, "but at a word from me, I think they would be very happy to invite you to preach, and then you could see where it leads."

Joseph was feeling more confident. His curiosity about the place and the challenge it represented were overcoming his hesitation. "I see no reason why I would not wish to preach there," he said. "These people certainly need the word of God more than many others."

"Indeed," said Gerrish, smiling. "I will write to Deacon Putnam. But I do warn you to be cautious. As I said, I think they will be eager to covenant with you. If you do it, make sure you have conditions that let you out of it if they begin to draw you into their feuds. You should perhaps insist that they maintain good fellowship with each other as well as with you. And be wary of allying yourself with one side or the other. I have only given you the broad outlines of the feuds among them. They are a very fractious people, always in the courts over one thing or another. Once the good will of fellowship is lost, that is what happens."

He looked at Joseph more earnestly than he had yet. "Try to be aware of the rifts among them so that you do not get caught up on one side," he said. "Your greatest task will be to change this habit of mind, this resentment and selfishness and suspicion, and to replace it with neighborliness and kindness and fellowship. Believe me, it will not be easy. I have struggled to do it myself these many years, and my flock is still by no means a model congregation, but if you can establish an ideal of Christian charity and a willingness to try for it, that will go far."

After a little more advice, Gerrish sent Joseph on his way so he could prepare for the afternoon service. "I cannot adequately express my gratitude for your help, Mr. Gerrish," said Joseph as he rose from his chair. "I will do my best to be worthy of your confidence."

"I cannot ask more, Joseph," Gerrish said, then smiled. "I think you may want to stop and have a word with Betty before you take to the road. She may be quite eager to hear what we have spoken about."

"Yes, I think so, sir," Joseph returned with a smile. "I shall do my best to satisfy her curiosity."

Elizabeth was at the parlor door by the time Joseph had reached the bottom of the stairs. "Come in," she said, "and do not keep me in suspense. What did my father say?" Her upturned face with its flushed cheeks and shining eyes was more eloquent than her words.

The bounds of polite address could not contain Joseph's excitement. "Elizabeth," he said, "he has given me such hope. He is to recommend me for my own ministry. He looks most kindly on our future hopes. And he called me Joseph." He laughed.

"Oh, Joseph!" She said his Christian name for the first time. "It is wonderful! But where is the church? Is it far away from Wenham?"

"Not far at all." He smiled. "Salem Village."

"Salem Village!" Her eyes widened. "It is very close to here, certainly, and that is good, but Joseph, Salem Village!"

"Yes, I know," he said. "It is a fearsome prospect, but still, it is a great chance for me. I am, after all, no prize-winning student or preacher. Your father thinks I did well today, though, and he thinks I have something of what they need there; a good dose of simple, plainspoken truth, I take it. It will be a great challenge."

He stopped and took her hands in his, letting his excitement show. "But Elizabeth, a chance for us!" he said. "I never expected we would have the prospect of marrying so soon."

She blushed at hearing her dearest hope spoken aloud. "Oh, if it could only happen! But Joseph, you must be careful. That place has destroyed much older and more worldly-wise men than you. And from what my father says, there have been several who have refused it this last year. I could not bear to see you preyed upon by vicious people."

He looked at her seriously. "Believe me, Elizabeth, I plan to go into this lion's den with my eyes open. I will consult several men who know about the witchcraft trials and can advise me, beginning with my old tutor, Mr. Brattle. He will tell me plainly if he thinks it is something I cannot manage. And if they do want me to come, I will make no agreements until I am thoroughly acquainted with the people, and I will make it absolutely clear that I will not tolerate their feuds and squabbles." He smiled at her. "It is not a dull place, at least," he said.

"No, it is not known for dullness," she said, returning his smile.

"And after all, I have not been offered a thing yet. First, they must hear me preach and decide they can put up with my sermons."

"They will," she said. "I have not the least doubt."

Chapter 8

1697

It was such a dark November morning that the boys in Joseph Green's class could hardly see to do their lessons by the paltry light from the window. In the afternoon, as it darkened even more, he did some grammar drills and heard some recitations, but there was no use in going on with the rest of the work he had planned, so he dismissed them a little early, with instructions to con their lessons well for tomorrow. As he sat at his desk working up the next day's lessons by candlelight, he was startled by the door opening. He looked up and saw two unfamiliar men entering the room. Peering at them in the dimness, he said, "Good afternoon to you. Can I be of help?"

As they came forward, Joseph made out two sturdy figures clad in the best broadcloth of a yeoman farmer. When they stepped into the circle of light from the candle, he decided that one of them, with his open, rugged face and rather heavy tread, was most certainly a farmer. The other was built on a less physical model. He was older, perhaps in his middle forties, and he was thinner, graver in countenance, and more reserved in manner. It was he who spoke. "Good afternoon," he said. "You are Mr. Green, I hope?"

"I am, sir, at your service," he said amiably.

"We come to you from Salem Village with an invitation," he said. "Might we speak with you?"

“Of course,” said Joseph, and he quickly got up and moved a bench over in front of the desk. “Please to sit down. I am sorry I have no refreshment to offer. You must have had quite a long ride from Salem Village.”

“Thank you, Mr. Green. This is quite comfortable,” the man said as he settled onto the bench. “We took some refreshment at the tavern nearby. When we saw the boys running by the window, we hoped we would find you free.”

“Yes, I let them go a little early today. It is so dark they could hardly see their lessons.” Joseph gave them a welcoming look. “But fortunately, it does leave me free to speak with you.”

“Let me introduce myself. I am Edward Putnam, Deacon of the Church of Salem Village. This is my cousin, Jonathan Putnam. We are here at the behest of the village to invite you to preach in our meetinghouse next Sabbath.”

Joseph gave a little bow. “I am honored by the invitation, sir. May I ask how it came about?”

“Of course, Mr. Green. Reverend Gerrish, our esteemed neighbor in Wenham, wrote to me and led me to understand that you might accept such an invitation. Some of us had heard from Reverend Walter and others what fine sermons you have been preaching here in Roxbury, and we would very much like to hear you. As I think you know, we have been without a minister for more than a year, and we are anxious for our pulpit to be filled. The congregation discussed the matter at a church meeting yesterday and voted to send us to invite you.”

Jonathan Putnam had been looking on impassively, but now he looked directly at Joseph, who saw a glint of amusement in his eyes. “We thought that if we could have a look at you, and you could have a look at us, perhaps we might learn if we want to see more of each other,” he said.

Aware of Edward shifting uneasily on the bench, Joseph smiled graciously and said, “I think that is an excellent plan, Mr. Putnam. I should very much like to come to Salem Village.”

After a little more discussion of the details of his visit, Edward Putnam said, "I pray you to excuse us now, sir. We are going on to Boston and hope to arrive there before it is completely dark."

"Yes, of course," said Joseph. "It is not a pleasant day for travel, certainly. I wish you a safe journey." He ushered them to the door. After it had closed behind them, he dropped onto a bench. *So it begins*, he thought. They had treated him like a real minister. He was happy that he had spent the money that fall for a good black coat so he might look the part, in dress if not in years, when he went to preach. He took some time pondering which sermon he should preach. There were several that had been commended at Roxbury, and of these, he thought about which text would most apply in Salem Village. He settled on Matthew 18:20, 'For where two or three are gathered together in my Name, there am I in the midst of them.' He would make no doubt from the beginning that if they chose him, they were choosing fellowship.

Sunday the fourteenth proved a bright and unseasonably warm day for November, so the meetinghouse was not excessively cold. To Joseph, it looked very small, the main room probably less than a thousand square feet, with little galleries projecting above it at either side. Although the windows were tiny, and some were boarded up because the glass had broken, they did admit some sunlight, which also streamed through the open doors. Joseph was certain that this had helped the congregation to be in a receptive and hopeful mood, and they seemed open to his message.

That night, Joseph was the guest of Jonathan Putnam, a most genial and generous host, not much older than Joseph was. His wife Elizabeth made her guest feel at home with the family from the moment he arrived, and she laid on a bountiful supper. In their company, Joseph felt completely at ease for the first time that day, and he began to think he could find congenial company in Salem Village. They all were surprised when a group of twenty or so men came to the door, led by Deacon Putnam. "Jonathan," he said, "can you spare us a few minutes to talk with Mr. Green?"

When the men had all filed into the large keeping room, the deacon said, "Please to pardon our intrusion, Elizabeth. So many members of the congregation came up to me after the service that I felt it was best to hold an impromptu meeting, and the consensus was so enthusiastic that we decided to come together to speak a word to Mr. Green." He turned to Joseph. "In brief, we felt that we have profited much from your sermon, and we very much hope that you will come again next Sunday and preach to us."

Joseph was overwhelmed. He could feel that he was blushing. "I am humbled by your kind invitation," he said. "I am very happy that you think my poor efforts have been of use, and of course I would be delighted to return next week." As he listened to introductions, he could see Edward take Jonathan aside. Mr. Gerrish seemed to be right. These people did indeed seem to be ready to move forward with good will, and they were a little desperate. But of course, he could not tell if he was seeing more than one side of the various feuds and factions. Certainly, there were a lot of Putnams here.

Should anyone not have seen the point in his first text, for his second sermon, Joseph chose Romans 12:5, 'So we being many are one body in Christ, and everyone one another's members.' He had not preached on this text before, and he had some late nights that week preparing his sermon, but he thought it was important to lay down just what ideals of fellowship he would bring to them. He was nervous as he rode to Salem Village the following Sabbath, but if any church members were put off after hearing the sermon, they kept their thoughts to themselves, or at least out of Joseph's hearing. The response was just as positive as the first week's, and he met more members of the congregation.

Joseph was once more invited to return, and that week, he learned that a majority of the men of Salem Village had voted to invite him to come and be their minister. He knew this was a legal formality and that what really mattered was the decision of the covenanted members of the congregation, but he was greatly heartened by this show of support from the people. The next week, after his sermon, the congregation voted overwhelmingly to invite him to assume the ministry.

Joseph had resolved that he would seek Reverend Gerrish's advice and also that of his old tutor, Mr. Brattle, before he would make any written agreement. He expressed his deep gratitude for the people's confidence in him and for the fellowship he had already experienced among them and told them he would give them their answer within the month.

It was a very busy month. On December fifth, the first Sabbath, he went to Wenham to share all the news with Elizabeth and to seek Mr. Gerrish's advice. The Gerrishes were very pleased to hear of the reception he had received. Mr. Gerrish said that, as long as he went into the situation with his eyes open, he saw no reason why Joseph should refuse, but cautioned him to get a written agreement about the ministry house and the salary, and any other details, such as the amount of firewood to be supplied, that might cause contention in the future, for there had been a great deal of wrangling over these things with Mr. Parris.

When they were alone, Elizabeth peppered him with questions about the people and the village, questions it would not have occurred to him to ask. He promised to be more aware of people in the future.

"I wish I could have you there to watch and observe," he said. "I know you would be far keener about the situation than I am."

"You must try to take in all you can before you are in the midst of things," she said. "I am most eager to hear about the people."

On the following Sabbath, Joseph had agreed to preach at Roxbury, and after the service, he acquainted Reverend Walter with the state of things. "Of course, I was expecting something like this, Joseph," he said. "You have made a mark with your preaching here that people have noticed. But I was hoping I might have you with me a little longer. Salem Village is not where I would send you if it were in my power, but I believe you can do much good there. You are right to bring the people's attention to Christian fellowship. If you can get them to take their duty in this to heart, it will go far to mend this broken congregation and village. Most of them are not bad people. They were caught up, as were many in this colony, in a great delusion of Satan five years ago. It made them fear and, it seems, hate each other. But I think you can show them that Satan has been banished and there is a way to God if they will try to love one another as Christians."

"I hope so, sir," he said. "It is certainly a worthy task. Someone must take it on, and if that someone appears to be me, I will humbly do my best."

Finally, after preaching once more at Salem Village on the nineteenth, he went to Cambridge to speak to his old tutor, William Brattle, now the Pastor of the Cambridge church, and laid out the situation and all his hopes and fears about it. He told him frankly that he was not sure he was capable of taking on such a responsibility.

"I know you suffer from self-doubt, Joseph," Mr. Brattle said, "but think of what you have overcome already. I remember well the condition you were in after that fever three years ago. You could hardly remember the English alphabet, let alone Latin and Greek, but you were undaunted. You rose in the morning and gave your best effort every day, and you regained the bulk of your intellectual power and earned your degree."

"With great help from you, sir. I could not have done that on my own."

"And you will have help with this great task as well. I will be happy to advise you at any time, and I hear that the neighboring ministers are all praying to see a healthy congregation in Salem Village. They will help when you need them. As you will not be able to administer the sacrament yourself until you are ordained, I suggest that you make sure you are able to go to another congregation periodically to participate in the Lord's Supper with them. This will help to keep in mind the greater fellowship as well as giving you spiritual renewal."

Joseph felt at peace with his decision when he left Mr. Brattle. He rode back to Roxbury, convinced that Salem Village was his future path. When Deacon Putnam and a delegation came to call him to the ministry formally, he agreed to come to the village on January fifth, but he first presented several carefully thought-out written conditions. The first and most important was that the members would continue in loving fellowship as a congregation, and if they began to quarrel and contend with each other, he would consider himself free from any obligation to stay with them. The second was that he was to be free once every month or two until he was ordained to go to another congregation in order to participate in the Lord's Supper. Finally, he was to have the ministry house and land for as long as he continued among them, with a salary of sixty pounds the first year, rising to seventy pounds if he stayed longer, as well as some land of his own if he were to be ordained and settle there.

When the village had readily agreed to his terms, he took his leave from Roxbury Grammar School, a sad occasion for him. He had been very happy there, and he had a keen sense that he was breaking his ties with the security and goodwill he had built up over the past year in the town as well as with the boys he had grown fond of. It was only the great promise of what lay ahead of him, his keenly longed-for marriage to Elizabeth and the great challenge of the ministry he was eager to meet, that made him joyful to see this day.

Joseph's brother-in-law, Zachariah, who was the chief carpenter at Harvard College, helped with his move from Roxbury in January, inspected the ministry house from top to bottom, and stayed with him the first night. After he had departed for Cambridge, Joseph slowly walked through the house, bigger than any he had ever lived in, including his parents' house, where he was one of fourteen children.

At the bottom was a good-sized cellar, empty, but ready for the storage of cider and vegetables. On the first floor, there was the large keeping room, with its enormous fireplace for cooking and heating. Some generous church members had given him a table and two benches for it. Across the hall was the parlor, looking cavernous without a stick of furniture. Upstairs were two chambers almost as large, one of which was the minister's study. It held his prized collection of sixteen books, bought with a legacy from his brother Edward, the small table he used as a desk, and the chair that Zachariah and his sister Ruth had given him. Still, it looked empty.

The other chamber held Joseph's clothes and a few other belongings. He planned to use it as a bedchamber when the weather got warmer, but for now, he would just spread his bedding out before the keeping room hearth. Fortunately, he need not worry about housekeeping yet, as he was to take his meals at Deacon Ingersoll's tavern, just down the road. As he walked through the house, he wondered how he would ever fill it. He imagined it full of children and activity and, especially, Elizabeth. "God willing," he prayed, "may it be so." He felt less alone as he thought of Elizabeth, at that very moment less than five miles away on the Wenham road. He could visit her every week and draw hope and sustenance from her presence. They could decipher the puzzle of Salem Village together.

Over the next few months, Joseph applied himself diligently to his ministry, especially his sermons. He was able to revisit many of the texts on which he had preached in Roxbury, but his consistent theme was peace and love and fellowship. Knowing that Elizabeth would be expecting his account each week, he observed his congregation closely and thought about the significance of their interactions. First, he had to sort out the various Putnams who made up half of the covenanted congregation. He was most familiar with Deacon Edward, who he knew, as the brother of Thomas, had had a substantial role in the witch trials. Edward was a rather silent man with a reserve that was difficult to penetrate, but he seemed very conscientious in carrying out his duties, and cooperative in working with the minister.

Jonathan Putnam, who was not too much older than Joseph and had a similar disposition, he came quickly to consider a friend. He was a straightforward fellow to whom good fellowship and fun came naturally, and they enjoyed the same things. Joseph was hard put to keep from laughing at church council meetings when he glanced at Jonathan's raised eyebrows and lively brown eyes, twinkling in amusement while one of his pompous cousins droned on and on about the wise expenditure of a shilling. Joseph loved the cold winter mornings when they went out fowling together, and his wife always invited him to dine with them and enjoy the results.

Jonathan's father, Captain John, the commander of the local militia, was another matter. A brusque and mostly silent man, Captain John and his brother, Nathaniel, held sway as the current patriarchs of the whole Putnam clan. Although Captain John was the de facto leader of the village, Nathaniel was much more interested in church matters than his brother and would often come to the minister's house on a Monday to take Joseph to task for some of the points he had made in Sunday's sermon. Joseph treated him with the deference due his age and tried to use Nathaniel as a bellwether to tell him how his flock was responding to his message.

Then there was Thomas Putnam. Thomas was a lieutenant in the militia, and Joseph had remarked his air of command during the drills he regularly took part in. He had also been keenly aware of him from the beginning as a central figure in the witch trials. Joseph understood that the strong sway Thomas had held over village affairs had diminished since 1692. He was still the village clerk, a position with power over village affairs out of keeping with its modest salary. He was privy to every official document, every vote of every committee, every financial dealing of the village. Joseph had the sense that he had always used the knowledge effectively to serve his interests, but in recent years, his close association with Samuel Parris had worked to his detriment as the village's attempts to rid itself of its former minister had dragged on and on.

Thomas's social status had also declined. As the eldest son, Thomas had expected to inherit the farm and the largest portion of the estate of his father, who had been the wealthiest man in the village. When the family farm went to his younger half-brother, Joseph, Thomas was left with the smaller farm his father had already given him, a thing he deeply resented. From what Joseph could gather, Thomas was not much of a farmer. He occupied himself with church and village affairs, leaving most of the farming to hired men and his young sons. His bad management had come to a low point a year or so before this, when he had been forced to sell a tract of land, including his fine home, to move to a smaller house built of used lumber on a more remote part of his farm. It was a most visible failure.

Joseph could tell that Thomas was a proud man, indeed a vain man. What other man of Salem Village carried a silver-headed walking stick to the meetinghouse? He usually spoke with an air of authority in meetings. But he was sometimes taken up short, as though he were realizing anew that he was no longer the eldest son of the richest man in town, but a middling farmer who had to watch his shillings and pence. At times, Joseph would see his lean face set in hard lines and his dark eyes fairly smolder. He was a man who felt himself much abused.

Thomas Putnam had a large family who always made a conspicuous presence in the meetinghouse on a Sabbath. At Elizabeth's urging, Joseph took careful notice of Ann, the eldest, and her mother, who had been central figures in the witch trials. While Thomas and most of the children were tall and lean and dark, Ann and her mother had light, almost colorless, blonde hair visible at the edges of their white caps, and, with their pale faces and very light blue eyes, they appeared fragile, nearly transparent. Ann was a few years younger than Joseph, perhaps sixteen or seventeen. She was slight and short in stature. He had only spoken to her in the company of her parents, when she always behaved as a demure and deferential young maiden. It was hard to imagine this frail-looking creature sending people to their deaths, a powerful reminder of the mystery of God's world and the need to be vigilant against the Devil's wiles.

On the other side of the witchcraft divide, there were several who had been accused and finally released from prison, as well as the families of those who had been executed. Joseph was learning more about the accused by the week. They ranged from Daniel Andrew, an uncle by marriage of Joseph Putnam and one of the wealthiest men of the town, to poor Dorothy Good, daughter of a laborer and recipient of the church's charity. Apparently, Dorothy had been accused as a small child and kept for months in the unspeakable conditions of the Salem and Boston jails, sometimes in chains. She had come out a damaged child and even now, at the age of nine or ten, was a dirty, disheveled, wild little girl who resisted all the well-meant attempts by the village women to take her in hand.

The most powerful of the 'anti-Putnam' group were the members of the Nurse and Towne clan, who had lost two of the three Towne sisters, Rebecca Nurse and Mary Esty—by all accounts, good and virtuous women and much beloved wives and mothers—to the witch trials. The church members Reverend Parris had described in the church book as 'the dissenters' mostly consisted of members of this family, led by Rebecca's son, the prosperous farmer, Samuel Nurse. They had worked tirelessly against the Putnam majority to rid the village of Parris and had finally succeeded.

Joseph knew that, with the anti-Putnam group, he was here on trial. They were watching closely to see if he would become a tool of the Thomas Putnam faction, as they thought Parris was. He was determined not to be this, and not to appear to be so. He made a point of spending time with the Nurse and Cloyce families, who were covenanted church members, and he found in Samuel a reasonable and intelligent man whom he could talk to about church matters, but he never broached the subject of the witch trials with him.

With Joseph Putnam, now the richest of the family, and his Porter relatives, Joseph had little to do. Most of them were members of the Salem Town congregation, and, although they came to his meetinghouse occasionally because it was convenient—and, he thought, to take the measure of the new minister—they did not figure in church matters. They were important in village matters, though, as the Village Committee tended to swing back and forth between this group and the group around Thomas and Captain John Putnam.

It was a complex web, to be sure, especially for a young man who had always been convivial and friendly to all, perhaps to a fault. His way had been to avoid conflicts among his friends and fellow students. Now, if he was to do any good in this community, even to survive here, he had to pay attention and find ways to move them from a state of truce to a true community.

Chapter 9

1698

In the winter of 1698, Joseph was able to see Elizabeth almost every week. Their deepening love brought him his greatest hope and joy. Like him, she was naturally endowed with wit and good spirits. The memory of her bubbling laughter and her warm golden eyes did much to get him through each week. She was also, he had come to see clearly, cleverer than he, and she had a greater insight into human relations. Considering her probing questions, he learned a good deal about the members of his flock and their interactions with each other. Every week, he described the incidents that he thought revealing of character, and they discussed how best to approach this one or that, although he was scrupulous about never breaking any spiritual confidence.

Joseph already thought of Elizabeth as his heart and his helpmeet, a most important part of his ministry as well as his life. He looked forward eagerly to the time when he could ask for her hand in marriage. Reverend Gerrish had made it clear to him that he did not intend to bless this union formally until he was sure of Joseph's future. Of course, that made good sense from a father's point of view. They were young to marry. Joseph had no financial resources beyond what he could earn, and Elizabeth's dowry would not be a large one. Considering Salem Village's history with ministers, he knew that Mr. Gerrish was right not to consider his position secure until he was ordained and the church and he had covenanted with each other. He could not help but be eager for this time to come, but with Mr. Gerrish's help, he tried to be realistic about the situation in the village and the church.

In June, Joseph's hopes for his union with Elizabeth were greatly lifted when the covenanted members of the church called him to a meeting at Deacon Ingersoll's tavern. There, in his presence, they took a vote on a motion that expressed their approbation of his ministry and their wish for him to continue with them permanently. This was the first step in the process that would lead to his formal ordination as pastor of the Church of Salem Village. A few weeks later, all the inhabitants of the village, church members or not, met to approve the invitation and to raise a subscription to encourage him to accept it. Joseph was delighted with this action. He would have agreed immediately, but he held himself in check, simply expressing his gratitude for the offer and his great love for the people of Salem Village.

The gift included a very much needed thirty cords of firewood, somewhat symbolic in that it was a provision that had been a matter of much acrimony in the village's negotiations with Samuel Parris. It also included some money that allowed Joseph to at last buy some furniture for the ministry house—some stools and benches, which were sadly lacking in a house where people were meant to gather, and a nice bedstead with a trundle bed. Goodman Goodale, the carpenter, gave him a knowing look that made him blush when he ordered the trundle bed, and he knew the news would make its way around the village in a day or two, but he did not care. They should know he was planning to marry soon, although it would probably result in a lessening of the many supper invitations he received from the mothers of the village maidens.

The public meeting where Joseph was to give his formal answer to the village was set for October ninth. He wrote a simple statement that placed the need for fellowship squarely at the center. "The answer I give to your invitation is this," he said. "If your love to me does continue and be duly manifested as hitherto it has been, and you do all study to be quiet and maintain peace among yourselves, then I am willing to continue with you, and in the fear of God to engage in the work of the ministry among you."

Two days before the ordination, Zachariah and Ruth brought Joseph's mother and his other sisters, Bethya and Mary, to Salem Village. It was a joyful reunion. Joseph rejoiced to have his new beds filled with his family, and what was usually an empty and rather gloomy house echoing with life. His mother and sisters wasted no time in cleaning the house from top to bottom, with many a comment on the slovenliness of bachelor housekeeping. He had to admit that he hardly recognized the place with the dust removed, the floors scrubbed, and the windows shining and admitting the sunlight.

After they had eaten a hasty dinner at noon, he drew his mother into the study and asked to speak with her seriously. He seated her in the best chair and sat down on a stool he had drawn up to it. Looking into her eyes, he said, "I want to ask your pardon, Mother, for all the trouble I have given you, and especially for the disobedience of my youth after Father died. It weighs on me that I gave such a poor return for so long to you and Father when you were always kind and loving parents who strove to teach us the way to God and righteousness."

His mother took his hands, and he saw tears in her eyes as she looked up at him. "Joseph," she said, "you never were aught but a blessing to us, though you were a young rascal. The fault is somewhat ours, I think. We may have spoiled you a bit, as you were our eleventh child and we were getting tired." She smiled through her tears. "Your father would have been very proud on this day, Joseph. You know it was his dearest wish to give a son to the church, and it was doubly hard on him when Percy died, that his ministry was cut short. When you were clever at your lessons, it was a rebirth of his hopes. He prayed every day that you would find your way to God."

Joseph found that there were tears in his own eyes now. "He often told me that. I wish I had attended more to him when I had the chance. It would have saved us all much time and trouble, and

I would have prepared myself better for this big task that I have before me."

"You will do it well, Joseph," she said. "And who knows if some of the experience you have had will not help others to find the path you have found. Sometimes I think there are ministers who are too saintly for this world. And you are hardly that, my son." She laughed. "I do not pretend to any learning, but one thing that raising children has taught me is that understanding and patience, with yourself and others, will go a long way in your search for a path to God."

"It is something I strive to imitate, Mother, although I am only beginning to understand how sorely tried your patience was."

"Joseph," she said. "As you well know, I have been mother to fourteen children, and there were but two Sabbaths when all the sixteen of us were alive and together to attend worship."

"I remember it, Mother," he said softly. "I was six years old. It is one of my earliest and most vivid memories."

She nodded and looked down for a few moments, and then she raised her head and said deliberately, "I have since lost three sons to the sea, and I pray every day, as I know you do, that our Benjamin will return safely to us. I have lost four sons to consumption, and my beloved husband and a son and a daughter to fevers. I know not where your brother Jonathan is. I only pray that he is safe. I have seen great sorrow in my life. You and my dear daughters are the comfort that God has seen fit to leave me in my old age, and I look to him and say that I am more than satisfied. I am blessed." She put her arms around her son and kissed him, a rare gesture for her, and one that Joseph felt deeply.

On the day of the ordination, the women were up with the dawn, beginning the preparation for the ordination dinner they were to serve to the church elders. As they worked throughout the early morning, women from the village arrived in a constant stream, bringing food, helping with preparations, and trading stories about the young minister with his family. Meanwhile, Joseph was at Deacon Putnam's house, where he met with the ministers from surrounding towns, convened as church elders, and was formally dismissed from the Roxbury church by Reverend Walter so he could become a member of the Salem Village church.

The little meetinghouse was full to bursting for the ordination service. Joseph was happy to see that church members had given their seats in the front benches to his family. Toward the back of the women's side, he saw Elizabeth sitting next to Mrs. Gerrish, her face fairly beaming. After Reverend Walter gave the prayer, Joseph preached on Colossians 3:15, 'Let the peace of God rule in your hearts, to the which ye are called in one body, and be ye thankful.'

Then Reverend Hale of Beverly came forward and, after asking the whole assembly if anyone objected, performed the ritual of renewing the call to Joseph to be ordained and take charge of the church. Reverend Hale spoke the words of ordination, with all the elders participating in the laying on of hands, and then Reverend Noyes of Salem gave the right hand of fellowship from the other churches to the Church of Salem Village in the person of Joseph, its new pastor. Joseph had chosen Psalm 133, 'Behold, how good and how pleasant it is for brethren to dwell together in unity,' for the congregation to sing after Reverend Peirpont gave the concluding prayer. The new pastor's voice rang out, clear and true, as he led the singing. He meant this psalm to be the keystone of his ministry. Then he gave the final blessing, and it was over.

After the ceremony, Joseph made sure that he spoke to every family in the meetinghouse before he left for the ministry house. He had been too overcome by the enormity of the occasion to think much about the ordination dinner beforehand. Now that it had come, it was everything he could have hoped for. Everyone was in a joyful mood. There were many prayers at the beginning and many toasts later on, wishing him and the church God's grace for a happy future. He was able to introduce the Gerrish family to his mother and sisters at last, and he could see that Ruth and Bethya and Mary were much taken with Elizabeth and very curious about their brother's relationship with her.

The dinner was a fine one, a real feast. Deacon Putnam had killed a lamb and other villagers had brought roasted and stewed chickens and their best vegetable dishes to go with the salted beef and pork that his family had brought, as well as all manner of pies and puddings. There was plenty of food left for the evening when the people of the village came to the ministry house to wish him well. Everyone who came was invited to supper, and as he looked around that evening at the rooms full of Putnams and Nurses and all those who had been caught between them, he felt that he had never seen Salem Village so much in harmony.

When Joseph and Elizabeth were able to steal a few moments together in a corner of the keeping room, they spent the first few of them just standing and smiling at each other. No words were needed to convey the joy they felt on that day, which was a momentous step in their quest to be together. Finally, Elizabeth said, "You are a pastor now."

Joseph laughed. "It would seem that I am," he said. "'Tis a daunting thought, but it gives me hope to see the members of the congregation here together in the ministry house."

Elizabeth looked around the room, crowded with groups of people engaged in animated conversation. "You must show me now, which are the people we have been discussing these many months. I know the deacons, but few others. Where is Jonathan Putnam?"

Joseph nodded toward a corner of the room where his friend stood in a group of men who were smiling over something that had just been said. "He is there, next to the wall, talking to his brothers, James and John, and his cousin, Benjamin."

She nodded. "He looks a very good-natured person, just as I had imagined him. And Thomas Putnam?"

"See that tall, rather grim looking man over there, looking as though he is laying down the law to the two deacons?"

"Ah, yes. Thomas Putnam in the flesh. And his wife and daughter?"

"His daughter is not here. I take it she never comes to public occasions. But her mother is there, the small, pale woman. She is talking with Jonathan's wife Elizabeth."

Elizabeth's mirthful expression was becoming more serious. "And where is Samuel Nurse?"

"He is there," said Joseph. "The big man. The smaller dark one is his brother-in-law, John Tarbell, and the others, Thomas Wilkins and Daniel Andrew."

Her brow furrowed as she looked at them, and back at Joseph. "They are the ones known as 'the dissenters,' are they not?"

"They are," said Joseph. "I am very happy to see them here today. I spent a good deal of time over the last week negotiating between Mr. Andrew and the congregation over the witch trials. I am most happy that he accepted the congregation's confession of its guilt for the treatment of him and others during those dark times and that he joined them once again in fellowship before my ordination."

Elizabeth nodded. "A very important step indeed. But Joseph, does it not strike you that the members of the congregation are not so much together in fellowship as next to each other in clumps?"

"Clumps?" Joseph looked around the room.

"Yes, clumps of Putnams and dissenters, like batter that is not sufficiently mixed."

"That is true," he said, looking a little downcast. "They are here, but they are not necessarily here together."

"Oh, Joseph," she said, "I am sorry. I did not mean to cast a shadow on this wonderful day. The important thing is that they are indeed here, and side-by-side if not together." She smiled. "We must make it our next task to break up the clumps so the batter may be smooth and wholesome."

Joseph returned her smile. "Indeed. I could not have said it better. It will be a big task for the two of us."

Then Joseph's sisters found them. "You must not be hogging Elizabeth for yourself," said Bethya, and the conversation became more general.

Later that night, to record the purpose he had set for himself, Joseph wrote in his journal that the great work before him was to bring the people of his congregation to be 'kind to one another, tender-hearted, forgiving one another, even as God for Christ's sake hath forgiven them.'

Joseph lost no time in pursuing his purpose. The first step in beginning to heal the profound breach between the accusers and the accused from the witch trials, he knew, was to complete the reuniting of the dissenters with the rest of the congregation. Although they now came to the meetinghouse on the Sabbath, a few of them still refused to receive the sacrament with those who had subjected their families to such suffering. He asked the church members to vote in favor of a statement that they were so satisfied with their brethren, Thomas Wilkins, John Tarbell and Samuel Nurse, that they were heartily desirous that they would 'join with us in all ordinances that so we might all live lovingly together.' Joseph was much relieved when everyone present lifted a hand in consent.

The difficult part was now in front of him, for he had to convince Rebecca Nurse's son and son-in-law to take the Lord's Supper with those who had been complicit in, or even directly responsible for, the suffering and death of their relatives. He communicated the contents of the resolution and the vote to all of them but was not surprised when none of them came to the first celebration of the Lord's Supper. He waited a few weeks for the idea to settle in, then he decided to approach the dissenters.

Joseph had already made friends with the Wilkins family, a large clan who lived on a number of farms in the northwest of the village, the Will's Hill area. Like him, they were avid fishermen and fowlers, and he had spent some very pleasant days with them on the river and in the woods. He rode out to Will's Hill and asked Thomas Wilkins if he had an hour or two to spend in the woods with him. Thomas was perfectly aware of what he was up to and was not at all surprised when he broached the subject as they walked home with their game bags.

"Thomas," he said, "you know the church has voted unanimously to ask you and Margaret to join in communion with us at the Lord's Supper. I truly believe it is a gesture of love and good fellowship."

Thomas looked at the ground as he walked along, his fowling piece on his shoulder. "I have been thinking much on this, Mr. Green," he said. "After all that has passed among us, it is a very hard thing to think of sitting down in fellowship to the Lord's Supper with them."

"It is," said Joseph. "I would not presume to say that I understand all that your family has suffered at the hands of some members of the church. But God calls us to something very difficult, and that is forgiveness, as he forgives us for our great sins against him through the intercession of his son Jesus Christ. This may be the most difficult thing you will ever be asked to do in the imitation of our Lord and Savior, but if you can do it, you will have done a great deed of healing for our church and our village. We will all be greatly in your debt, and you will make manifest the spirit of God among us."

"I will think on it, Mr. Green," he said. "I will talk to my wife, and we will pray on it."

Joseph put his hand on his shoulder. "Let me pray with you today," he said. "We will ask God for his guidance."

When they returned to the house, Thomas called Margaret into the parlor and explained what Mr. Green was asking. They kneeled together and prayed with him for the spirit of forgiveness and love and fellowship, and then he rose and thanked them for their hospitality. He had a good feeling as he rode home from Will's Hill that day. Thomas and Margaret Wilkins were good people with a generous spirit. He thought they would seize the opportunity to do something important for the church.

With the Nurses, Joseph had a much bigger task ahead of him. Not only was their mother the beloved matriarch of a large family, she had become the symbol of those falsely accused and executed, largely through the efforts of her sons and sons-in-law. Samuel was the eldest of those sons, and, from what Joseph had seen, was by no means ready to reach out a hand to those who had been responsible for hanging his mother. Joseph decided to talk to Samuel and John Tarbell together, after a meeting of a committee they all served on. He thought that John, who was of a milder disposition, might temper Samuel's reaction, but he did not have great hopes.

When Joseph asked Samuel and John to tarry a few minutes with him, he saw a knowing look flicker around the circle of men who were preparing to leave his study. Of course, everyone knew what was afoot. "Brother Samuel, Brother John," he said after the others had departed, "you know what I would speak about today. The church members have voted, without a single objection, to extend the hand of fellowship to you and ask that you participate with us in the Lord's Supper. I am particularly desirous of having you there. I think you know what weight your actions and opinions carry in the congregation and the village. If you were to join with us, you could do much to heal the great breach that still divides this church and this village against itself."

Samuel looked at him, his honest face showing the deep distress he felt. "I understand you, Mr. Green," he said, "and I fully appreciate your good will in trying to bring us together. But you are asking us to sit at the Lord's Supper with those who are responsible for killing our mother and destroying her good reputation forever."

Joseph looked him in the eye. "It is a great wrong," he said softly. "Forgiveness of a great wrong against us is one of the most difficult things the Gospel calls us to. 'Love your enemies; bless them that curse you; do good to them that hate you, and pray for them which hurt you, and persecute you, that ye may be the children of your father that is in Heaven.'"

Samuel's face reddened, and he looked down at the table. "The Sermon on the Mount. I struggle with it often," he said. "But to sit among these people who have neither confessed to their great crime against my mother nor suffered its consequences and to feel fellowship with them, that I cannot do."

John turned a troubled face to Joseph. "You must help us, Mr. Green," he said, "if we are to find a way to forgiveness. It is very hard to think that God would allow for this great wrong, where all of the suffering has been ours, and then to lay the burden of forgiveness on our shoulders, too. Are those who have afflicted us to suffer nothing? Are we to offer them our hands as if naught had come between us?"

"It is a most difficult question," Joseph said frankly, "and one I have thought and prayed about very hard. I cannot say I have the answer for you. I am not Cotton Mather. I am no theologian. I do not have the kind of mind to decipher the word of God so as to explain all that we have to suffer on this earth. I can only say that God calls us to do this. And he has laid this great burden on you and your family for his own reasons in his great wisdom. It is my duty as your minister to urge you to it, and to tell you I am confident of your joy in Christ once you have fulfilled what he has demanded of you."

When they had prayed together, the two men departed, still deeply troubled. Joseph was much less sure of his ground than he had allowed himself to appear. He could not have said why so much was asked of these poor people who had suffered so much when those who had inflicted the suffering, although perhaps under the Devil's deception, seemed to have paid so little. He wished he were able to explain the theology better and felt frustrated at being such an inadequate instrument to do the work of the Lord for his people. As he prayed fervently over the next few days for guidance in this first difficult challenge of his ministry, a plan slowly formed in his mind.

When the day for the February celebration of the Lord's Supper came, Joseph was delighted to see Thomas and Margaret

Wilkins, John and Mary Tarbell, and Samuel Nurse's wife Mary among the communicants. That Samuel Nurse was not there he was not surprised, but it was heartening to have seen him in the congregation that day. He decided to move ahead with his plan.

Over the next two weeks, whenever Joseph saw members of the Village Committee, he made sure to talk with them about the committee for reseating the meetinghouse. It was important, he said, for there to be representation on the committee from all parts of the village, which they easily understood to mean both factions. They generally agreed with him, for the Village Committee was trying in its way to heal the breach, just as he was. When the seating committee was named, it included two members from each side—Samuel Nurse, John Tarbell, Jonathan Putnam, and Deacon Edward Putnam—and Joseph Green.

When the committee met, Joseph was more assertive than usual, beginning the meeting by expressing the hope that the seating in the meetinghouse could help to advance the renewed fellowship that was being felt in the church. The principles for seating the meetinghouse were already set, to a point. Age was the first criterion. On the men's side, the eldest among them, whether the patriarch of a powerful family, like Bray Wilkins, or an impoverished old man who could hardly keep body and soul together in the winter, like George Buckley, sat on the first bench.

The second criterion was status in the church and village. Seats on the front benches went to the minister's and deacons' families, the magistrates, constables, members of the Village Committee, and the officers in the militia. Those remaining were ordered primarily by the taxes they paid to the village—in other words, in order of wealth. On the women's side, the order was similar. The servants and the children sat up in the galleries. There was room to manipulate within these categories, and in the last six years, that flexibility had been used to keep the members of the two factions apart. When they came to this point in the process, Joseph proposed to use it to bring them together.

"I know this is a very hard thing for you to hear," he said. "I have spoken to several of you in this room about it already, and I know the deep disquiet it brings to your souls to think back on those horrifying events six years ago. I know that you have preserved the peace between neighbors by staying aloof from one another and keeping to the divisions that were set in that dark time, but I ask you today to try to step beyond those divisions, to reach across that deep gulf between you and accept one another as brothers and sisters in Christ. If the village and the congregation are to have a future, we must all strive to achieve true harmony in Christian fellowship. We must be able to sit together and hear God's word as one people. I ask you to take the first step now."

Joseph indicated the next bench on the seating chart and turned to his friend, Jonathan Putnam. "This is where you have been sitting, Brother Jonathan," he said. "Who would you have with you?"

Jonathan nodded. He knew exactly what was being asked of him. "I suggest my brother, James, and Thomas Wilkins," he said evenly. "We pay similar rates."

Joseph gave him a grateful look. "Are there objections?" he asked. When all were silent, he turned to John Tarbell. "And you, Brother John?"

"I will sit with Nathaniel Putnam's son, John," he said. "We are near neighbors."

Joseph nodded. "Thank you," he said. With his heart in his mouth, Joseph turned to Samuel Nurse. "Brother Samuel," he asked quietly, "who will you join in fellowship?"

Samuel grasped the edge of the table. His open, honest face grew red, and Joseph could see his jaw working as he glared down at the table. *It is too soon*, he thought. *I have moved too fast*.

"I will sit with Thomas Putnam," Samuel said.

The effect was palpable. Everyone in the room felt that a momentous thing had been said, and they acknowledged it with silence. "God bless you, Brother Samuel," said Joseph simply, and they went on with the seating. They did the same thing on the women's side, with Samuel's wife placed next to Ann Putnam Senior and Sarah Houlton, who had also accused Rebecca. The mother of accuser Mary Walcott was placed next to Rebecca Nurse's daughter, and so on, until the whole meetinghouse was seated.

As the meeting drew to an end, a stillness came over the room. Looking around the table at the men gathered there, honest farmers and neighbors who had struggled to do what they believed to be right despite the great burden it brought to them and their families, Joseph felt the weight of that day's proceedings. Deacon Putnam turned to him and said, "Perhaps you would offer a prayer, Mr. Green."

It was not customary for Joseph to pray after a village committee meeting, but he saw that it was the fitting thing at that moment. The men around the table, Nurse and Tarbell and Putnam, kneeled and listened with bowed heads to his prayer of thanks to God for helping them find a way forward toward fellowship. Then they rose and joined him in singing his beloved Psalm 133, 'Behold, how good and how pleasant it is for brethren to dwell together in unity.' The men were solemn as they filed out of the room, the sense of that day's importance permeating the air. The last to go was Joseph's friend Jonathan, whose lips noiselessly formed the words 'well done' as he passed with a nod. Joseph fervently hoped so.

The new seating was posted, and if there was a rebellion, it was a silent one, for Joseph never heard of it. On the next Sabbath, he was anxious as he walked the short distance from the ministry house to the meetinghouse. He had stepped out of the house just at the time the service should begin so he would not be engaged in superficial conversations along the way, and when he stood at the door of the meetinghouse, he looked at the backs of the people of Salem Village all sitting quietly on their benches, together.

Joseph steeled himself to walk slowly up the aisle and take his place in the pulpit. From there, he looked out over his congregation. Before him was the concrete image of his dream for the church. Putnam and Nurse, Walcott and Tarbell, accusers and victims; they all sat next to each other in stillness. The room was not a large one and Joseph could easily see the anger smoldering in Thomas Putnam's dark eyes as he sat next to the stolid Samuel Nurse, the instinctive shrinking from each other of Mary Nurse and Ann Putnam Senior as they kept their eyes straight ahead and held their babies on opposite sides of their bodies, John Putnam's set look and tightly folded arms as he sat next to a rigid John Tarbell. There would be much to tell Elizabeth about this day.

Joseph smiled a little to himself as he took up his sermon, thinking there was not a great deal of Christian love on display in his church at the moment. But the village had done its part. Now it was his turn. He looked slowly around the room and then he read out the text for his sermon, Colossians 3:14–15, 'And above all these things put on love, which is the bond of perfectness. And let the peace of God rule in your hearts, to the which ye are called in one body, and be ye thankful.'

Chapter 10

1699

In December of 1698, Joseph formally asked Reverend Gerrish for his daughter's hand in marriage. The negotiations did not take long. Mr. Gerrish was not wealthy, but he made Elizabeth as generous a dowry as he could. Joseph would have married her joyfully with none at all. There was never any doubt of Elizabeth's response. She and Joseph spent an entire afternoon in the Gerrish parlor simply marveling at their good fortune in finding each other and in having their future secured. It was the last quiet afternoon they spent together. The marriage was planned for March, which gave less than three months for the preparations. Anna Gerrish was determined that the young couple would begin housekeeping with everything they needed and that her daughter would have the appropriate clothing for a minister's wife. This meant a constant bustle of sewing, quilting, and knitting by herself and her daughters.

It seemed that every week, Elizabeth had something new to show Joseph—a quilt that she and her sisters had made together, a beautiful pillow cover embroidered by her mother, a new jacket or skirt that she had just finished. He knew there were other garments that he was not being shown, but he did his best not to dwell on them. The Gerrishes also saw to it that the young couple would have the kitchen supplies they needed. The ministry house had the basic pot and kettle and roasting spit, but cups and plates and knives and spoons were lacking, as well as wooden things like a bread trough and kneading board. Some of these things had to be ordered from the tray maker well in advance, and Mrs. Gerrish wanted everything to be there when they started housekeeping.

All this activity spurred Joseph to make needed repairs to the ministry house and to make it a fit place for his bride. With help from two of the village men who had requested that they pay their tax for the minister's salary in labor, he whitewashed the inside of the house, which had become quite dingy with soot. When they were finished, it had lost its gloomy air, and seemed ready for the young couple to begin a new life there. Joseph consulted with Elizabeth and Mrs. Gerrish about the furniture they thought necessary for a functioning household and made some careful investments. He was very heartened to see how many of the villagers came with their congratulations when they heard of his engagement and brought a gift, which was usually something they had noticed the ministry house was sorely lacking. The closer the day came, the more excited Joseph felt about the home that he and Elizabeth would make there.

March sixteenth proved to be a beautiful, clear day, with a hint of spring in the air. When he looked back on it afterward, Joseph could not remember a single thing he had thought about on the ride to the Gerrish house. It was all one ecstatic blur. His sister, Bethya, told him he had grinned like an idiot the whole time he stood waiting for Elizabeth to take her place by his side. He remembered Reverend Hubbard addressing some words of wisdom to them about their future state, but for the life of him, he could not remember what they were. The marriage vows he did remember, and Elizabeth's lovely low voice reciting them. Then all was a happy blur again, with Gerrishes and Greens congratulating them and wishing them well, and a delightful dinner with prayers and toasts and cake.

At last, they were alone together, in a small upstairs room of the Gerrish home that had been cleared out and made into a bedchamber for them. Both were virgins, and Joseph was very glad he had managed to resist the temptations of his student days.

As he had reflected on his upcoming marriage, he had had to admit that the thought of keeping his body chaste and pure for his future bride had been the last thing on his mind in college. His chastity was owed to the public whipping and heavy fine that were the legal penalties for fornication, along with the fear of a pregnancy and the constant reminders to the students at Harvard that public exposure of such sins would destroy any hope of a ministerial career before it began.

Regardless of the cause, the wonder of that first night was something Joseph would remember vividly to his dying day. They were a bit clumsy and fumbling the first time they made love, but there was no doubt of the great joy they felt in each other. As well as he thought he knew Elizabeth, he had never imagined anything like this intimacy, this closeness. "I hope you are not hurt," he whispered. "I am sorry it was over so quickly."

"Do not worry, my love," she said in his ear, "a small hurt. And we have a lifetime to devote to achieving perfection."

They stayed with the Gerrishes for a month, a little respite before they moved into the responsibility of the ministry house. During this time, Joseph felt they were coming close to achieving perfection. Elizabeth was an ever-unfolding delight to him. Each day and night brought the promise of something new to be learned about each other and about themselves together. With the welcome release of pressure from church duties other than preaching, and with the regular rhythms of family life, he began to feel peaceful and content in a way that he had never felt.

At the end of the month, they had moved all their new belongings into the ministry house and it was time to bid the Gerrishes farewell and bring his bride to Salem Village. Joseph could sense a little sadness in Elizabeth along with the excitement of coming to a house of their own and building their life together. "Do not worry," he said, "it is not far. We will see your family often."

"I know," she said, looking into his eyes with her open smile. "'Tis time we made our own home."

Within a week of his bringing Elizabeth to Salem Village, Joseph hardly recognized the ministry house. With its fresh coat of whitewash and the thorough cleaning the village women had given it, the house seemed fresh and new, needing only Elizabeth's touch to make it theirs. And so she gave it, with bright bed curtains and quilts and towels and bits and pieces of sewing and embroidery as well as the wonderful food she cooked. Joseph had never felt so cared for. Even when he was a boy at home, his mother had had so many to look after that she rarely had time to attend to just one unless he was sick. Elizabeth consulted his taste in arranging this or that about the house and always asked his preferences as she cooked. Most of the things he had never thought about. He had always taken his surroundings for granted and eaten what was placed in front of him. She took pleasure in pleasing him, which was easy for her to do.

After the months of preparation in Wenham, Elizabeth was well supplied with clothing as well as sheets and towels and other linens, but she was aghast at the state of Joseph's clothing. As the son of a tailor, he was conscious of the presentation his outer clothes made to the world and had always taken pains to keep them clean and decent. But he paid no attention to the clothing underneath, other than to get it washed occasionally. Elizabeth found his shirts and underclothes in such a pitiful state that it was all she could do to keep herself from throwing them on the fire before she had been able to make replacements for them.

Elizabeth spent most of the chilly April evenings by the fire when the regular housework was finished, sewing for Joseph and darning stockings. Often, he read to her as she worked, mostly from the Bible, but also sneaking in some very secular poems from the single volume of verse that he owned, *Shakespeare's Sonnets*, brought to him from London by his brother, Edward, when he was just starting at Harvard. When Elizabeth presented him with a snowy white linen shirt, he felt that he had never known such luxury.

Both Elizabeth and Joseph wasted no time in seeing to the garden and the dairy. As part of Elizabeth's dowry, the Gerrishes had given them a sturdy young milk cow as well as a few chickens and a rooster. Having done this work since childhood, Elizabeth was well prepared to tend to the cow and the dairy. The ministry pasture would have been ample for many more animals than the single horse and cow they owned, and Joseph planned to invest in a heifer or two and some pigs when he had the chance. They had come to the village and planted some early things before they moved in, but they were getting a late start on the work of gardening, and they were still planting through the rest of April. In August, they were able to harvest sufficient Indian corn, peas, cabbages, parsnips, carrots and turnips to see them through the winter, as well as enough apples for Joseph to make eight barrels of cider and enough barley for Elizabeth to brew three barrels of beer.

Joseph added plum and other fruit trees to the apple trees because Elizabeth wanted them to make preserves, but he knew little of orchards, and for the first two years, he gratefully accepted Jonathan Walcott's offer to prune his trees for him. Watching and learning, he was soon able to do it himself. He eventually became so good at grafting that he received requests to help the Gerrishes and some of the neighbors with their trees. Between what they raised themselves and the meat and vegetables some villagers gave them to pay their share of the minister's salary, the Greens lived very comfortably that first year and were able to give a good deal of food to those in the village who needed it.

It was barely a month after the wedding that Elizabeth told Joseph she thought she was with child. They both were elated at this good fortune, and when, after another month, they felt sure, they shared the good news with his mother and the Gerrishes. There followed a flurry of sewing and knitting that rivaled the wedding preparations, although of smaller garments this time. Watching Elizabeth as the summer went on, Joseph marveled at his strong, healthy young wife, whose constant activity did not abate as she grew big with child. All summer, she worked in the garden and the dairy and the house, and when the fall harvest came, she brewed her wonderful beer and made sure the vegetables were stored well for the winter.

Joseph decided that the time had come for Elizabeth to have help in the house, and they began to search for a maid. This was not an easy task in a small village where the farm families mostly needed their daughters at home, and few were looking to work out. It was not like ten years earlier when there were so many girls coming to Salem from Maine after they had lost their families in the Indian Wars. One Sabbath in September, they were very happy to hear that Ava, a quick and willing girl of fourteen with a sunny disposition, was looking for a place. Within a week, she had been installed in their house and was quickly learning Elizabeth's ways with the housework and the dairy.

Late in November, when the time came, the swaddling clothes and the cradle were ready. Still, when the pains started in the early morning, Joseph was seized with a great fear, and could hardly bring himself to leave his wife for the time it took to ride the mile or so to fetch Mrs. Buxton, the midwife. She came with him immediately, and after examining Elizabeth, told Joseph it was still hours from her time and he should go downstairs and get some breakfast.

Joseph sent young Nathaniel Putnam to Wenham after Mother Gerrish. He tended to the animals and then went to his study and tried to do some work, but the sound of Elizabeth's muffled cries was too disturbing for him to concentrate. He sat listening to her cries of pain and the soothing voice of the midwife until Jonathan Putnam and Deacon Ingersoll arrived, ostensibly with an errand about church business. They were there to distract him, he knew, and he received their company with gratitude. When Mother Gerrish arrived in the afternoon, Joseph immediately felt less anxious. She went right to her daughter, and after a while came to Joseph with the good news that all was well, and Elizabeth would deliver before too long.

Joseph had never felt anything like the relief of hearing those first little cries. Before long, Mother Gerrish came in and told him he could see his wife and baby. Elizabeth was pale and exhausted, but she looked at his anxious face and smiled. “Come and see your daughter, Joseph,” she said.

He bent over the bed, carefully examining the tiny red face peeking out from the tight swaddling roll. Elizabeth gave a little laugh. “Do not worry,” she said. “She is all in there, and she is perfect.”

“A perfect little gift from God,” he said, his face still close to the baby’s. With a smile, he raised his eyes to meet Elizabeth’s and then looked at Mother Gerrish. “We have decided to call her Anna,” he said, “after her grandmother.”

Anna Gerrish’s face was the picture of pride and joy in her daughter and granddaughter, but she only nodded modestly and smiled at him.

Mother Gerrish stayed with them for the first week, caring for Elizabeth and Anna until she was sure they both were thriving. Joseph rode to Cambridge and brought his mother to stay for the next week. With winter coming on, there was not much for the women to do beyond the house and dairy, and they all enjoyed this time, doting on the baby, eating good meals together, and sitting by the hearth in the evening.

Chapter 11

1699

Joseph's spirits were high as he mounted his horse to ride out to Thomas Putnam's house on a sultry morning towards the end of May in 1699. All was well in his home. He felt he was making good headway with the congregation. The theme of unity and fellowship he stressed in the church services seemed to be seeping into the culture of church and village, and his efforts to pay as much attention to the Nurses and the Tarbells and the Wilkinses as he did to the members of the omnipresent Putnam clan were noticed and appreciated.

As he rode, he prepared himself for this morning's visit, which he did not expect to be a happy one. Passing the fine house that Thomas Putnam's father had given him in the 1680s, now the home of Samuel Braybrook's family, Joseph reflected on the fleeting character of earthly wealth and position. The house he rode up to was further out on the road to Will's Hill. Much smaller than the family's original house and constructed with used lumber, it was a visible sign of Thomas Putnam's sunken fortunes. In addition to the land that was sold to Braybrook, he had recently sold a plot of land along the Ipswich River to some prosperous neighbors from Topsfield who were building a mill. Joseph could only imagine how it must have rankled Thomas Putnam that two of the group were nephews of Rebecca Nurse and her sisters.

Now Thomas and Ann Putnam and their ten children lived in this modest house and tended the farm, which was considerably reduced from its original 200 acres. For Joseph, a good indicator of a family's fortunes was whether they paid their share of his salary in money or in labor. Thomas had paid his last share by helping to whitewash the inside of the ministry house.

As he walked up to the door, Joseph saw the two eldest boys, Tom and Eben, hoeing in the field behind the house. Betty and Deliverance were feeding the animals, trailed by several smaller children. Everything was behind time. If their father was seriously ill, Joseph would have to see about getting them some help. It was Ann Junior who answered his knock. "Good morning, Ann. God bless all here," he said in his usual greeting. Ann bowed her head and ushered him inside the keeping room, lit only by the open door, one small window and the hearth. "I hear your father is not well," he said.

"'Tis a fever," she said. "Some of the children had it and came through well, but he seems to have been taken harder."

"When did he sicken?"

"He has been ill this week and more, I think."

"Is he well enough to speak with me, or shall you and I pray together?"

"Let me ask my mother." She slipped quietly through the door into the small sleeping parlor, and he could hear voices murmuring. As his eyes grew used to the dimness, he noticed the long table next to the hearth and the stools and chairs—not enough for a family of twelve to sit at table together—along with a bed that seemed to fill the room. He was reminded of his own family home, which was always bursting at the seams with people. There was never room for everyone to sit at table there, and as one of the youngest, he had waited his turn impatiently while his big brothers ate their dinners and got on with their business in the world. He was always eating with his mother and sisters after the men had departed.

Ann's head appeared at the door. "Please to come in, Mr. Green," she said.

Thomas Putnam looked much worse than Joseph had expected. His skin was yellowish and waxy, his cheeks hollow, his eyes, which appeared black in the dark room, seemed sunken in their sockets as they were fixed on him. "Good morning, Mr. Green," Putnam said hoarsely, "have you come to strive with me?"

Joseph was careful to speak cordially. "Good morning, Brother Thomas," he said. "I have come to pray with you if you wish it. No doubt we are both in need of God's mercy."

"I am afraid that God has not turned a kindly face to me these seven years. You can see how reduced in circumstances we are here. You would never guess that I was once the presumptive heir to the wealthiest man in the village. You know that the Devil invaded my family with the scourge of witchcraft seven years ago. The affliction of my wife and daughter seems to have ended, but we have not recovered from his curse. I have had nothing but ill fortune in the years since."

"That is not true, Thomas," Joseph reproved him, though his voice was gentle. "God has blessed you with many children, some of whom have just come through this illness. And you have a fertile farm here. You are blessed with much more than many have."

"But they have not suffered the tortures of witchcraft as my wife and daughter have, and as I have, watching them."

It seemed that he wanted to talk about witchcraft. Joseph was reluctant to go into the subject with this man who was very likely to die soon. But if some kind of confession was in the offing, it was his duty to pursue it. "Do you have any doubts that it was witchcraft afflicted your family?"

Thomas stared at him. "Why would I doubt it? What do you know of it?"

Joseph spoke quietly. "I know nothing directly," he said. "But there are many, including ministers who are much more learned than I, that say it was all great a delusion of the Devil and there were no witches, only the Devil practicing delusion on the witnesses by transforming into the shapes of those they did accuse."

Thomas lifted his hand as if in protest and let it fall. “I know they say such things,” he said hoarsely. “But they are wrong, or they are lying. The Devil has a plot to destroy God’s Kingdom in New England, and he has enlisted many of those who are enemies to God to destroy those of us who are his loyal subjects. It is a hard thing, Mr. Green, to be the father of a family Satan has chosen to attack, but it is a glorious thing as well. We have suffered for the Lord. My wife and daughter have suffered greatly, and I through them. But we did not give in. God will reward us for that.”

Joseph saw no desire to confess anything here. He was sorely tempted to let this twisted and deluded man slide into death with his grandiose notions intact, but he steeled himself and prayed silently to the Lord to support him in his duty to try to enlighten this member of his flock. “Brother Thomas,” he said gently, “I sincerely hope and pray for your recovery from this fever. But it is in times like this that we must call to mind that God can take us at any time and hope to go to him with a clear conscience and a joyful heart. I would not tax you further, for I can see your strength is failing this morning, but you seem to have this witchcraft matter on your mind. Is there anything about it that you want to tell me? Are you satisfied that you acted in good faith and in obedience to God throughout this ordeal?”

The man looked at him, his eyes burning. “Why do you tax me with this?” he rasped. “Did I not tell you? I have instructed some of the greatest ministers and officials in this land about this matter. Do you think I would take instruction from an ill-educated boy like you? I will answer to God for all that I did. He knows that I am a much beset and earnest soldier in his cause.” His voice had risen in intensity if not in volume during this speech, and he lay back gasping when he was finished.

“I can see you are exhausted,” said Joseph. “I will not strain you further today. Let us pray to God together to forgive us for the sins we have committed and for God’s peace upon this house and upon this family.” The two women knelt with him as he offered his prayer. Neither of them raised her eyes to his.

When Joseph came to visit the next day, Thomas Putnam was in a stupor, apparently hearing and seeing nothing. He died on May twenty-fourth, at the age of forty-seven. A week later, his wife fell ill with the fever. There was no deathbed confession from her either, for she was out of her head, probably delirious with fever, when he visited her. On that day, Joseph saw fear on her daughter's face, and offered to pray with her. "We must ask God to look mercifully upon your mother," he said. "Perhaps he will spare her. She has many children who need a mother's care."

Ann looked him in the eye, something she seldom did. "He will not spare her," she said, "and he will not spare her children." She was right. Ann Putnam Senior died on the eighth of June, just two weeks after her husband. Ann Junior, at nineteen, was the eldest of the ten children they left behind.

Joseph was prepared to rally the congregation to help the Putnam children. He knew that the presence of Ann would restrain their free exercise of charity and good will, but there were nine others to think of who had had nothing to do with the witchcraft trials. As it turned out, he need not have worried. He had not reckoned on the Putnam and Bayley families. During the funeral observances and the meal afterwards, Joseph noticed a great deal of earnest talk among Thomas Putnam's relatives and in-laws. A few days afterwards, Jonathan Putnam asked if he would accompany him and Deacon Edward to Thomas's house to talk with the children. "We need to speak with them about the future," he said, "and it would be helpful to have you there."

Joseph did not have a great deal of hope as he rode up to the house. Jonathan had told him they had a plan for the children, but they wanted to see how they would react to it before anything was made public. Ann looked exhausted as she opened the door to him, but she and all the children were well groomed and dressed in their somewhat shabby but immaculate Sunday best, as though the family had sensed something momentous was about to happen to them. "Please to sit down, Mr. Green," she said. "My uncle and cousin will be coming soon."

Joseph looked around at the anxious group of children, ranging from Thomas and Ebenezer, boys who did the work of men, to little Seth, just three or four years old. Joseph had catechized most of them. He greeted each child, placing his hand in blessing on the heads of little Susanna and Seth. "Let us all pray together a little," he said. "And ask for God's blessing upon this day."

His prayer was not interrupted by the arrival of Edward and Jonathan, who stood with respectfully bowed heads until he was finished. Eben and Thomas placed chairs for the three of them and the children all waited silently for them to begin. Seeing them standing there, Jonathan broke out in his cheerful manner, "Pray do not wait on us so solemnly, children. Sit down and be easy. We only want to talk with you about what to do next."

This broke the tension a bit, and the children moved from the stiff formation they had unconsciously formed to sit on stools and benches, giving Ann the remaining chair. Instinctively, everyone looked at Edward, who was now the patriarch of the family. In his quiet way, he explained to them what the family had been discussing. "Children, your father left shares of the farm to his sons and Ann, but only Ann is of legal age to claim hers. We think it best to rent the farm for the time being and for you children to come to live with some of your relatives. "

Tom sat up like a ramrod at this. "Uncle," he said, "there is no need to rent the farm. With father away in the village so much, Eben and I have well-nigh farmed it ourselves this last year and more. Ann and Betty and Dell can take care of the house and garden, and even the little ones help. We can manage by ourselves."

Edward had expected this. He spoke evenly and reasonably. "I understand you, Tom. We all know that you and Eben do a man's work on the farm and have surely kept it going this last year. But you are not yet master of all it takes to run a farm and a household. You need more time to learn before you take on such a responsibility, and Eben is not yet fourteen. We are not suggesting that you abandon the farm forever, just that you take some time to learn."

Tom knew that he was right. Often in the last year, he had been frustrated by his father's unwillingness to discuss problems with the animals, or to think out what was best to do about planting and harvesting and selling their crops. His idea of what to do when money was short had always been to sell some more land, something that Tom could see was the very worst thing to do. A farmer should never sell his land. His father was not a good farmer in the best of times, no better than he was a father. Tom knew he still had a lot to learn about the right things to do. But a great deal depended on who would do the teaching. "Who would we live with?" he asked.

Edward looked at Jonathan, who said, "Of course that is not a fixed thing. We would want you to have a say in it, but there are family members who are eager to have each of you come to live with them. Your uncle has made a list."

The children seemed to draw together as they looked nervously at Edward. Tom spoke for them. "Please tell us, Uncle Edward. We are most anxious to hear."

Glancing at the piece of paper he had taken from his pocket, Edward said, "This is what the family proposes. If you do not agree, we can think some more and with God's help come to a satisfactory arrangement." He spoke gently. "Your cousin John Junior and Hannah would like to have Tom come to live with them." Tom looked up and nodded, surprised and pleased with the news.

Edward continued, "I would like to ask you, Eben, to come to us." A quick smile passed over Eben's face as he met his uncle's eyes and nodded. He looked like a thirteen-year-old boy for the first time that day.

Edward smiled and nodded back before continuing. When he said, "Jonathan and Elizabeth would like to have Betty," she raised her eyes to Jonathan's with a blush and a smile and nodded.

"John III and Hannah would have Abigail. Your Aunt Elizabeth and Uncle Joshua Bayley, having no children of their own, would like to have Timothy, Experience, and Susanna come to them."

"And Seth?" asked Ann, her arms around the little boy on her lap.

"Your Uncle Joseph and Aunt Elizabeth would like to care for Seth."

Ann looked at Edward Putnam, her pale blue eyes wide with surprise. She cast them quickly down before she said to him, "Do you think my father would wish it?"

Edward spoke in a kindly but authoritative tone. "We are one family, Ann. We have been torn apart for several causes these seven years and more. The rest of the family feels as Jonathan and I do that we can make some good come of this very sad time by healing what breaches we can. Joseph wants to care for his nieces and nephews just as I do. Seth knows nothing of the past. Placing him with Joseph's family can be a good beginning for our family and a fine opportunity for Seth."

Ann tried hard to control her voice. "But Uncle, Seth does not know Uncle Joseph."

"You can help him, Ann. Bring him to visit. See if everyone is suited. It need not be done immediately, and we can shift another way if the boy is not happy, but I think he will be."

"What of Ann and Deliverance?" asked Tom. The unspoken question was whether anyone in the family was willing to take Ann in.

"As Ann is of age," said Edward, "she may stay here on the farm. She can look after the house and garden and keep an eye on the farmer who will be renting. We thought that Deliverance would be good company for her. She is old enough to help with the housekeeping and the garden." Ann and Dell exchanged glances. They had always had a special understanding, from the time that Dell was a little girl. Ann thought it beyond her uncle to have seen this, but perhaps Aunt Mary had suggested the arrangement.

Looking around the room, Ann suddenly felt a sense of shock and bewilderment that she might be losing her brothers and sisters, whose care had been the work of her life until now, and at the same time an enormous relief from the burden of responsibility that had weighed on her since her father's death. She saw Tom and Eben trying hard to look grown up and stoical, but she could tell they were experiencing feelings similar to her own. No longer bearing the whole responsibility of the farm on their young shoulders, they would be living with family members they liked and working with men they admired. Tom had always looked up to their cousin John, who was an excellent farmer, and Eben had been a special pet of Uncle Edward's since he was born. Betty looked happy. She loved Jonathan and Elizabeth, as everyone did.

The younger children looked dazed. It would take some explaining before they understood what was happening to them and to the family. What she would not explain to them was one thing that was becoming very clear to her. This was the end of the family of Thomas Putnam. Her relatives had succeeded in splitting them up and blending them into the large mass of Putnams and Bayleys like berries into batter. In the eyes of the world, she and Dell would be the last remnants of this embarrassing issue, and they would be more or less hidden from view.

Ann's instinct proved accurate in the next few years as her brothers and sisters gradually cut themselves off from Thomas Putnam. In September, Tom went to Joseph Green and asked to be baptized.

"But you were baptized as an infant, were you not, Tom?" asked Joseph. Rebaptism was not common in the Congregational Church, and in fact could smack of the Anabaptist heresy.

"Yes, I was, Mr. Green," he said. "But I wish to be baptized by my own desire as a person of age fourteen and upwards."

"But why, Tom? Was there anything amiss about your first baptism?"

"No, Sir. I was baptized in the First Church of Salem, I believe by Mr. Higginson. But I would like to be baptized anew and to seal my bond with my cousin John by having him recognized as my guardian in the eyes of God as well the court. He is willing that I should do it."

Joseph began to understand. He spoke gently. "Why do you wish to do that, Tom?"

"To be frank, Mr. Green, I would like to cut myself off from the line of Thomas Putnam and begin anew."

"And why is that?"

"Mr. Green, there is a great deal that happened in this village before you came here that was simply evil. People hated each other and brought each other great harm. You brought a new way of seeing things. You taught us to put the past behind us, and to look to a future of community and fellowship. You know that my father was a big part of the witchcraft doings. But you do not know what went on in his house. He was a hard and a cruel man, and I think, deluded. He hurt all of us, Ann most of all. His house was a house of pain and fear, and, I have come to see, of evil. It is only since I have been living with John and Hannah that I see how a loving Christian family behaves. That is how I want to be. I want to leave the evil and cruelty behind me and be truly baptized in the name of Jesus Christ."

It was the longest speech Joseph had ever heard Tom Putnam utter, and the most consequential. "I understand, Tom, and I am willing," he said. "I myself had a crisis of the soul that was similar to yours but for very different reasons. This is the time of your conversion, and I truly believe you will be born again."

Tom's rebaptism took place on the fourth of September. Eben, now fourteen, followed his lead by being rebaptized in October, appointing Edward as his guardian. Betty followed in 1702, appointing her cousin Jonathan. The younger children were not rebaptized, but they were formally adopted, Abigail by John Putnam III in 1702, Timothy, Experience, and Susannah by

Joshua Bayley, and Seth by Joseph Putnam in 1704, when Thomas and Ann Putnam Senior's estate was finally settled and closed.

The estate had been inventoried by John Putnam Junior and Jonathan in June of 1699, two weeks after Ann Putnam Senior's death. Its value was accepted by the Court of Wills at £437, including about 160 acres of land, with the recently built house and improvements, the animals, several beds and bedding, a table, four chairs, four stools, two pine chests, an old cupboard, and a cane with a silver head, the one remaining symbol to the world of Thomas's former pretensions and hopes, and to his children of his cruelty. Few had escaped his angry blows with this cane.

Thomas's brother Edward and half-brother Joseph were appointed administrators of the estate. Their final account in 1704 explained that they had had to sell some of the land in order to pay Thomas's debts, which amounted to almost £200. Since his death, part of the farm had been rented for £12 a year, which, with hard work and careful housekeeping, was enough to support Ann and Deliverance on the remaining land.

Thomas Putnam, whose fierce defense of what he considered his own right as first-born had sown such dissension in the family, of course left the lion's share of his land to his eldest son Thomas Junior. The unusual thing was that, apparently recognizing that his eldest daughter would be unmarriageable without a substantial dowry, he had left her a share of the remaining land equal to those of her other three brothers and the right to live in the house for the rest of her life if she did not marry. Young Tom considered that right to extend to his sister Deliverance as well.

After the estate was closed, Tom moved back into the house, and the three of them made an amicable but quiet household before the addition of Tom's bride Elizabeth Whipple the next year, soon to be followed by their quickly growing family. They had eleven children in all, six of whom lived to adulthood. From the beginning, Tom was determined to be the father of a loving and happy family. This came naturally to his wife, who had grown up in such a home. Ann eventually transferred her share of the land to Tom by virtue of a deed of labor. She said that, as it was he who worked the land, it should belong to him and his family. In the end, he had a farm of seventy acres, nothing like the grand estate of his grandfather, or even the substantial farm of his father, but with a lot of hard work, it was enough for this large family to live on.

Chapter 12

1699-1700

The misfortune that had visited Thomas Putnam's family in the spring of 1699 proved to be something of a blessing for the congregation of the Salem Village church. The absence of Thomas and Ann Putnam Senior from the meetinghouse removed two of the most visible reminders of the witch trials, and Ann Junior, who in those days many considered the central figure, shrank from view. Although she attended services with her sister, Ann was not a covenanted church member, and she took no part in the church community. Joseph Green still thought it his duty to visit the sisters from time to time. He always felt his heart sink as he rode up to the little house by the road, built with used lumber as Thomas Putnam's fortune declined visibly. In the time before young Tom was to return from his cousin John's, Ann and Deliverance tended the house and garden and dairy and kept to themselves. Joseph was happy to see that the large Putnam clan had not deserted them. They never seemed in want. Still, there was an air of misery and isolation about the place.

With the spirit of peace somewhat restored, the congregation was gaining in size. Many of the village inhabitants who were not covenanted church members had simply stopped coming to services during the witch trials and all the wrangling over Samuel Parris as he tried to keep his hold on the ministry, gave sermons about the money owed him, and laid claim to the deed for the ministry house. Once Joseph became pastor, the people gradually began to appear on the Sabbath, and some applied for church membership. With the tiny meetinghouse full to bursting on Sundays now, Joseph thought it would be a practical as well as a symbolic good for the village to come together and build a new meetinghouse. When he began talking about it in the winter, he found a majority of the villagers enthusiastic about the idea of escaping the crowded, unheated, gloomy building that had been hastily constructed in 1672 when Salem Village was incorporated.

In March of 1699, a committee was chosen to look into the possibility of building a new meetinghouse. After much discussion and negotiation, the committee proposed a building fifty by forty feet with a true second story for the gallery where children and servants were to be seated, big fireplaces, and ample glass windows. On July first, at a village meeting, the inhabitants agreed to finance the new building. As with anything in the village, the financing was the biggest obstacle to the venture. Joseph devoted a good deal of time and energy throughout the summer and fall to persuading people to pledge the funds. Most everyone agreed in spirit, but it was slow going.

At home, Joseph and Elizabeth were doting parents to their baby Anna. Every small accomplishment was greeted with wonder, and Joseph looked forward all day to the half hour he would spend with Anna while her mother and the maid Ava got the supper together. One summer evening after she had laid the sleeping baby in her cradle, Elizabeth came up to Joseph as he sat reading in his study and said softly, "I have a surprise for you, Joseph."

He looked up. "A happy one, I hope."

"I think it is, yes." She smiled down at him.

He drew her onto his lap and put his arm around her waist. "Out with it then," he said.

"I think Anna will have company in your heart soon."

His face broke into a happy grin. "Ah, my love! Another child so soon? Our Anna is but seven months old."

"Yes, it is soon."

"God be praised. You are a wonder. We shall have to get another cradle."

"And we shall have to wean Anna a little early. That will be your job."

"I had not thought of that," he said, frowning. "It will not harm her to lose her mother's milk?"

"Not to worry, Joe." She smiled. "It need not be for months yet. She will be well over a year old and able to take cow's milk and solid food." That night, they lay awake for a long time talking and planning.

With the harvest and beer and cider-making, Joseph's campaign for the meetinghouse, care for Anna, and the preparation for the new baby, the fall was a busy time for the Green family. It was a happy time for Joseph, who surveyed his life on his twenty-fifth birthday, and felt that he could only be grateful for God's bounty to him and his little household.

On the eleventh of January, a Saturday afternoon, as he was in his study preparing for the next day's service, Joseph heard Elizabeth come slowly up the stairs and shut the door to their bedroom across the landing. With an instinctive sense that something was wrong with his wife, Joseph got up immediately and went to her. She looked up at him from the bed, where she lay on her side, her hand pressed to her belly.

"Something is wrong, Joe. The pain is terrible."

"Is it the baby?"

"I do not know. This is not like any birth pains I had before."

"Shall I fetch Dr. Griggs or Mrs. Buxton?

"Just sit with me and let me lie here." He sat down on the bed and laid his hand on her back, which was rigid with the pain.

Silently, he prayed, 'Dear God, make her better. Take away this pain,' over and over.

They sat like that for half an hour or so until, slowly, she began to relax. "It is better now," she said, taking his hand. "If you cover me up, I think I will sleep a little."

He pulled the quilt over her and put his hand to her forehead. "You have a fever," he said. "Your face is hectic. I think I should go for the doctor."

"All right," she said. "Pray, do not be long. If the doctor is not there, just come back home."

He ran down the steps, calling to Ava to watch Anna, that he was going to fetch the doctor for Mrs. Green. When he came back with Dr. Griggs, Elizabeth was awake and again rigid with pain. Dr. Griggs examined her quickly and said that the baby was coming soon. "Fetch Mrs. Buxton, Mr. Green," he said. "I may need some help."

Joseph was off before he had finished talking. Luckily, Mrs. Buxton was at home. Having just returned from a lengthy delivery at one of the remote farms, she was about to get a little sleep. But one look at Joseph, and she asked, "What is wrong with Mrs. Green?"

"The doctor thinks her time has come, although it is at least two months early. He said he would need your help. There seem to be difficulties. She is in a great deal of pain." Mrs. Buxton said no more, but checked over her midwifery gear and then led the way out the door. He helped to lift her onto the pillion seat and they were off. It had been less than ten minutes.

Elizabeth had a very hard delivery, but a fast one, and between them, Dr. Griggs and Mrs. Buxton did their best for her. They told Joseph to leave the room. He went to the kitchen to help Ava, who was boiling water and getting the things for the baby together.

They sat together, just waiting, until Anna woke up, hungry. Joseph took her in his lap and talked to her, but she began crying for her mother. "Try this, Mr. Green," said Ava, handing him a cup of milk with cornbread broken up into it. "'Tis what my mother gives the little ones." When he put a spoonful in her mouth, Anna was a little bewildered at first, but she soon got the idea.

At the sound of a stifled cry, she suddenly looked around.

"Mama is resting, Anna," said Joseph. "We must wait until she wakes."

Ava stood up. "Shall I take her to the Ingersolls', Mr. Green?"

"I think that would be best. I will come for you later."

Ava quickly bundled up herself and the baby. "We are going to see Goody Ingersoll," she said to Anna. "Come, we will have a pleasant time with her."

Joseph went upstairs and tapped on the door. In a minute, Mrs. Buxton opened it, her face carefully set. "The doctor is coming to you, Mr. Green. Please to sit in the study."

Joseph paced up and down in the study for what seemed like an eternity, imagining the worst and praying the same simple words over and over: "Please spare them. Please let her be all right."

When Dr. Griggs came into the study, he took one look at Joseph and said, "Please to sit down, Mr. Green."

When Joseph was sitting in his chair, Dr. Griggs pulled the room's other chair up next to it. "First, let me say that your wife has survived this childbirth. She is feverish, and we must watch her carefully, but I think she will recover." He looked at him kindly. "I am sorry to say that the child was stillborn, a boy, about a seven months' baby."

Joseph felt as if a blow had been struck. "Stillborn? He never lived at all?"

"No."

"Can I see him?"

"Of course."

"And I want to see my wife."

"Let me ask Mrs. Buxton if your wife is ready. This was a very difficult birth for her."

Mrs. Buxton came to Joseph with a little bundle. He took it in his hands and marveled at its tiny lightness. He could have held his son in one hand. He opened the wrap and looked closely at his features, at his tiny fingers and toes.

When he went into the bedchamber, Elizabeth lay back on the bolster, sick and exhausted. He took her hand, and she turned, eyes filled with desolation, toward him. "He never lived, Joseph," she said. "Our little boy."

"It is God's will," he said. "We must try to accept it." He could not summon anything more eloquent than that to say.

The next day was the Sabbath. It took all of Joseph's strength to come to the meetinghouse that day. He put aside the sermon he had planned, and instead preached one he had given several times before. Salem Village being what it was, word of his bereavement had already gotten around the congregation, and he had a most sympathetic audience. He told them that he did not feel well enough to preach in the afternoon and asked them to read the Bible and pray in their homes. After the service, Deacon Ingersoll went to Wenham himself to fetch Mrs. Gerrish, and Joseph sent young Nathaniel Putnam to Cambridge for his mother. The next day, Captain John Putnam went to Salem for wine and gloves for the funeral and a group of men dug the little grave in the frozen dirt of the burial ground. Joseph asked Reverend Gerrish to pray over the grave.

Mrs. Gerrish remained with them for several weeks, nursing her daughter, who was very sick. After the worst of the danger had passed, Elizabeth continued weak and ill for months. Under the direction of his mother and Mother Gerrish, Joseph took the best care he could of her and of their little Anna. The grief and fear he felt during this time were the worst thing he had faced in his twenty-five years, eclipsing even the loss of his father when he was sixteen.

Even after Elizabeth had recovered from the birth and her fever, she was troubled by headaches and various other ills. She made a valiant effort to carry on as always, making a happy home for her husband and daughter, but Joseph could see what it cost her. He did what he could to bring comfort to her but was at a loss himself. From the depths of his own sorrow, he realized how hollow the things he said to people who suffered such losses must ring.

It was the sorest trial of Joseph's faith yet, for he could not find a reason why God would take their little one, except their own failure to deserve him. This was something he was prepared to face for his own sins, but not for his beloved wife, whose goodness was not something he could doubt. He took the guilt fully upon himself. It was several months before he was able to write a sincere prayer in his journal. 'I desire to acknowledge the hand of God in all and quietly to submit unto him,' he wrote, 'and I think that I never did once murmur against God for this stroke, but have cause to say that God has punished me far less than I deserve. I desire to bless God that he has taken me into that covenant which includes my seed also—and that he spared and restored my wife. O that I could walk more humbly, circumspectly and thankfully before God all my days.'

Part Three

Light Breaks Through

1701–1706

Chapter 13

1699-1705

Unless they had known their parents, people who saw Ann and Deliverance Putnam together in 1699 would never have taken them for sisters. At twenty, Ann was very like her mother. Although she was not what most observers would call pretty, her pale blue eyes, the bands of smooth ash blonde hair that were visible at the edges of her cap, her very fair skin, and her small, slight frame suggested a delicate and fragile young woman. At first glance, Deliverance recalled her father. Like his, her tall, thin frame masked a surprising physical strength. At the age of twelve, she could do an adult's work in the garden all day with no apparent effort, and she could do many a task in the barnyard that was usually assigned to boys or men. She had her father's dark coloring and his prominent nose, but unlike her father's grim countenance, her face was open and inviting, and often illumined by a contagious smile. She loved to laugh and make others laugh.

Throughout the grim days during and after the witchcraft outbreak, it was Deliverance who kept the members of the Putnam household from descending into total darkness. With advice from their wives, Edward and Jonathan Putnam had chosen carefully when they had suggested her as a companion for Ann rather than her older sister, Betty, although they had not known that she and Ann had always had a special bond and an unspoken understanding about the life and the people they saw before them.

The loss of their parents within weeks of each other had wrenched the sisters' world off its axis. They had lost the mother who, although not always stable or reliable, was the emotional center of their lives. They had lost the father who was their unquestioned authority, who regularly delivered the edicts that directed their lives and meted out whatever punishment he chose for perceived failure to execute them. When their relatives acted to break up Thomas's children and blend them into other families, not only were they doing the normal thing for young orphans, they were doing what they knew in their hearts was necessary for the healing of those damaged souls. They were hoping that Ann and Dell could heal each other.

In the blaze of activity and emotions that followed their mother's death, the girls tried not to think of anything beyond the work that was before them, getting all the members of the family ready to move to their new homes. This meant mountains of washing and mending for Ann, Betty and Dell, for they were determined that their brothers and sisters would go off to their new families neat, clean, and decently clad. On the appointed day for each departure, they made sure that water was heated, and they oversaw a thorough washing of each child, especially the boys.

When the time came and the designated guardian rode up, all of the family fought back tears and reminded each other that they would be together again soon. Ann told the older ones she knew they would uphold the family honor by their behavior at Uncle Edward's or Cousin John's or Cousin Jonathan's. To the younger three, she had tried to explain that Aunt Elizabeth and Uncle Joshua would be making a new home for them, and they must try to love and obey them as their new mother and father. Dell had told them stories of the big, beautiful house and yard, and the animals. Although they managed to keep their resolutions to be cheerful and smiling when they sent them off, each of the small figures on a big horse with an adult they hardly knew, the sisters collapsed weeping into each other's arms when they had closed the door after them.

Little Seth was the hardest. Edward Putnam had acted deliberately when he had urged his half-brother, Joseph, to take in the youngest of Thomas's children. "There has been an unnatural rift in our family for too long, Joseph," he said. "It has led to dark things no one would think to see in a lifetime. We have the chance to do something that might join it back together now. This little child knows nothing of his father's enmity. He has done you no harm, nor you him. What an act of healing this can be."

In the end, Joseph had agreed, and his wife Elizabeth was eager to welcome the little boy who was to serve as peacemaker. Edward had charged Ann with bringing Seth to meet them, knowing that she would feel it her duty to the child, no matter how she felt about it herself. His strategy had worked well. Elizabeth Porter Putnam was a warm, maternal woman and Seth was a well-behaved, bright little boy who took well to the kind attention of his aunt and uncle and cousins from the beginning. Under Elizabeth's influence, the stiff and wary meetings between Ann and her Uncle Joseph gradually gave way to something like cordiality, and when the cheerful Dell was added to the mix, the transformation was complete. In the end, as he had hoped, Edward had created a familial support for Ann and Dell as well as for little Seth.

Alone in the family house, it took a long time for the sisters to fully realize that everyone else was gone. They continued to sleep in the attic room up under the eaves, although they would have had a much better bed in the sleeping parlor or could even have had their own chambers if they had wanted to. After cleaning the house carefully from attic to cellar, they closed off most of it and lived in the keeping room, the lean-to pantry and dairy, and their bedroom. It made the house seem less empty when they kept to the scenes of their daily life and work.

At first, the sisters carried on as they always had, operating the household of a large farm family, which included running the dairy, keeping up the substantial kitchen garden, and caring for a number of animals. The Putnam men and boys all helped to keep up the farm for the rest of 1699 and did the harvesting. For the next year, the fields were rented with the arrangement that a certain amount of hay, wheat, corn and barley was turned over to Ann and Dell. This took care of feed for the horses and cows, and flour and meal and malt for brewing beer.

With advice from their uncles and cousins, and some resistance from Tom, who would have kept the whole farm intact if he could, they gradually sold off most of the stock. Once the farm was rented out, they kept just one horse, the sheep, two milk cows, a heifer and a calf, a few pigs, and a few chickens. They found this was manageable for them and more than enough to supply their meat, eggs, milk, cheese and wool for the year. For the next summer, the vegetable garden was reduced considerably in size, although they continued to grow the same variety of things to cook and preserve. There were plenty of peas, beans, turnips, onions, squash, cabbage, carrots and greens. One thing that occurred to them was that they only had to grow what they wanted to eat. Dell hated parsnips. After 1699, there were no parsnips grown in the Putnam sisters' garden.

They made butter whenever the milk was rich enough, and cheese in the spring, enough to last through the year. In the summer, they gardened and took care of the animals, and in the fall, harvested apples for cider and sheared the sheep to make wool for spinning. Dell became quite good at this, so that soon there was no need to ask anyone to do it for them. She also became adept at killing chickens and small pigs. Before long, they only needed to ask their uncles and cousins for help in the annual winter butchering and salting of a swine and a heifer to last the year.

As they gradually shaped their household, the sisters built a life that fit the two of them. If Ann had been left to herself, she probably would have given in to her profound sadness over the loss of her family and fallen into deep melancholia. She might have become a recluse, never straying further than her well-kept house, barnyard and garden. But Dell was of a much more sociable and adventurous disposition. She insisted on their keeping a riding horse, ostensibly so they could conveniently go to the meetinghouse for services every Sunday and see the family. But as she grew into her teens, she used the horse more often for visiting than for worship, keeping up a close connection with both family and neighbors. She could always entice Ann away from the house for an hour or two with the promise of spending time with one of their brothers or sisters.

At the meetinghouse, Ann did her best to be invisible. She was keenly aware of the shift in the village's sympathy away from the 'afflicted children' and toward those who had been accused of witchcraft and their families. During the early stages of the witchcraft trials, the prevailing belief had been that the girls were bewitched and tormented. As witchcraft was a grave sin and a capital crime, the village willingly participated in imprisoning, excommunicating, and executing the accused. But with the doubt that was cast by the ministers and others on the use of spectral evidence, the allegiance of the people began to shift. In October of 1692, when Governor Phips expressly forbade the court to take spectral evidence or the charges of the afflicted that an accused person was harming them in court as sufficient evidence of guilt, the juries began dismissing all the complaints.

Most people believed that the girls had suffered, but the prevailing view came to be that they were afflicted by 'a delusion of Satan,' subjected, like Saul in the Book of Samuel, to Satan's appearing to them in the shape of an innocent person. In March of 1692, Ann and her companions had been considered special persons, continually assaulted by Satan and his minions, but gifted with special sight into the spirit world. By the end of the year, they were mostly thought of as victims of Satan's delusion, because of which they had brought great suffering, misery, and death to their community. And of course, there were those who had never believed in the witchcraft outbreak at all. Ann Putnam was not welcome company to either group.

Ann did her best to stay out of the public view when she could. Arriving at the meetinghouse on the Sabbath, she immediately went up to the gallery and sat with the children and servants. Besides keeping her away from the villagers, this gave her the chance to keep watch on her little brothers and sisters and see that they were happy and well cared for. At first, she paid little attention to the service that was going on below. She had long since lost confidence that anything that went on there could be a help to her. But as time went on, she found the sermons of Reverend Green, so different in tone and substance from those of Samuel Parris, to be surprisingly comforting. She began to look forward to listening to him, and she and Dell often talked about what he had to say on the ride home.

Chapter 14

1701-1705

The presence of their Anna was a consolation and a quiet joy to Joseph and Elizabeth in the midst of their sadness in the spring of 1701. They attended to her every milestone as though she were the first child ever to accomplish such a thing. When she began to walk without leading strings, Joseph proudly recorded the date, as he did the date of her first words. The sight of his daughter toddling toward him with a delighted smile never failed to lift his spirits, and each day her little accomplishments gave him and Elizabeth something pleasant to talk about. Slowly things began to seem, if not normal, then familiar again. In April, when Elizabeth told Joseph she was expecting another child, they both were able to take the news as a blessing. Privately, he thought of it as a sign of redemption for himself. How much more precious would this child be to them now that they took nothing for granted in this world?

While Joseph and Elizabeth were enduring their private sorrow, some of his friends in the congregation were doing what they could to help fill his days. Toward the end of January, Joseph's friend, Jonathan, and his cousin, Benjamin Putnam, came to the minister's house with a plan.

"We have been talking of your proposal to build the new meetinghouse," said Jonathan, "and we have been to a number of men in the village who would be willing to subscribe to a building fund if you were to give the word. Deacon Ingersoll would donate land on Watch House Hill for it."

"Most certainly, I will support the effort," Joseph said. "What do you think it best to do first?"

Jonathan grinned. "Well, with church business as with any other, there is always the matter of money to be dealt with first. It would go a long way with the village if you were to subscribe yourself."

Joseph nodded. "Of course," he said. He sat back and thought for a minute. He knew that it was important for him as pastor to make the kind of grand gesture that would set an example for the village, and especially the church members, to make a substantial sacrifice for this vital project. He also knew what Jonathan was getting at, that this kind of gesture from the minister would set the wealthy men of the village to competing, which could only be good for the meetinghouse fund. The question was how much to give. Five pounds would be a very generous donation, but not a grand gesture. If he were to give ten pounds, a seventh of his annual salary, it would put a serious burden on the family finances for the year, but it would be the kind of gesture that was needed to show the importance of this building. He sat up in his chair and placed his hands on the table.

"I shall subscribe ten pounds," he said.

Both of his visitors were clearly taken aback.

"A good deal of money," said Jonathan.

"Yes, it is," said Joseph, "and Elizabeth and I shall have to scrimp this year to afford it, but I believe we must build this meetinghouse." He looked at the two men, good, honest farmers and devout Christians both. "We all know that this village was torn apart by the witchcraft delusion nine years ago. I think it is slowly healing, and we did a good deal to help that along when we re-seated the meetinghouse, but, as long as we meet every week in the same gloomy building where those wretched scenes played out, the memories will be staring us in the face as a congregation and as a village. They are especially painful for those whose families were most deeply affected. A new meetinghouse will give us something to work at together, to build a new foundation for our little Israel and new hope for a future of living in true fellowship with each other."

"Well," said Jonathan, smiling, "that was pretty much what we had in mind, but we could never have described it with such eloquence."

Joseph blushed a little. "You will have to forgive my being carried away with enthusiasm for your plan," he said. "I am truly beginning to believe it is something that can happen. Now tell me how much we will need for a master builder and carpenters and lumber."

Joseph was still in a state of excitement when he bid goodbye to his visitors. He sat for a long time thinking about the building and making plans for the parts of the fundraising that he had agreed to take on, but he was worried about the effect his decision about the donation would have on his wife. Elizabeth was an excellent housekeeper, and a far better manager of money than he was, but the loss of that much money would take a toll even on her resources.

When he told her about the new plan, she caught his excitement. "Oh, Joseph," she said, "your greatest hopes for the church may finally take shape now."

"I do hope so," he said. "It would mean so much to this congregation to meet in a new building they had built together with none of the horrors and the sadness the old one harbors." He looked at her in open appeal. "Betty, I hope you will not think me too rash in subscribing us for a large sum. It is so important for the pastor's family to lead in this and spur the rich men of the village to dig deep in their pockets."

He hated to see the look of trepidation that came into her eyes, but she responded quietly. "How much did you pledge, Joe?"

"Ten pounds."

Her eyes widened, and she took a sharp little breath before she answered. "It is a good deal of money."

"It is, I know, and believe me, I also know that the greatest burden will fall on you to manage with so much less, but I did not promise this lightly. I believe that the success of this plan, and the future of our congregation, depends on our standing up and taking the lead in the village. We must show how committed we are to building a community of loving fellowship here, and I know you agree with me that ridding ourselves of that accursed building is the best way to begin anew to build the community."

"I do agree with you, Joe," she said, "and I think this is a critical time for your ministry if your congregation is to flourish. It is the right thing to do. We will both have to make sacrifices this year if we are to fulfill the pledge, but I am ready to do my part."

"My beloved, what a wonder you are!" he said with a smile and an expression of great relief. "I promise to do everything I can to save money. The farm is doing well. I will be able to sell some meat this year and some cider and corn, perhaps even a load of hay. I can plant more crops than we usually do and sell some of the excess rather than giving it all away for just this year. If worse came to worst, I could borrow of my brother, Jonathan. He is doing very well in Newton now."

"We will manage, Joe," she said, "but there will be no new clothes, except for Anna and the new baby, of course."

"We have no worries there," he said. "I know their grandmothers will keep our little ones well clothed all on their own."

In the next few days, Joseph could tell that Elizabeth was more worried about managing than she had let on, and he suggested that they sit down together and go carefully over the household accounts. Counting the shillings and pence, they worked out a plan for living on sixty pounds for the year, and he resolved to be much more careful with money than he usually was.

The fundraising for the meetinghouse proceeded more quickly than Joseph had ever dreamed. The deacons not only subscribed impressive sums themselves but enthusiastically joined Jonathan and Benjamin in canvassing. Joseph was careful to make sure the plan did not become a Putnam project in the eyes of the village. He enlisted his friends at Wills Hill and members of the Hutchinson and Nurse clans to join the effort as well. Deacon Ingersoll was as good as his word in donating the land. The builder's plans, for a heated building forty-eight by forty-two feet with a true second story for the gallery and many big windows, met with enthusiastic approval in both the church and the village meetings.

By early April, the carpenters were at work. As Joseph had hoped, the village men joined in the work willingly, some in lieu of monetary donations and some just to be part of it. He did have an hour of worry when a meeting about the building began to show signs of the village's old contentions and resentments. Some of the village residents complained that the Watch House Hill site would make it more difficult for them to get to church services, implying that Deacon Ingersoll was favoring a particular group of villagers by donating that site rather than one closer to the old meetinghouse. They pointed out that the hilly site would have to be made level before the building could be raised, adding to the cost. As the discussion descended into wrangling and threatened to become personal, Joseph thought of a compromise.

"It is clear," he said, "that the site must be leveled before we build. Would it not be fair to say that the work should be done by those who will have their way to the meetinghouse shortened by our adopting the new location?" Since all were really in agreement about their desire for the new meetinghouse to go forward, the contending parties were able to save face by voting for a resolution based on his idea.

In early May, the designated villagers leveled the site where the building was to go, and soon others joined them to dig the foundation so that, when the carpenters finished the frame on the nineteenth of May, all was ready for the raising. Two days later, Joseph walked with Betty down to the building site and was greeted by a scene he had spent four years hoping for but was never sure he would see. It seemed that the whole village was there, ready to join in the communal effort it took to raise the frame.

Joseph stood next to his wife for a few minutes, just taking in the sight. Then he went over to join his flock as they worked together under the direction of the master builder, Captain Flint—Putnam and Nurse and Wilkins and Tarbell and Hutchinson and Houlton, working with their fellow villagers to raise their new meetinghouse. For Joseph, it was a glorious three days, with everyone joining in the feast the village women provided at midday, and all the families mixing, if not in loving fellowship, at least in peace. *It will come*, Joseph thought, *God willing*.

The village still had to pay for lumber and plaster and the precious window glass, as well as skilled craftsmen to direct the volunteers and do the finish work, and the pledged money came in slowly after the first burst of enthusiasm. It was not until the following summer that the building was finally finished. In early July, a group of men whitewashed the inside, and on the fourteenth, many turned out to see the first glass installed in the big windows. It was a matter of great pride.

The building had five windows on each side, three on the second or gallery floor and two on the first, as well as a door in each wall, to provide ample light and a cross breeze when the doors were opened in the summer. The hipped roof also had a gable with a window on each side and, Captain Flint's bit of extravagance, a cupola at the center with windows on each side. Each of the big windows was leaded to contain eighteen diamond-shaped panes of glass.

A few days later, when the glass was all installed and the workers had gone home to their suppers, Joseph walked to the new meetinghouse by himself and stood looking at it from the road. The afternoon sun hit the windowpanes, causing them to glisten as though they were indeed so many diamonds. He stood for a few minutes just taking in the accomplishment that Salem Village had achieved. This beautiful building where they would gather in fellowship to praise God had risen out of the sacrifice, the good will, and the skilled hard work of the people of this village.

Joseph walked up the short path and the two stone steps. He stepped inside the new building and walked to the very center, beneath the cupola. There, he looked up to the galleries on the second floor, then to the lofty ceiling with its gables and windows, and finally straight up to the light-filled space at the peak of the roof. With the sunshine streaming through all the windows and reflecting off the white walls, it was a space full of light. It was truly a place for a new beginning, a place that would inspire him to preach and his people to hear a message of love and hope. In this place, he felt that Salem Village at last had a house of worship.

Joseph's hopeful state that summer came from his private as well as his public life. Betty had given birth to a son in December, a big, healthy boy. They named him John for Joseph's father, and Joseph joyfully recorded his prayer of thanksgiving in his journal. 'The Lord bless it and own it as one of his children,' he wrote, 'and let it be born again of the spirit of God. And O that we might be thankful and learn to trust God for the future and live more to his praise for the time to come.'

Mrs. Moulton, the new midwife, had stayed with them until Joseph was able to bring Mother Gerrish from Wenham the next day. Betty had recovered quickly that time, and their son was nothing but a joy to them. When Joseph looked at his family in the evening, Betty peacefully asleep in their bed, Anna next to her in the trundle, and little John in the cradle, he felt that God had blessed him far more than he deserved.

The years that followed brought some sorrow but also great joy, with the births of their sons Joseph in 1703 and Edward in 1705. For Joseph, those years, his late twenties, were the time when his life found its natural rhythms and he at last felt at ease in his world. The rhythm of the year came from his newfound love of farming. When he had come to Salem Village, Joseph was determined that he would not be the kind of pastor who held aloof from his flock, but a true member of the village as well as the church. In a village of farmers, this meant entering enthusiastically into the work of growing his family's food and raising their animals. He knew about growing vegetables, having helped his mother in the kitchen garden that supported her large household since he was big enough to walk. He could milk a cow, and he knew about chickens. He had worked his share of harvests in his teens and was a good hand at mowing hay.

Joseph had basic skills, but he had never had the experience of managing a farm that provided for all the family's food throughout the year. For this, he needed more knowledge, and he learned gratefully from his neighbors, who were pleased and a bit amused by the young minister's enthusiasm for the work. They helped him to prune his orchard and plant new trees that would produce apples for pies and cider as well as plums for Betty's rich preserves. They taught him to make the barrels of cider in the fall that would last throughout the year. They showed him how to shear his sheep and how to slaughter, butcher, and salt down his own hogs and calves so the household would have meat throughout the year.

In the first year, the farm work had been a blur. It had seemed that there was always someone coming to the ministry house to help him with pruning or plowing or butchering or harvesting. But as the years went by, it was the seasons that gave them shape and rhythm. For Joseph, the year began in April with the plowing and planting. He always had John Goodale to do the plowing, for this good farmer preferred to work off his minister's tax that way, and he liked to keep an eye on Joseph to make sure he got things right with his oats and wheat to start off with. There were also two days in late April or early May when Joseph and Betty and that year's maid and Ben Putnam, who worked for them, all turned out to plant the garden. May was also the month for sheep shearing and marking the lambs. In June, they set the two or three hundred cabbages that would be harvested in October and last them through the winter.

Joseph enjoyed the early summer the most, when the crops were all planted and growing, which for him was a powerful sign of God's bounty. He always preached on this at least once during the summer, a heartfelt sermon the congregation responded to enthusiastically. It was also the season when he stole some time to go fishing in the streams at Will's Hill, with his little sons accompanying him as soon as they could sit on a horse and hold a fishing pole. He came to feel that one part at least of his misspent youth was worthwhile after all, for he was a good fisherman and a good shot with a fowling piece and well-respected by his neighbors on that account.

In the heat of August, the hard work of the harvest began with the oats and hay, and then the Indian corn in late September and October. And then there were carrots and beans and turnips and apples and cabbages to be harvested and stored in the cellar for winter. His favorite part of the fall was picking apples and making the cider. He became known for the quality of his cider and was proud to bring in eight or nine barrels that would usually last them throughout the year.

In the winter, there were the animals to see to and the meat to put up. Betty and the maid took care of the chickens and the dairy, but the meat was Joseph's responsibility. By 1711, he was producing eight hundred pounds of pork, and they usually had about a hundred pounds of beef in a year as well as lambs from their flock. They were able to give away a good deal to villagers in need and to friends in Salem, as well as selling some. Joseph was raising so many animals that he soon had to buy additional land to supplement the meadow that went with the ministry house.

In February and March, Joseph and young Ben were usually hard put just to keep paths dug through the snow to the barn and the road and to keep the family and the animals warm and well fed and safe from the elements. But as March came to an end, and the trees began to come to life, it was time for Joseph to think once more about the orchard, and to set to work pruning and grafting. It gave a profound meaning to the spring that Joseph thought only a farmer could appreciate fully. He believed fervently it was God's plan that the land came to life and bloomed and died every year, and that his children lived off the land by virtue of God's great bounty and the sweat of their father's brow.

If the rhythm of the year was Joseph's participation in God's plan for the earth, the rhythm of the week was the rhythm of his ministry. It, of course, revolved around the Sabbath. Joseph reserved Fridays and Saturdays each week for preparing the two sermons he would preach on Sunday morning and afternoon. This was sacrosanct. The smallest of toddlers knew better than to disturb their father when he was in the minister's study with the door closed. The Sabbath itself was an exhausting day for him. Not only did it involve preaching for hours, but, because it was often the only time he saw the more remote members of the church, it involved a great deal of pastoral care as well. He often spent the time between sermons and after the day was officially over in deep conversation in his study.

After seeing to the animals and the house, Joseph and Betty usually visited the Gerrishes on Mondays, or made visits in the village that were more friendly than pastoral. Tuesdays were generally reserved for church business. He made his rounds visiting the sick and those in need, and often saw the deacons or other church members in his study. Wednesdays were the days for church lectures. In the early years, Joseph did not give a lecture himself, but usually went to one in Salem or sometimes Boston, and often Betty went with him. Thursdays were days for Joseph to spend at home, seeing to the farm, and then his week began again with preparation for the Sabbath.

Joseph's daily rhythm, his soul's heartbeat, was his family life. It began at the crack of dawn when he heard the maid of that year stir in the keeping room to make up the fire and go outside to milk the cow. Then it was usually the baby in the cradle who stirred and fussed, and Betty who awoke to feed it. They sometimes had some quiet talk for a few minutes until one of the children in the trundle bed woke the others and the day began.

The mornings were a whirlwind as children were dressed and breakfast was prepared and eaten. A short interlude of quiet came as Joseph led the household in morning prayers, and then they all were off to their business, tending the animals, gathering eggs, making butter, working in the garden or the fields, writing sermons, washing clothes, baking bread or pies, or cleaning the house. On the days he was at home, Joseph felt the house as a living thing. He relished the sounds that filtered through on mornings when he worked in his study, the little voices of the children proudly crowing their newly-mastered words, the murmuring back and forth between Betty and the maid as they went about their work, punctuated by hymn singing and laughter, their good-natured teasing of Ben as he stomped about downstairs with the wood or came on an errand from the barn.

Noonday dinners were the time when everything paused, and the household sat down together to enjoy the bounty they were blessed with. Joseph loved to watch his wife at this time, her cheeks glowing pink with the heat from the cooking and the last rush of preparations, her warm golden eyes looking carefully over her children to make sure they were well fed and practicing the rudiments of table manners. In the afternoons, if it was not planting or harvest time, they often had visitors, the household pausing for a while in its business as their little domestic circle enveloped friends and relatives.

Suppers were usually quick and simple meals followed by evening prayers, during which Joseph tried to think of an apt verse from the Bible related to the events of the day. The children were put to bed after that, usually so tired that they dropped off to sleep immediately. Joseph and Ben saw to the animals as the women made their preparations for the next day. And then, if they were lucky, some peace and quiet followed when Joe and Betty could sit by the fire. Her hands, of course, were never still. She always had sewing or mending or knitting to do. But they could talk, or he could read aloud until they very soon could no longer stay awake and joined the sleeping children.

Walking home from the meetinghouse after he had quelled a contentious village meeting one summer evening in 1705, Joseph thought about how different his interaction with his fellow villagers had been when he had arrived eight years earlier as a young schoolteacher, hardly more than a boy, with a dream of bringing peace to Salem Village. He reflected that in the time since, each realm of his life had affected the others, and what he had once seen as the separate roles of father, pastor and farmer were all deeply intertwined. He had made inroads with his congregation as his growing competence as a farmer had gradually engendered the respect and trust of his neighbors. They were far readier to trust in his pastoral counsel and reveal the secrets of their souls to him than they would have been to confide in someone like Samuel Parris. On the other hand, his growing influence as a pastor led to greater influence in the village, and he was often looked to for the last word in a dispute or quarrel. Over the years, the village had fallen in with the general theme he had set for his ministry from the beginning—peace and fellowship and tolerance in their community. It had become as much a consideration in the actions of the Village Committee as in those of the church.

Most profoundly, Joseph thought, his life with his beloved Betty and their children had deepened his understanding of what it meant to love, and what the members of his congregation, men and women, lived through every day. The combination of overwhelming love, great joy, and constant care and worry that was part of raising children was something he knew intimately. The worry and fear when Betty and the children had been very sick and the grief at the loss of their stillborn son had had a redeeming element for the pastor. Those wrenching experiences had helped him to understand that, while he could never fathom what others were going through, it was important to offer the comfort his faith could give. At the age of thirty, Joseph knew that he was not and never would be the kind of learned minister that Cotton Mather, or even Reverend Walter was, but he knew that he was a good pastor to his flock, the kind of pastor they needed, and he worked very hard to serve them well.

Chapter 15

1702

In early December of 1702, Joseph had his customary meeting with the deacons to distribute the money that had been collected for the poor on Thanksgiving Day. They had a good amount to distribute: three pounds, seven shillings and five pence. After much discussion, the three of them agreed to specific amounts for the Widow Sheldon and the Widow Richards and to the Stacy, Wyatt, Case and Good families. Afterward, as Joseph stood at the door of his study talking with Nathaniel Ingersoll, Edward Putnam sat at the table, carefully placing the shillings and pence into packets made of folded paper and marking them with the names of the families so he could distribute them the next day. Out of the corner of his eye, Joseph saw Edward reach into his pocket and take out a small purse, from which he took some money, adding it to the last packet. When Ingersoll left, he stepped quietly over to the table and asked, "Brother Edward, do you think we have been insufficient in our charity to one of the villagers?"

Edward looked up, uncharacteristically flustered. "No," he said, "I think we have been most judicious in dividing the money."

Joseph picked up the packet marked 'William Good' and took out the money. He looked down at his deacon in surprise. "This is three pounds you've added to his three shillings, more money than William Good might see in a year. It is most generous. But why do you hide your gift in the packet instead of giving it to him in Christian fellowship?"

Edward looked increasingly uncomfortable. "I would prefer that he did not know the donor."

"It could cause resentment and bad feeling in the village if the others hear that Good's portion of the money is so much greater than theirs," Joseph said gently. He knew that Edward was fully aware of the scrutiny and comparison the donations received.

The deacon, usually so calm and reserved, was now actually blushing. Looking down at his hands folded on the table, he said quietly, "There is no need to worry, Mr. Green. I do this every year. Good has the sense to keep quiet about it."

"'Tis a very kind act of charity, Brother Edward, but if I may ask, why William Good?" Good was a famously lazy man who did the bare amount of farm work and whatever else came to hand to keep his family alive.

"'Tis not so much for Good as for his daughter, Dorothy," Edward said softly.

Joseph began to see. "Ah, yes," he said, "poor child of God. It is kind of you to think of her." Dorothy Good was one of the most notorious victims of the witchcraft outbreak, and he had heard her story several times. The daughter of William and Sarah, who was hanged as a witch, the child was accused of witchcraft at the age of four, and, prattling away as four-year-olds do when she was questioned by Judge Hathorne, she said that her mother was a witch and had given her a little snake to suckle at her finger, things she had heard other people say in the court. She was confined in the jail and later taken from her mother and moved to the Boston jail along with a number of adult prisoners, where she was chained to the wall.

Dorothy remained in jail for eight months, until her bail was paid by a donor from Salem Town and she was given back to her father. By that time, she was unrecognizable as the healthy, fanciful child who had been imprisoned. She was like a wild animal that had been chained up, out of control and terrified of any adult other than her family who tried to touch her. With no mother to care for her, she had been left to her father and the charity of the neighbors ever since. Now she was fourteen and still not in full control of her behavior or her wits.

At Joseph's praise, Edward flinched as though he had been dealt a blow. "No, it is not kind at all, Mr. Green," he said, "not kind." He looked up at the young minister, who stood regarding him with an expression of deep concern. "You must not praise me, Mr. Green."

Joseph sat down across from him. "Brother Edward," he said, "is there something you would like to tell me about?"

Edward looked into his eyes and seemed to make a decision. "There is," he said. "It has been the great burden of my soul these ten years. I seek forgiveness with every breath I draw."

Joseph nodded. "You know that forgiveness is not mine, but the Lord's," he said, "but if it will ease your soul to discourse about something, I am here to help share your burden."

"We have never talked together of the witchcraft doings here, and I am not sure how much you know of them."

"Not a great deal. I know, as everyone does, about the executions and the families torn apart, and neighbors falling into enmity with each other, but I have tried not to dwell too much on the past in my ministry so that we could look to creating a future together in Christian fellowship."

"I understand that, Mr. Green, and you have been precisely the pastor we had hoped you would be when we asked you to come. But I must tell you something of the past if you are to understand me."

"Of course, Brother Edward. You must tell me what you need to tell."

Edward looked down at the table and began to talk. It was clear that he had dwelled on every detail of this story many, many times, and it came out in a single rush of talk. Joseph was attentive, responding from time to time, but he felt that it really did not matter if he was there or not, except as a vessel to receive this pent-up confession.

"The witchcraft doings began here in this house, with the strange behavior of Reverend Parris's daughter and niece," Edward said. "He held his silence about it until he had to call in Dr. Griggs to see if he could tell what ailed the children. Dr. Griggs is not a discreet man, as you know. When he saw no explanation except witchcraft, the village knew about it soon enough.

"My brother, Thomas, was a close companion of Mr. Parris's, and both were very interested in witchcraft." Edward glanced up at him. "Do you know Mr. Mather's *Late Memorable Providences*, about the bewitching of the Goodwin children?"

"I have not read it, but I have heard it discussed," Joseph said. "It includes detailed descriptions, does it not, of the children's behavior when they were bewitched, crawling about and falling into fits, speaking gibberish and so on?"

Edward nodded. "That book was published in 1689. My brother and Mr. Parris read it closely. They spent hours discussing the workings of Satan and witchcraft and their manifestation and effects on the victims. When it became clear that Thomas's daughter, Ann, and then his wife, were showing the same effects as the children in Parris's house, he was greatly aroused. His view of what must be done was different from Mr. Parris's. The minister was quite naturally concerned with the spiritual dimension. He often preached about Satan's assault on New England and his determination to destroy this small Kingdom of God that we have erected in the wilderness. He called on us to defeat the Devil by prayer and days of fast.

"Thomas saw a more earthbound battle. His thinking was that Satan had chosen to work his evil by earthly means, through those who served him in his design to destroy God's Kingdom by attacking his people. He believed that Satan's grand design was to destroy New England, and so bring down the people who were most determined to keep him from taking dominion over all. He believed that Satan was working through people who were already enemies of God's people. He thought their targets included ministers and deacons, of course, but also those who maintained civil order. Thomas believed that the Putnam family was a particular target of Satan in Salem Village because we have had great influence in both the church and the village.

"When the women in Thomas's own house, his niece and his maid as well as his wife and daughter, began to be tortured before his very eyes, he was quick to address it through legal means. As witchcraft is a capital crime, it took complaints by two adult witnesses to have those accused arrested and charged, the testimony of minors not being sufficient. That was why Thomas often sent for me to watch when one of the girls would have a fit, to serve as a witness when she called out the name of the person whose specter was afflicting her. I would then join Thomas or another witness in swearing out a complaint, and the person would be arrested and confined for examination by the magistrates. I did this many times through the months of March and April in 1692."

"Did you believe them guilty?" Joseph asked quietly.

Edward looked startled. "Yes, I did at the time," he said. "The girls, Ann especially, seemed in great pain from the bites and beatings and other tortures they suffered. Their limbs were wrenched about so much it seemed they must be out of joint. And they often showed bruises and bite marks when they came out of a fit." He stared ahead of him for a moment. "Once, I remember, Ann displayed her back to me, and it clearly showed the purple imprints of chain links on her skin, as if someone had given her six lashes with an iron chain."

"But you have come to doubt?" Joseph's tone was even, encouraging.

Edward nodded. "I have come to doubt. I have thought on this many times and listened to those who are skeptical. I realize that these things I witnessed, and that later took place in public, could possibly have been dissembling. There is a physical explanation for each of them. No one actually saw the bare skin of the afflicted until they exposed it after their fits. But what child or young woman inflicts such pain on herself in order to accuse someone she hardly recognizes? There is also the possibility, as Mr. Increase Mather has said, that what the girls suffered was not witchcraft, but all a great delusion of Satan."

Joseph looked at him intently. "I have heard this spoken of. What do you mean, exactly?"

"Just as Saul was deluded by the Devil into thinking he saw the specter of the Prophet Samuel, the Devil could simply have made them *think* they saw the specter of Goody Nurse, let us say, but it was all just a fancy, and Goody Nurse did not send out her specter at all, but it was the Devil using her shape."

"And you believe this?"

Edward looked down at the table. "Some days I believe one thing, some days another. I know what I saw, but I also know that what we see is not always what it seems. The afflicted could have been telling the truth, or they could have been lying. They could have told the truth for the most part but lied on occasion. If they were telling the truth, either witchcraft or a delusion of Satan could explain it, and again, it could have been one thing at one time and the other at another."

"All of this is true," said Joseph. "If you did what you thought was right at the time, why does your conscience feel so burdened with guilt?"

Edward lifted haunted eyes to his. "Because I swore out a complaint that accused a four-year-old child of witchcraft. I saw the bite marks on my niece's arm, the imprints of little milk teeth, and I saw her fall to the floor, screaming, in court and accusing the little girl of biting and pinching her and bringing her the Devil's book to sign. And because I believed these things made her a witch, that little girl is the poor distracted child of God you see today. I cannot shirk it."

Joseph nodded. "I understand," he said simply. "You can but bring it to God, pray for forgiveness, and do what good you are able to, as you are doing. Only you and God can judge the sincerity of your effort. But, Brother Edward, do you believe this child was a witch?"

Edward looked him in the eye. "No, I do not," he said. "I think my niece was lying about this and at least one other."

"Who was the other?"

"Martha Corey."

"Why do you think that?"

"I think Ann played us for fools at that time. You see, Goody Corey was a church member, and when Ann began to call out her name in her fits, Ezekiel Cheever and I were appointed to go and discourse with her about witchcraft. This was in the middle of March, about two weeks after the first complaints were sworn. We noticed that the magistrates were asking the witnesses what clothes the specters wore to help identify them and thought we would try a test to make sure Ann was not mistaking Goody Corey's identity, she being the first church member to be accused.

In the early morning, I went to Thomas's house and told Ann to notice the clothes Goody Corey's specter came in that day, and we would come back and ask her about them before we went to the Corey house in the afternoon, then we could compare the clothes of the specter with the clothes Goody Corey was wearing. When we returned to Thomas's house, Ann told us that she had not been able to see the clothes because Goody Corey had come shortly after we left and blinded her to the spirit world, saying she should not see her again until it was night."

Joseph could not suppress a smile at this. "Somewhat convenient," he said.

Edward nodded. "It sounds like a childish lie to me now, too. When my niece was a child, I more than once chastised her for lying. At any other time, I would have probed her to make sure of the truth, but so convinced was I of this witchcraft that I took what she said without question."

"What did Goody Corey say?"

"Goody Corey asked us almost immediately after we arrived what my niece had said about her clothes. She had heard that the witnesses had all talked in court about the clothing people wore. When I told her what Ann had said, she just smiled, as though she had shown us a pretty trick."

"And what happened?"

"We took her action as evidence of *her* guilt, not Ann's. We assumed that the Devil had informed her that we would ask about the clothes and that she had sent out her specter to go and blind Ann. When we got back to Thomas's house, they told us that it had been as Ann had said, and Goody Corey had not been there all day. Later, Thomas told me that after we had gone, she came once more to afflict the child. When the time for her trial came, the judges used my affidavit with the story about the clothes against her, taking it in the same way I had. It was not the main piece of evidence against her, but it was something they dwelled on. I swore the complaint against her and supplied the deposition. I bear a grave responsibility for her suffering and death. If I had been less blind, less arrogant, less convinced of my own righteousness, I might have saved her."

Joseph reminded Edward of God's infinite capacity for forgiveness and of Christ's atonement for the sins of those who repented, but he knew there was little he could do to ease the conscience of his deacon. He carried his own burden of guilt, and he knew what it was like. They prayed together to God for forgiveness, and Joseph ended with a plea for mercy to his faithful servant, Edward, who had done so much that was good in his name.

Joseph sat at the table for a long time after Edward had left. He had been able to maintain a calm and ministerial demeanor while he was there, but he was deeply shaken by these revelations. How could this good man have been drawn to do such a horrific thing? An excellent father to his children and a generous and kindly uncle to his brother's orphans. Joseph thought of his own little Nanny, the joy of their household, the same age Dorothy Good was when she was chained to the wall in the Boston prison. How could anyone think a four-year-old could covenant with the

Devil? She could not yet tell the difference between the truth and a lie or fantasy. He thought of Nanny's little tales of fairies in the garden and animals speaking, her imaginary friend, her terror at night of nightmares and shadows in dark corners that had to be illumined before she could be calmed enough to sleep. Did the judges have no children? And how could a reasonable man like Edward Putnam be brought to believe so intensely that a little child had made a covenant with the Devil that he felt compelled to sign a complaint he knew would send her to prison and possibly death?

Joseph believed the Devil must be in this somewhere, but he was fairly certain it was not in the person of Dorothy Good. Had the judges interrogated the witnesses at all? Everything else aside, did they believe a four-year-old, whether in body or specter, could torture a girl who was twice her size with biting and pinching and the girl not be able to fight her off? The whole thing sounded nonsensical, but so many people he knew to be reasonable and well-meaning seemed to have believed it. How had this happened?

Chapter 16

1702

In the evening after Joseph's discussion with Edward Putnam, he and Betty sat together in their bedchamber in the unusually quiet house. Everyone else had gone to bed. John was asleep in his cradle next to them, and Nanny was curled up under her quilts in the trundle bed. This was their usual time for talk, a time Betty looked forward to all day, when she could have Joe's comforting presence all to herself. But tonight was different. Joseph sat staring into the fire for a good long time before his wife finally spoke.

"Is there something worries you, Joe?" she asked. "You are so quiet tonight."

He started as if awakened and turned to her. "'Tis church business, beloved," he said. "Nothing I need worry you with. It concerns discourse with a church member."

As the daughter of a minister, Betty knew well not to probe further. Joseph would never speak of a conversation with a church member held in the confines of the minister's study. "I hope it is not too much of a burden to you," she said. "I would share it if I could."

A warm smile lit his eyes as he looked at her in the firelight, and she felt he was back with her. "I am just trying to work out how to help with it, and what is best for the congregation." He looked down for a moment. "There *is* something you can help me with. Your father has never spoken to me about the witchcraft outbreak except in very general terms. Can you tell me what he thought about it?"

Betty was silent for a few moments, thinking back on her father's talk about the witchcraft trials ten years earlier. "I think it was deliberate, his not telling you his thoughts," she said. "He was probably afraid to scare you off by talking about the past. The present in Salem Village was frightful enough at that time." They exchanged a look that spoke volumes about their experience of the last five years. "And he did not want to say anything that would hinder you in your efforts to bring the people here together."

She spoke deliberately. "My father never approved of the trials. He was present for some of the earliest examinations by the magistrates, and he did not like the way they accepted anything the 'afflicted children,' as they called them, might say. He thought Judge Hathorne was particularly harsh with the accused and dismissed their attempts to defend themselves. I remember he was angry that Hathorne ignored it when people used the example of the Prophet Samuel as someone the Devil impersonated against their will. The judge said in court that those whose shapes appeared to people must have covenanted with the Devil."

Joseph nodded. "I have sensed Father Gerrish's disapproval of the trials over the years, but we have avoided speaking of them much directly. 'Tis such a tender subject." He suddenly sat up straight, as if he had made a decision. "I think I will go to Cambridge to see Mr. Brattle this week," he said. "His brother, Thomas, wrote a very influential account of the trials that has never been printed but was only circulated as a letter because of the danger at the time. I have great respect for him as a disinterested observer and a rational man." He spoke with growing confidence. "You know he is not just a merchant and Harvard official. He is greatly esteemed as a mathematician and astronomer. If anyone could give a straightforward and unprejudiced account of the trials, it would be he. I am certain Mr. Brattle can explain his views to me in detail, and we can discuss the subject without the burden of personal emotion it carries here."

Betty smiled. "'Tis a good idea, Joe. It will help to keep you from prejudice toward one side or the other. And you can lodge with your mother in Cambridge and see how she and Mary are getting on. It has been too long since you visited them."

When Joseph left for Cambridge very early on Tuesday morning, he could feel the promise of a rarely mild December day and said a little prayer of thanks that his journey would not be an especially difficult one. When the sun came up, it did indeed prove to be one of those rare New England December days when the sun seemed impossibly bright and warm, even on a road carved through the forest. He made very good time, arriving at the Cambridge ministry house by mid-morning. In Mr. Brattle's study, he found his old tutor sitting before the fire, glancing over the text for his Wednesday lecture. When he saw Joseph, he was out of his chair and across the room in a moment, his face lit with a happy smile as he grasped his hand.

"Joseph, what a welcome surprise," he said. "Take off your cloak and come sit by the fire while I heat you some cider to warm you. What brings you here on this beautiful day?"

Joseph laughed as he removed his cloak and hat. "Why, of course, I come to Cambridge to see you, sir. And as usual, I come in search of good advice."

William Brattle's broad smile faded. "I hope you are not troubled, Joseph," he said.

"Oh no, sir. For once, it is not me who is the problem. I seek your advice about Salem Village."

He nodded. "Ah yes, Salem Village. But you are doing well there, Joseph. Everyone speaks of the change you have wrought in the place. You have been there five years now, is it not, without a single major quarrel among the villagers?"

Joseph smiled. "The village is all right, and the congregation is healthy and growing. I am here to seek advice about the past, or rather, the past that is now the present."

He nodded again, as if he had been expecting this. “The witchcraft trials. Sit here by the fire while you explain.”

Joseph sat down and held his hands toward the fire as his old tutor heated the poker in the flames. “You see, I have been very careful to avoid speaking directly of the witchcraft trials with my people because I determined that if I was going to lead them out of the horrible enmity of the past and into a community of Christian fellowship, I should try as best I can to be a neutral party between the two sides. I think this has been successful as far as it can go. We have built a new meetinghouse and the people sit together as a congregation and a village now instead of as two warring sides. And most everyone has come back to worship.”

“A great accomplishment, Joseph. You should not belittle it.”

“No, I do not. I thank God every day for the newfound peace upon our little Israel. But there is still that ugly thing that festers at the center of our life together. I do not think I can ignore the horrors of the witchcraft doings any longer if we are to get past this state of truce into a genuine peace and fellowship together.”

William nodded slowly, a concerned expression on his face. “No doubt that is true. How can I help you?”

“I come to you as always, for knowledge and wisdom. Any account I get of the witch trials in Salem Village, even from people I trust and respect, will be tainted with bias or loyalty toward one side or the other. I know that your brother, whom I respect greatly as a highly intelligent and rational man, wrote an influential account of the trials that has not had general circulation. I am certain it is disinterested and most rational, and I would be very grateful if you could pass on the substance of it to me.”

William jumped up, his warm smile transforming his blunt features. “I can do better than that, Joseph,” he said. “My brother is here in Cambridge today for a meeting at the college. I am dining with him, and you will be most welcome. Now warm yourself by the fire and we shall talk together until it is time to go.” He poured a tankard of cider, pulled the poker from the fire, and plunged it in, filling the room with the rich apple fragrance.

For a young man of twenty-seven with humble origins, Joseph had considerable experience of dining with important men. He was often invited to dine by the most esteemed minsters in the colony when he went to Boston or Salem for Wednesday lectures, and he had dined with members of the General Court and the Governor's Council, and even with the governor. He was at ease with these men now, but he was still a little intimidated at the thought of sitting down with Thomas Brattle. The Treasurer of Harvard College as well as a wealthy Boston merchant, he was also greatly respected by students and faculty alike for his expertise in mathematics and astronomy. When Joseph had been at the college, the boys who had not aspired to be Increase Mather or his son, Cotton, had aspired to be Thomas Brattle. He knew that Brattle had contributed to the fund for his own education, doubtless at his brother William's request, and he had seen his confident, imposing figure at a distance, but had never met him.

When his old tutor introduced him at the Pig and Whistle, Joseph bowed rather lower than was his custom, and was surprised when Thomas Brattle grasped him firmly by the hand. "It is a pleasure to meet you, Mr. Green," he said. "I have heard much of the wonders you have wrought in keeping the peace in Salem Village. I am told it is hardly recognizable as the place where I spent some considerable time ten years ago."

His brother stepped in and spoke for the still reticent Joseph. "That is just what Mr. Green has come to talk to you about, Tom," he said. "He has heard of your account of the witchcraft trials and he would like to get the benefit of your observations."

"Then we shall have a long meal," said Thomas, sitting down at the table he had chosen in a relatively quiet corner of the room. As they joined him, he looked at Joseph and said, "You must understand, Mr. Green, that my view of the witchcraft episode is not a theological one. I leave that to the ministers. I am just a hard-headed observer who attended the court as a private citizen with an interest in the legal proceedings."

"I understand that, sir," said Joseph. "I know of your important work in mathematics and science, and it is just that rational approach that I seek. I am somewhat familiar with what the ministers have written on the subject, but frankly, I am not naturally of a theological turn of mind myself. I came to the ministry late, after I had finished at Harvard, and Mr. Brattle will tell you that I was much more attuned to mathematics and navigation than to theology. I had planned to use my education in a practical way at sea, following in the steps of several of my brothers. You may have heard of my brother, Edward, who was captain of the *Eagle*."

"Ah, yes," said Thomas. "The hero of the naval battle of 1695. I have heard great things of him. He fell in the battle, did he not?"

"No, sir. He died of consumption a few days later."

"A great loss."

"I try to honor him by doing the best work I can. I had written to him just before he died about my newly formed ambition to become a minister and he left me a bequest so that I might acquire my modest library."

Thomas nodded, settled into his chair and leaned forward slightly, ready for business. "What is it you would like to know about the witchcraft trials, Mr. Green?" he asked.

"I have heard about them in a general way, Mr. Brattle, but I do not have a clear sense of what took place. Any account I hear of one incident or another is always highly colored by the experience and the loyalties of the person telling it. Your perspective on it as a neutral observer who is committed to an unbiased and scientific way of considering things would be invaluable to me."

Thomas nodded. "Many a day I sat in that little meetinghouse marveling at what was taking place before me. I can tell you that the witch hunt very quickly took on a ritualistic form. The 'afflicted children,' as they were called, although some were mature women, would complain that someone tortured them. A complaint would be sworn out against the person in their names, along with the names of two adult witnesses if they were not of age, and a warrant would be issued to apprehend the accused."

Warming to his topic, Thomas Brattle spoke with increasing energy. "The accused person was then brought before the magistrates for examination, the afflicted children also being present, along with a meetinghouse full of spectators. The judges asked the accused person why she afflicted those poor children, to which the accused replied that she had not afflicted them. The judges ordered the accused to look upon the children, and at the time of that look, the afflicted were cast into a fit. I do not say it was *by* that look, as the judges did, but that one thing followed the other. The accused was then blindfolded and ordered to touch one of the afflicted persons, and at that touch, the afflicted came out of her fits. The afflicted persons then declared and affirmed that the accused had afflicted them, upon which the accused person, though of ever so good repute, was forthwith committed to prison, on suspicion of witchcraft."

"Was it as cut and dried as that?" asked Joseph.

"I reduce it to the frame of the ritual," said Thomas, "but in truth, it varied little in its outlines. Likewise, what followed varied in detail, but the procedure was the same. During the weeks or months they were in the jail, evidence was collected in the form of testimony by the complainants about their particular afflictions, usually biting, beating, and pinching of them by the specter of the prisoner, as well as any testimony that might be gathered up from the neighbors or others, accusing them of curdling the butter, killing the cat, spoiling the ale, or coming to men's chambers at night and sitting on their stomachs. As an incubus, you see. The grand jury then made out an indictment accusing the prisoner of using 'detestable arts, called witchcraft and sorcery, wickedly and feloniously' against one or more of the afflicted children, by which they were 'hurt, afflicted, pined, consumed, wasted and tormented,' which is the language of the statute."

A look of disgust crossed his face as he continued. "After more weeks and months in that loathsome jail, the case would be brought before the court of Oyer and Terminer established by the governor and the prisoner would be examined by the same judges as before, now as justices of the court instead of magistrates, along with a few others. The same procedures would be used with the afflicted children, which the justices took as evidence that witchcraft was being practiced in that very courtroom, and then the testimony of the neighbors would be introduced. The jury would be sent out with instructions from the justices, and almost without fail, would come in with a Guilty verdict. Then the prisoner would be sentenced to hang."

Their dinner had been placed before them, but now that Thomas Brattle had engaged with his subject, there was no stopping him. "I expect you see a few flaws in this procedure, Mr. Green," he said as he tucked into his boiled beef and vegetables.

Joseph nodded. He said, "On the matters of the touch test and the use of spectral evidence, the ministers have spoken clearly. Increase Mather said the touch test is but folklore and should not be used at all, and almost all the ministers have endorsed what he wrote in *Cases of Conscience* and have spoken against the use of spectral evidence in other ways. Even Cotton Mather, in his official account of the witchcraft trials, wrote that it should never be used as the sole evidence of guilt. I believe that their speaking out, along with the views of a few influential men like you, was behind the governor's finally forbidding the court of Oyer and Terminer to convict on spectral evidence alone, causing the Grand Juries to bring in all the future indictments as having insufficient evidence and dismissing them."

Thomas gestured toward Joseph with his knife. "Right you are, Mr. Green," he said. "The touch test was nonsensical. It all comes from the folk belief in the evil eye. The idea is that the witch sends forth her spirit through her eye to wreak evil upon the victim, but if she is forced to touch the one who is bewitched, her spirit will be drawn back into her body. If the judges thought the prisoner was causing fits in court simply by looking upon 'the afflicted,' they would force the prisoner to touch one of them, and suddenly they would all be cured of their fits, forsooth."

He smiled slightly. "Early on, I suggested that Judge Hathorne make an experiment to see whether there was not as much power to cure by a touch in his own hand as there was in the accused person's. All it would have taken would have been to blindfold the person in the fit and then I would venture two to one that the afflicted person would have come out of her fit upon the touch of the most righteous hand in Salem. Of course, this was never done. But when he was being interrogated, Mr. Alden stared at Judge Gedney and asked directly how it came about that his look would cast the afflicted girl into a fit but not the judge. The judges ignored this because there was no answer. I am fully persuaded that this test is pure sorcery and superstition, and there is no justification for it from law, reason or religion."

"What is your view of 'spectral evidence' from a scientific point of view?" asked Joseph.

Thomas shifted in his chair and sat up straight. "I will leave it to the religious authorities to say whether these specters or spirits, or shapes, or what you call them, do exist, and if so, whether they come from witches or directly from the Devil himself. But I will say that the *afflicted ones* often spoke of talking directly with the Devil, and at the request of the judges, they asked him many questions. If this is not holding correspondence with the Devil, I know not what is. What's more, if someone, say a judge, believes that an afflicted person is informed by the Devil, and he acts upon that information, then his act may properly be said to be founded upon the testimony or information of the Devil. In my view, such testimony is not only unreliable but probably felonious, as it is based on illegal congress with the Devil himself."

Thomas sat back in his chair and took a draft of his ale. "All of this is interesting to talk about," he said, "but you know it is not the central problem with the trials themselves."

"What is that, sir?" asked Joseph, who had been riveted by his account so far.

"It is the indictment," he said. "What people were accused of was afflicting those specific girls and women, causing them to be 'hurt, afflicted, pined, consumed, wasted and tormented,' as the statute says. Now these 'afflicted persons,' who might have twenty strange fits in a day, were, in the intervals between, hale and hearty, robust and lusty, as though nothing had afflicted them at all. When Chief Justice Stoughton gave the charge to the first jury, he told them they were not to mind whether the bodies of the afflicted were *really* pined and consumed, as expressed in the indictment. He said they should consider whether the afflicted suffered such afflictions as might *tend* to their being pined and consumed, wasted, and so forth. This, said he, is pining and consuming 'in the sense of the law.' I think I need add nothing to this."

Joseph looked at him, incredulous. "No indeed," he said. "'Tis as though one were to be accused of murder after punching some-one on the nose because people have been known to die from a blow to the head."

Brattle nodded appreciatively and leaned forward. "The matter of evidence is important too, though. There was much testimony introduced in the Court of Oyer and Terminer to bolster the spectral evidence given by the afflicted girls. This was where the stories of spoiled butter and ale, strange animals appearing in the night, horses and cattle suddenly taken ill, incubi and so forth came from. They were supposed to be evidence that the accused person was practicing witchcraft. But they did not speak to the crime for which the accused was in fact indicted, causing the pining away and consuming and so forth of these specific girls and women.

"This testimony was admitted in court and taken as evidence that the accused person was guilty, and that is the basis on which Cotton Mather and others claimed that those executed were not convicted on spectral evidence alone. They were in fact convicted on spectral evidence plus additional evidence that had nothing to do with the crime they were charged with. If I am charged with murdering B, and evidence is introduced that I have in fact murdered C, that may show me to be a murderer, but it does not prove that I have murdered B and can legally be executed for that crime."

"This is most enlightening, Mr. Brattle," said Joseph, "and, I am afraid, a severe indictment of our court. There seems to be either deliberate deceit or gross incompetence at every turn."

Thomas looked at him and nodded. "The first is right, I think. Deceit at every turn. My concern has always been with the court, and so I look to the judges, whose duty is to see that the law is upheld. They clearly did not do this, but from the beginning were strongly biased on the side of the accusers. I am not able to offer a rational judgment on the accusers. I saw them fall down in their fits and tumble about on the floor. I saw them accuse clearly innocent people of torturing them. I saw them use childish deceptions—bruises that were covered by clothing until introduced in court, pins that they pulled from their heads and their hands or found in their clothing, the pretense of suddenly being struck blind or dumb when asked a question they could not answer.

"I thought many of their ploys transparent, ridiculous. To take just one example that I remember vividly, when Elizabeth Proctor was being examined, Abigail Williams and Ann Putnam suddenly turned on her husband and began to say that John Proctor was a wizard, which had not been suggested before this. Immediately, the others fell down and tumbled about, crying out that John Proctor afflicted them. At length, presumably when they had exhausted themselves, they got up again, and one of them called, 'There goes Goodman Proctor to take up Mrs. Pope's feet.' Mrs. Pope's feet shot up into the air. The judges told Proctor to explain these things, and when he protested that he knew nothing about them, Abigail Williams cried out, 'There is Goodman Proctor going to Mrs. Pope.' Mrs. Pope fell to the floor in a fit.

"Judge Hathorne's response to this was to say to Proctor, 'You see the Devil will deceive you. The children could see what you were going to do before the woman was hurt. I would advise you to repentance, for the Devil is bringing you out.' I would laugh at such a thing, but the effect was that several days later, John Proctor was imprisoned for witchcraft, and we know the rest. Now someone might believe, as Hathorne said, that the Devil was bringing him out, but for what reason I cannot imagine, for why would the Devil be exposing his own henchmen in court?"

"Indeed," said Joseph. "Do you have a hypothesis about what was actually happening in the court?"

"From what I observed of the behavior before me, I most strongly believe that those girls staged this thing, in a premeditated way, to accuse John Proctor. Why? I do not know. The human heart is not my specialty, nor is the human conscience. I am also certain that they were not acting alone. Thomas Putnam was everywhere in those proceedings, swearing out complaints, writing out the testimony of his wife and daughter and others, taking down testimony during the hearings. He also kept a tight rein on his daughter from what I could see. He was always there, hovering about her, whispering in her ear. Parris was similar with Abigail Williams in the beginning, although he seemed to keep his distance later. And there were other men about, whispering in those 'afflicted' ears, and a number of mature women among the afflicted, including Putnam's wife. There could be a myriad of motives among all these people, including the accusers themselves. But that is your line of country, Mr. Green, not mine."

"Yes, it is," said Joseph. "You are talking about some of the members of my congregation. Ann Putnam is not a church member, but she comes regularly to worship. Her parents are dead now, but I know the family fairly well. She is very motherly toward her brothers and sisters. It is hard to imagine her doing these things."

William Brattle, who had been listening quietly throughout their dinner, spoke up. "Now comes the hard part, Joseph. You must imagine it. If you are going to help these people, you need to learn not only what they did, but what they thought they were doing and why. The truth involves both."

"Yes," said Thomas. "I may not believe this was witchcraft, but I have the feeling that the Devil was in it somewhere. I think we must hope that human beings, especially children, are not capable of generating this much evil all by themselves."

Chapter 17

1702

Joseph was able to forget all about the witchcraft trials when he reached his mother's house. He began to feel peace descend as soon as he stepped inside, surrounded by the familiar objects of his childhood home. He was happy to find that all was well with his mother and sister, and they had plenty of firewood and provisions. He split some kindling for them, more out of sentiment than need. Then they spent a pleasant hour talking of the family, of the little accomplishments of Nanny and John, of the news of Zacharia and Ruth, of the hope that Benjamin would be sailing home soon. His mother made his favorite codfish pie, a treat for supper, and she and Mary praised the plum preserves that Betty had sent.

As he fell asleep in the familiar chamber he had shared with many of his brothers through the years, Joseph reflected that once again Betty had been two steps ahead of him. She knew he would be deeply distressed by the talk of the witchcraft trials, and that the best thing he could do would be to spend that night under his mother's roof.

As he rode home from Cambridge the next morning, Joseph pondered what he had learned of the witch trials and what he ought to do next. Sitting with Betty that night, he asked, "Would it please you to go to Wenham if the weather is mild on Monday? It would help me to have a talk with Father Gerrish." Betty was always happy to visit her family, and they set off with the children on two horses for the five-mile trip. There was a joyous meeting with the Gerrish clan, with lively talk and much laughter before the dinner hour brought a meal of roast turkey, provided fresh by one of the congregation and done to a turn on the spit, along with root vegetables from the cellar. Afterward, Joseph asked his father-in-law if he had time for a quiet talk in his study. They retired upstairs, where they could still hear the happy din of the keeping room as the women cleared the dinner away and put things to rights.

As they sat down in the two chairs by the fire, Reverend Gerrish took a keen look at Joseph under cover of his genial manner. “Is there something on your mind, Joseph?” he asked. “You seem unusually quiet today.”

Joseph laughed. “I know not how you would notice, Father Gerrish, in the noise of this crowd. But ’tis true. I do have something particular I would like you to advise me about, if you will.”

“Of course, I shall be happy to help if I can.”

“I do not think you will like the topic. It is about the witchcraft doings.” Joseph spoke frankly. “You know I have kept myself from delving much into the past because I wanted to concern myself with building a loving community in Salem Village for the present and future and to avoid preconceived prejudices as much as I could.”

Gerrish nodded. “Yes, and it has been a good plan. Your congregation has been remarkably peaceful with one another these last few years.”

Joseph smiled. “Of course, we have our disputes, but we are learning to deal with them without the spite and rancor of the past. I think everyone recognizes now that it will take a long time, and we must all approach it with good will. What has been troubling me is that church members are beginning to come to me to discourse about their roles in the witchcraft trials. I am finding it hard going, for while I am encouraged that they trust me with their spiritual burdens, I feel that I am too much in the dark about the events to offer worthwhile advice. I am trying to learn a little more now, and last week I was able to talk with Mr. Thomas Brattle, who is the brother of my old Harvard tutor."

Gerrish looked up with interest. "That must have been very enlightening, Joseph. I have heard of the letter he wrote about the trials, which is said to have been influential in the governor's decision to shut down the court."

"Yes," said Joseph, "it was most helpful. Mr. Brattle is a man of science, you know, and his view is based on the legality of the thing and the specific events that took place in court. It helped me to form a picture of the trials and also to understand the vexed issues from a legal point of view, rather than only the theological view we have from the minsters."

"Did Mr. Brattle give you his opinion of the validity of the trials?"

Joseph smiled. "He most certainly did. He believes they had no validity whatsoever."

"Why? Is it the question of spectral evidence?"

"That comes into it, certainly. He classes it with the touch test and other things they did in court as folklore amounting to sorcery and roundly condemns the judges for using it. But he goes to the heart of the legal matter in saying that, aside from spectral evidence, almost none of the testimony introduced in court was relevant to the indictments, which were specifically for causing 'pining and consuming and wasting' of those named, and so it should have been thrown out and the accused should not have been convicted. This contradicts Cotton Mather, as you probably know, who maintains that the executions were legal because none of those executed were convicted on spectral evidence alone."

"Does Brattle think any of them guilty?"

"He would not give his opinion on guilt or innocence. He says that is our line of country, not his. But he says that the trials did not prove it. He did make it clear that he did not believe the 'afflicted children,' who he said were lying and performing childish deceits, and I must say that the examples he gave certainly suggest that. He suspects there is guilt that goes beyond the young girls. 'The Devil is in it somewhere,' as he says."

"I see," said Gerrish thoughtfully.

"What I would like from you, Father, is the opinion of a man I most greatly trust and esteem, who is eminently qualified to approach the religious question. I realize that you were not involved, and that Wenham was, thanks be to God, spared from accusations. But that is perhaps all the more reason to value your opinion. Am I right in thinking that you did see some of the court proceedings?"

"Yes, I did."

"And what do you think of Mr. Brattle's characterization?"

Gerrish looked at the young man before him, so eager to learn, so anxious to help his people, and made a decision. "This is not to be bruited about, Joseph, but I will be frank with you because I consider you a son and trust you implicitly." He shot him a meaningful look.

"Of course," said Joseph. "You may rely on me to keep this between us."

"It may surprise you, son, that I agree completely with Mr. Brattle."

"You did not believe the 'afflicted children?'"

"No, I did not. I attended some of the early examinations—not as many as Mr. Brattle, but enough to see that there was more performance than affliction about it. The judges were so eager to believe the accusers that they did not apply the most basic skepticism to their testimony. I have not thought about the indictments before, as I had not seen what they said specifically. Like most of the spectators, I thought the trials were to prove that the accused were practicing witchcraft, not that they caused specific physical effects to those particular people. Of course, Mr. Brattle is right that all of the supposed corroborating testimony should have been thrown out. Those people should never have been convicted." He slowly shook his head, struck anew with the enormity of it.

"I tell you, Joseph, I have my own burden of guilt to carry. I wish I had done more to try to stop it. I signed the findings of the ministers against the trials, and I helped to prepare petitions for Sarah Cloyce and Mary Esty, but seeing that all of that had no effect, I decided to concentrate my efforts on my own congregation."

"You clearly did some good here. There were no accusations in Wenham."

"'Tis true. I determined early not to ignore the trouble to the west, but to preach about it. Instead of harping on the war with Satan, like Reverend Parris, I spoke often of the duty we owed one another as members of a community to exercise Christian charity in both our treatment of one another and our thoughts about our neighbors. When there were a few suggestions of trouble brewing, I went immediately to the source and discoursed with the persons involved, emphasizing the great harm that an accusation of witchcraft could wreak on the accused and their families, and admonishing them to be absolutely certain before they accused anyone of such a thing and took a possible burden of guilt for murder upon themselves. We prayed together for enlightenment, and each time, the person said she had been confused or perhaps deceived by the Devil, or it had been a dream.

"I am afraid I abetted the sin of pride in my congregation, encouraging their belief that they were a more Christian community than their neighbors to the west, but it was a relatively small fault in the circumstances. They were determined not to become another Salem Village, or worse, as Andover did."

"I have heard that you were a great help to Reverend Hale when they accused his wife."

"That was providential, I think. Mary Herrick, a member of his congregation, accused Mrs. Hale's specter of torturing her. Mr. Hale asked me to come with him to discourse with her, and eventually she told us that she had come to believe it was *not* Mrs.

Hale's specter that had appeared to her, but that she had been deluded by the Devil into thinking it was. Mrs. Hale was never accused in court, but the experience greatly unsettled John Hale, who up until that time, was a supporter of the witchcraft trials. He changed his mind then, and wrote against it, his belief being that it was Satan himself who appeared to the afflicted in the shapes of the accused. His account was published after his death these two years ago."

"I have heard of it. His change of heart was late, but still useful in changing public opinion. Most people now seem to believe that it was not witchcraft by individuals but a delusion of Satan that caused people to see specters. They believe that the accused were not guilty, and the accusers were deluded."

"Yes, but it was all of it too late. We did not save the lives of twenty innocent people, nor stop the untold misery for many others." Reverend Gerrish looked down at the floor for a few moments, and then raised his head with a characteristically hopeful expression on his face. "But what do you think of doing now, son?"

Joseph straightened himself in his chair and spoke with energy. "I am thinking this. As you said, the members of my congregation have found their way to peace with one another, at least outwardly, over these last ten years. But I fear that peace does not go deep. This thing still sits festering among us. As long as it is not spoken of, it will be there, and could erupt to the surface at any time. My desire is to bring it into the light. I want us to look at the past and acknowledge it, and move on from it, but I am hoping to do it without digging up the old enmity and resentment, which would only make things worse."

Gerrish nodded. "That is a laudable but very delicate process that could easily go wrong."

Joseph went on eagerly. "I fully agree, and that is one of the things I would like you to advise me about. I am thinking about Martha Corey, one of the first to be accused. She was a member of our church and was excommunicated by the congregation for witchcraft a few days before she was hanged. It sits heavily upon many in my flock that they sent her to her death an uncovenanted soul, and some have spoken to me about it. I am thinking of proposing that we revoke her excommunication and reinstate her membership in our church. I think we owe it to her if we now believe in her innocence. And what is more, it would be an important symbolic act, an acknowledgement of the wrong that was done by the village and the church without making accusations against anyone in particular."

Gerrish thought for a few moments. "I think it may be inspired, Joseph. It could accomplish a great deal. But you would have to be careful that the church members do not fall back into familiar warring sides over this if there is still feeling in the village that the witchcraft trials were just."

"That is my worry. But I think the support for the trials has weakened considerably. Thomas Putnam and his wife are dead, and I am certain that his brother Edward, my deacon, would approve of this, as would Deacon Ingersoll. Several others who participated as witnesses and signed complaints have said things that suggest to me they would welcome such a move. Most of the 'afflicted girls' have left the village in one way or another, with the notable exceptions of Ann Putnam, who lives very quietly with her sister, and Mary Walcott, who is married to the grandson of one of the victims. Neither of them is a church member."

"Perhaps if you spoke discreetly with key persons, like Jonathan and Captain John Putnam, to see if they would be in favor, you could get the lie of the land before you broached it at a church meeting."

"I can do that and talk with several others as well." He looked searchingly at his father-in-law. "Do you think this is a good idea?" he asked.

Gerrish nodded. "Yes, Joseph, I do. It is a matter of whether this is the right time. Only you, and Betty," he smiled, "can gauge the general feeling in your congregation, but if they are ready to take an action like this, it could help enormously to heal the breach they have suffered."

"Depend on it, I shall be consulting Betty. She often knows what is going to happen from the women long before I get wind of it from the men."

"I find the same to be true of your Mother Gerrish. We are lucky men, Joseph."

"Agreed."

Joseph did, of course, consult Betty, who made discreet investigations into the feelings of the village women about the witchcraft trials. What she heard corroborated what Joseph learned by talking with his friend, Jonathan Putnam, as well as other influential men in the village. He also asked Edward Putnam, who was enthusiastic about the idea of reinstating Martha Corey, to sound out the rest of his family, with good results.

On December twenty-seventh, Joseph broached the idea at a church meeting. Speaking simply and straightforwardly, without laying blame at anyone's door, he said, "Brethren, I find in your church-book a record of Martha Corey's being excommunicated for witchcraft, and, the generality of the land being sensible of the errors that prevailed in that day, some of her friends have moved me several times to propose to the church whether it be not our duty to recall that sentence, so it may not stand against her to all generations. I myself being a stranger to her, and being ignorant of what was alleged against her, I shall now only leave it to your consideration, and shall determine the matter by a vote at the next convenient opportunity."

There were a few questions about the theology behind it and the timing, which he tried to answer clearly and honestly. Then he let the congregation do its work, as the idea quickly made its way around the village and out to the surrounding farms. He asked Betty and the deacons to keep their ears to the ground as they went about church duties and functions, and Jonathan and Elizabeth Putnam to monitor the gossip in their wide social circle. There seemed to be little objection and a general feeling that it was a thing the church ought to do.

On the fourteenth of February, 1703, Joseph brought the matter of reinstating Martha Corey's membership before the church meeting. The resolution noted that Martha Corey had been excommunicated on September 14, 1692, 'she being, before her excommunication, condemned, and afterward executed, for supposed witchcraft.' It went on to say that the members of the congregation 'do freely consent and heartily desire that the same sentence may be revoked, and that it may stand no longer against her, for we are, through God's mercy to us, convinced that we were at that dark day under the power of those errors which then prevailed in the land, and we are sensible that we had not sufficient grounds to think her guilty of that crime for which she was condemned and executed, and that her excommunication was not according to the mind of God, and therefore we desire that this may be entered in our church-book, to take off that odium that is cast on her name, and that so God may forgive our sin.'

While no one made any serious objections, the vote was not unanimous. Joseph noticed six or seven dissenters in the meeting-house. But it was a strong majority, including Edward Putnam, Nathaniel Ingersoll and Ezekiel Cheever, who had figured importantly as witnesses against Martha Corey. It was a crucial step forward on their church's road to Christian fellowship.

Chapter 18

1706

It was a very hot Sunday in July, one of those brutal New England summer days when the humidity hung down heavily and every movement caused the sweat to trickle. Joseph had just finished preaching the second of two sermons in the sweltering meeting-house and he was soaking wet and worn out as he stood outside the door, bidding goodbye to his congregation. As the last few families came up to him, he noticed the little figure of Ann Putnam standing off to the side, looking as though she were doing her best to be invisible in the unforgiving sunlight. When the last of the families were readying their horses for the ride home, Ann came up to Joseph by herself, something she had never done before. She usually waited near the road as he spoke to Tom and Elizabeth and Deliverance. This time, they waited for her.

"Good morning, Ann," he said. "It is a pleasure to see you."

She looked up at him, blinking in the sun. "Thank you, Mr. Green," she said. "I think you must be very tired, and I will not keep you. I have something particular to ask you. Would it be possible for me to come and talk with you sometime this week?"

Joseph tried not to show his surprise. "Of course, Ann," he said. "You are always welcome at the ministry house. I will be away in Wenham tomorrow, but at home on Tuesday. Can you come on Tuesday afternoon?"

"Yes, I am most grateful, Mr. Green," she said, and turned and walked off quickly before he could ask her any more about it.

As they strolled back to the ministry house with the children, Betty asked Joseph what Ann Putnam had spoken to him about.

"I truly do not know," he said. "She asked to come and speak with me next week. 'Tis most unusual. I do not believe she has ever been in the ministry house before, at least not in our time."

"No," said Betty. "I would certainly remember that."

On Tuesday afternoon, Betty watched as Deliverance Putnam rode up to the ministry house, her sister on a pillion behind her. After helping Ann to dismount, Deliverance rode off toward the village and Ann walked slowly up to the door and knocked. To Betty, she looked like a bashful child screwing up her courage to talk to adults. She opened the door immediately, greeting Ann in a way that she hoped was welcoming without being overwhelming.

"Please to come upstairs, Ann. Mr. Green is expecting you this afternoon," she said, leading the way to the minister's study.

Joseph had, of course, heard them on the stairs. He called "Come," when Betty knocked lightly on the door, and looked up with a smile.

"Here is Ann," said Betty. "Nanny will bring up some cider to cool you both."

They were soon settled in the room's two most comfortable wooden chairs, looking at each other across Joseph's small table, their cider between them. "It is good to see you, Ann," said Joseph. "How can I help you?"

Ann glanced at him and then dropped her eyes, her usually pale face pink with the heat and possibly a blush of embarrassment. "I have a question to ask."

"I will do my best to answer it," he said amiably.

She glanced at him again and then spoke a sentence she had obviously prepared carefully. "I have come to ask whether it would be possible for me to petition to join the church."

Joseph tried not to show his amazement and to speak with pastoral kindness. He relied on a little speech he had given many times before to prospective church members. "Most certainly, you may petition for membership, Ann. I welcome all God's children in this study. I realize that you probably know what is required for membership. You have been coming to the church all your life and many of your family are members. But let me remind you that you first must examine your past life and make a full confession of your sins to God. Then, if you have a conviction of his forgiveness and accept Jesus Christ as your savior, you can be propounded to the congregation for a vote on your joining our church. You must make a shorter public confession to the church members before they vote to receive you into the church."

She had fixed her eyes on him as he spoke and answered quickly. "I understand, Mr. Green, and I am ready to do it."

Joseph's look was encouraging. "May I ask why you have decided to take this step now?"

She reddened a little but did not drop her eyes. "Mr. Green," she said, "I am twenty-six years of age. You know that I have been living with a great burden of guilt for more than half of my life. I feel that the time has come for me to face my God and ask forgiveness. I must find out whether what I have done is forgivable."

He looked into her eyes. "Ann, everything is forgivable to God," he said earnestly. "He has the power to forgive all sins. And his son, Jesus Christ, freely offered to undergo the punishment our sins deserve, and by his suffering and death, did infinitely satisfy divine justice for the sins of those who believe in him. As church members, we believe this is the only way we can be saved, from the guilt and from the dominion and power of sin. But we also believe that Christ came into the world to save only a certain number of souls, chosen by God, from their sins and bring them to eternal glory. The Lord Jesus is fully able and abundantly willing to save those who show that they are of this number by truly repenting of all their sins.

"For you, Ann," he said, leaning forward, "the most important thing is faith. It is not enough to repent for our sins. We must have faith that Jesus Christ can intercede with God for us. It is through God's grace alone that we are offered this path to salvation, but God justifies freely for his son's sake all those who believe in him and perform the duties they are called to as well as they are able. He absolves them from the guilt and condemnation their sins deserve and accepts them to eternal life as righteous. But first, the sinner must acknowledge his guilt. I will tell you frankly that this can be a very difficult and painful thing. For you, it would mean going back to revisit the dreadful events of 1692."

Ann had been listening closely to Joseph's explanation of the doctrine, and she nodded. "Thank you, Mr. Green," she said, "I think I understand the church's teachings and I do my best to believe in the infinite mercy and grace of God." With a clear effort of will, she met his eyes. "And be assured, there is not one day these fourteen years when I have not revisited the dreadful events of 1692."

From his ten years' experience of serious discourse with the members of his congregation, Joseph could sense the sincerity in those words. He nodded. "I understand. And I can tell you from personal experience that revisiting your sins with the thought of confessing and being forgiven is not nearly as bad as reliving them only to feel the guilt for them over and over without end."

She gave him a brief, intense look. "May it be so," she said.

Now that the terms of the discourse had been laid out, Joseph relaxed a little in his chair and took a drink of cider. "I am most ready to be of help," he said, "and I suppose the way to begin is to begin. Can you read and write, Ann?"

Ann answered uncertainly. "I read a little in the Bible and enough to do the business of the farm, and I can write my name, but I cannot write script. My father believed that writing was a thing for men. He wrote a beautiful hand himself and saw to it that my brothers learned, but not the girls."

Joseph nodded. This was the case with most of the women in his church. "There are two ways we can approach your private confession, then. You can dictate it to someone and then show it to me, or you can tell it to me. In either case, you can dictate your public confession to me, and I will read it out to the congregation with you standing in witness."

"I see," she said quietly. She looked at him, an appeal in her eyes. "If you are willing, I would prefer to tell it to you. There is no one else I would want to talk to about this."

"We shall do that, then," he said decisively, straightening himself to show he was ready for business. "And I assure you that nothing you tell me in this room will go beyond its walls."

Looking at her with warmth in his eyes, he asked in a lighter tone, "Tell me, though. Have you spoken to your family about your wish to join the church?"

"Oh, yes," she said, smiling for the first time. "Tom and Deliverance and Elizabeth have all encouraged me to come to you. Tom especially. He says you are very kind and sensible."

He smiled back at her. "I am happy he thinks so. I certainly try to be." The memory of the anguished face of young Tom Putnam during the discussion they had had years earlier about his rebaptism came into Joseph's mind. There certainly were depths in this family that he had never been eager to plumb. He spoke carefully. "I know little about the events of 1692. I was a boy myself then, and since I have come here, I have tried to look forward rather than backward in my ministry."

"I know that, Mr. Green." Ann spoke eagerly. "It is one of the things that gives me confidence you will hear what I have to say. I see how careful you are not to stand on one side of the village or the other, but to listen to all voices and draw your own conclusions about things. There are many in this village who think they know all about the witchcraft doings, but I can tell you they know only the outside of things. They know nothing of what really happened in 1692." She looked directly into his eyes. "I have never told my part in it to anyone except God, and now I want to tell you, as a man of God I trust to be honest with me, to see if I can find forgiveness."

Joseph was impressed with her frank response. "I do my best to keep an open mind until I know something about things," he said. "Let us begin at the beginning and see where it takes us. I understand that you were among those who first made accusations of witchcraft. Can you tell me how it came about?"

Ann closed her eyes briefly. "I was twelve years old," she said, opening them. "My friend Abby, Abigail Williams, who is Reverend Parris's niece, a year younger than me, was angry at the way she was being treated at home. They were training her into service, and making her answer to the servant, Tituba. She found a way to change things when she heard Mr. Parris talking with Mr. Noyes about Reverend Cotton Mather's first book about witchcraft, the one about the Goodwin children. Do you know it?"

"*Late Memorable Providences Relating to Witchcrafts and Possessions*? I have read it."

She nodded. "That is the one. Abby was much taken with the effect the Goodwin children had on adults, and she determined that she and her little cousin, Betty, could do the same. They began to do the things the Goodwins did, running through the house screaming, flinging firebrands about, feigning fits and such. Reverend Parris was deceived by all of it, and they had great sport, wreaking havoc in the house and receiving solicitude rather than chastisement. They spent their time as they liked and there was no more talk of sending Abby out to service. Reverend Parris was afraid for anyone to hear of such doings at the ministry house, so he kept it quiet at first."

"How did you learn of it?"

"Abby had told me about it from the beginning. They showed me what they did and trained me in it, so that I became as convincing as they were, and better at some things, like falling down in fits and trances. Abby was too healthy-looking to be very convincing in a trance, but my pale skin could make me look almost dead, they said."

There was a certain pride of accomplishment in the way this was spoken that disturbed Joseph. “Tell me,” he said, “when did you begin to use these arts to deceive?”

Ann seemed to come back to the occasion and blushed a little. “Mr. Parris finally called in Dr. Griggs to diagnose the girls. It was always Abby’s way to go too far, and the Parrises were frighted by the states the girls got themselves into. When the doctor said it must be witchcraft, Abby told me I must try it at home, as my father was a great believer in witches and often talked of witchcraft with Mr. Parris. I had been reluctant before, expecting that it would only bring me a severe beating, but I decided to do it.”

He looked at her gravely. “And do you remember your motives?”

Looking down, she slowly shook her head. “I have thought about it many, many times, but I regard myself at that age and am still amazed at it. I think it was mostly the sin of pride. I believed I had an art I could practice and fool these adults, including my father. There was excitement in it and risk. My father was a stern disciplinarian. He fervently believed that sparing the rod would spoil the child. If I failed, I would pay a heavy price, but if I succeeded, I thought it would be a wonderful thing to have the place in the household that Abby had at the ministry house.”

She looked at him frankly. “In the end, I suppose I did not think much at all. It was just a thrilling thing to do. We were thoughtless girls who never considered consequences beyond our own households at that time. And it succeeded. My father was much interested in my doings and what I had to say, and my mother never bothered me about the housework that was being neglected.”

Her face turned grave. “But then they began pressuring us to tell them who was bewitching us. If there was witchcraft, there must be witches. And that is where it all went horribly wrong.”

“You lied about the witches?”

She looked at him. “We lied and lied and lied.” She dropped her eyes and took some time to think, to remember, and then continued. “It did not seem so bad to us at first. Abby named their slave Tituba, who was already suspected because she was an Indian from Barbados, and I named Sarah Good, the wife of William Good, who begged food and money at people’s doors. Many heard her muttering curses when they disappointed her, and they already called her a witch. I also named Sarah Osborne, a distant relation who was thought very wicked in our household because my father believed she had stolen money from him out of his cousin’s estate. At first, we did not think of them being arrested and examined by the magistrates. That is how ignorant we were.

“Soon enough, though, we found ourselves in the meeting-house testifying.” She looked at a point beyond Joseph as if she were watching it unfold. “The first to be examined was Sarah Good. The magistrates made us stand up in front of all the people and they asked, ‘Did this woman hurt you?’ and then they bade Sarah Good look upon us. Abby fell to the floor then and went into a fit, and so we all did it. They did the same thing to every one of them.”

“How did the women respond?”

“At first, the women all denied the charges and accused each other. But then Tituba confessed to covenanting with the Devil and being a witch. She told many things we would never have thought of. Our accusations were all childish stories about being pinched and bitten. Tituba said she had made a bargain with the Devil, and that she used a cat and a bird and other animals as familiars. She said she rode on a pole in the sky with the other two witches to go to hurt people and talked about seeing the Devil’s book and about the appearance of the Devil as a hairy animal with wings. Abby told me later that was a picture in one of Mr. Parris’s books.”

Joseph had seen such images in King James’s *Daemonologie* and other books. With Samuel Parris’s interest in witchcraft, it did not surprise him that he had owned such things.

Ann went on. “The things that Tituba described all became regular parts of the proceedings after that. The magistrates would ask those accused about them, and then often they would confess to the same kinds of things."

"Why did you not confess to your lies at the beginning?"

Again, Ann seemed mystified by her younger self. There was a certain detachment in her response. "I confess I do not know the answer to that," she said. "I think we were staggered by the court proceedings. We were much impressed by the magistrates and the constables and all the people who had come to watch. They had to move the hearing from Ingersoll's tavern to the meetinghouse because there were so many people. I like to think that, were it just a simple hearing in a room with the magistrate, I might have confessed it then, but I fear I am deluding myself."

Joseph was quiet while she took time to remember. She looked up at him again. "By that time, my father and uncle were involved in swearing out depositions and filing formal complaints on our behalf, and my father would have been furious at being made to look foolish. I feared my father more than the lie. And we were stunned by Tituba's stories. We thought she must really be a witch to have known about all those things. Of course, the thing she was formally accused of, hurting us, she never did do, but we thought if she confessed to witchcraft, she must be guilty of witchcraft, which was what the magistrates were after her to confess. And she accused the other two as well. We were very ignorant at that time. We did not know that conviction of witchcraft was a death sentence."

"I have never understood how it spread so far. Why did you not end the accusations with these three?"

Ann explained easily, as though this was well-traveled ground for her. "At first, there were people in the village who spoke out against us because they did not believe us or did not hold with the witch trials at all. Martha Corey was one of the loudest of these, and because she was a church member, her voice was more influential than many. This infuriated my father, who often denounced the Coreys in our house as enemies of our family who wanted our land and would use any means they could to attack us.

He kept after me, asking if I did not see Goody Corey coming to attack me. Finally, I said yes. I performed my tricks and my father sent for Uncle Edward to come and serve as witness."

She stopped to reflect for a moment. "I think Uncle Edward could have sent the whole thing clattering down at that time," she said. "He caught me in a lie about Martha Corey. In examining the others, the judges had asked us what clothes the witch's specters were wearing. Uncle Edward and Constable Cheever, going as church members to discourse with Goody Corey about witchcraft, asked me what clothes her specter had on that day, so that they could observe her clothes and make sure I was not mistaken in her identity. I made up a childish lie about Goody Corey coming and blinding me to the spirits that day so that I could not see her clothes. Uncle Edward had caught me in lies before and was very good at spying them out. I was surprised and greatly relieved when he let that pass.

"When the men visited her, Goody Corey was wearing some unusual clothes, and knowing this would be remarked on, she asked them if I had described them. They took this as evidence that she had indeed come and blinded me to avoid identification. They reported it so to the court, where it was used as evidence to discredit *her*, not me. That is how much they wanted to believe us. Even a wise and honest man like my uncle was deluded. After Goody Corey, there were very few who spoke their minds if they did not agree with the trials."

Joseph showed a touch of the impatience he was feeling. "But why did you continue with the accusations? Could you not have stopped it then?"

She looked at him earnestly. "I tell you truthfully, Mr. Green, we wanted to. Or at least I did. Abby was for keeping it up as long as we could. By this time, there were many of us involved. Several older girls had joined us and even some married women. Abby was no longer in control of it as she had been. Then my mother began to have fits and all of us children in the family were greatly frighted. I did not know if she was feigning or not. I thought that my playacting might have brought the fits on her.

"My mother and father kept asking me if Rebecca Nurse afflicted me. I wondered at this, as I did not know Goody Nurse by sight, although I knew the name. I knew she was a member of the Salem Church and came rarely to our meetinghouse. Finally, I said that someone appeared who I did not recognize, and my mother asked if it was Rebecca Nurse. I began crying out that Goody Nurse did hurt me. I accused her in the court during Goody Corey's trial."

Ann needed no time to reflect now. Her story came out in a rush of words that could hardly be stopped. Joseph simply sat still and listened. "Then my mother had a grievous fit that lasted for two days, sometimes in a fury while she seemed to fight off Rebecca Nurse, screaming and arguing with her, saying she would not sign her book, she would not serve the Devil, and quoting scripture, and then lapsing into a trance."

Ann's face reflected the fearful sight that appeared in her mind. "It was dreadful to watch. It was very like what I did, but far worse in degree and effect. I became certain that she was not imitating us but was really being tormented by some horrible dark spirit. I feared that we had unleashed the Devil on her with our lies. My cousin, Mary, and I tried to keep the children away, but I was as terrified as they.

"Goody Nurse was arrested, but my mother continued to have grievous fits. During the trial, she had a violent fit such as we had never seen before. At the end, she was lying on the floor of the meetinghouse, unable to move. The magistrates told my father to carry her outside. She slowly came back to herself. Rebecca Nurse was put in jail, and after that, my mother seemed to recover and saw her specter no more for months.

"Then my father called me to him and said he had something very serious to tell me." She paused, her eyes riveted to a point in the room beyond Joseph. "I can still see the awful look on his face, the burning in his eyes. He said that my mother had been afflicted because of the evil intent that Rebecca Nurse had long harbored for our family. He said she was just one of many people who wished us harm. He said he himself was a powerful figure in Salem Village, the place that Satan had chosen as a battlefield for his attack on God's people. He said Satan's plan was to divide New England eternally by enlisting those who were willing to practice witchcraft against God's people. He told me I was one of those chosen by God to resist the Devil's plan, as was my mother, but that my mother was not strong enough for this battle and it might kill her. It was my responsibility, he told me, to take up the mantle and fight for God's Kingdom and for our family by helping him to cleanse New England of the witches who served Satan. He asked me whether I was ready to take on that responsibility and help him to search out those who served Satan."

During this horrifying rush of words, Joseph tried hard not to reveal the shock he was feeling. Aside from the self-delusion, the overweening arrogance of this man, the thought that a father would demand such a thing of his child was incomprehensible to him. Thomas Brattle had been right. There was most certainly evil here, but it had nothing to do with witchcraft. He did his best to control his voice and speak calmly. "What did you think about this speech?" he asked.

She looked at him as if a little surprised to find him there. She took a moment, and then answered. "I think I was relieved, somewhat. If I was part of a bigger plan of my father's and God's, I thought it meant that I was not at fault. Perhaps our original deception had also been part of a larger plan to reveal the truth about Satan and his followers. But I was also much frighted. I already felt that what Abby had begun had spun far beyond our control, with dreadful consequences. My father was talking about something even bigger. And I was worried about my mother and whether she could be lost to us if I failed to live up to my duty in this."

"And so, you agreed to it?"

She looked up in surprise. "Of course. What else was I to do, Mr. Green?"

He met her look honestly. “I confess I do not know, Ann,” he said. “I will have to think and pray on all of this a good deal.” He sat back in his chair and looked at the floor. Both were quiet, occupied with their own thoughts. After a few minutes, he asked, “What exactly did your father bid you do?”

She answered promptly. “After that, he would tell me which of Satan’s minions were revealed to him and who I should call out in court. By that time, my cousin, Mary Walcott, and our servant, Mercy Lewis, had joined the ‘afflicted girls,’ as we were called. They looked to me and Abby at first and helped to accuse whoever we called out. My father was serving sometimes as the recorder for the magistrates as well as village clerk. He took down our depositions and then wrote complaints on behalf of himself and Uncle Edward or Mary’s father and others of our relatives. That was *his* part in the battle, he used to tell me.

“From that time on, there seemed to be a never-ending stream of names to call out. My father soon went beyond Salem Village to our neighbors in Ipswich and Topsfield, and then to Salem and to the other towns around, and even Boston. At first, we called out the wives of men who had opposed our family, but after we called out John Proctor, another of those who spoke against the trials, there were many men too. We called out men who were more and more important. There was Reverend Burroughs, who had been our minister, and wealthy Salem men like Captain John Alden and Mr. Philip English.”

“And the magistrates believed everything you said?”

“Almost everything. At the beginning, they sometimes warned us against lying. And there were a few among those accused they would not touch. Mrs. Thatcher was spoken of, but never called to be examined. She is sister-in-law to Judge Corwin. Abby was sent from the court at the end of June after she called out Reverend Samuel Sewall’s name, and she was never called back. And there was the governor’s wife, Lady Phips. I really think that was what led the governor to shut down the court in the end.”

“How many did you accuse yourself?”

She looked at him steadily. "Forty-three."

He looked her in the eye and asked quietly, "How many did you send to their death?"

She looked down. "Seventeen."

He continued to look intently at her. "Tell me straight now, did you believe what your father said, that you were acting for God?"

That time, she met his eyes. "I did then. Now I do not know."

"Why do you doubt it?"

She spoke fluently, as if she had thought a good deal about this question and knew the answer. "I think my father confused his own petty affairs with God's. I do not know if this was part of a larger plan in God's war with Satan for New England at that time. I heard sermons from several ministers who said it was so, and they know better than me. But I do not think that Satan was interested in our farmland or in the political affairs of Salem Town and Salem Village that my father cared so much about. In the end, from what I can see, many of those he accused were people he had grievances against from long before 1692. I believe he used me and my mother as instruments of his petty vengeance."

"Do you think he did this knowingly?"

"I cannot know his heart, or his soul. I have thought about it very much these fourteen years, and I have come to think that he was very confused in his mind. Perhaps this was the delusion that Satan used to set his plan in motion."

"Perhaps," said Joseph, "but our concern is with your soul, not his."

After a few moments, he straightened himself in his chair and spoke in something like his normal congenial tone. "It grows late, Ann. I believe I heard Deliverance arriving a while ago to carry you home. Can you come again on Thursday? We can continue our discourse then."

She nodded.

"Let us both pray for God's light in the meantime. I would like you to think specifically about what particular sins you would confess to God. It is when we confess our sins that we can move from guilt to repentance and forgiveness."

"I will think on it, Mr. Green," she said, "and I will pray." She rose slowly from her chair and started toward the door. Halfway there, she suddenly stopped and turned to him. "Thank you, Mr. Green," she said. "You have given me hope. Something I have not truly felt these many years."

"It is a good sign. God be with you, Ann," he said.

Joseph sat for some time in his study after Ann had left. Of course, he had known the general story of the witchcraft trials and had learned a good deal from the observations of Thomas Brattle and his father-in-law, but now he had heard the intimate details of the evil that lay beneath the thing. It had almost overcome his well-honed pastoral demeanor.

Now that he was alone, Joseph could admit that he was shaken to the core by what he had heard. That what had begun as a game, albeit a dangerous game, by a group of children could grow into this dark and horrific web of evil, that a father and husband could use his wife and his young daughter in what appeared to be a hideously calculated scheme to destroy everyone he hated, was incomprehensible to him. It simply was not in his nature to understand how men could act such evil.

Joseph did not for one moment believe that Thomas Putnam had been acting in God's name or that the evil he wrought was in the service of the church in New England. Perhaps God did allow such things to happen in order to execute his grand scheme. It was a complex theological question. But if truth be told, it occupied him less than the question of why God allowed the Devil to be in the world at all, or why he allowed men to do evil to each other.

Joseph had read what some learned men had written about these things, and he had heard them debated among his Harvard classmates by much better minds than his. He had sometimes offered explanations he had read or heard to church members who were troubled by doubts, but in truth, he had never seen an explanation that satisfied him. He had long ago decided to take his

God on faith and not try to understand what was ultimately unfathomable to men. But in this case, he saw no complexities to be debated. He had seen Thomas Putnam on his deathbed, had seen the anguish and torment of his children. Whether the Devil was in it or not, that man was evil, and he had done great damage in this world, damage that Joseph had to try to address. That was the sum total of his concern.

In Ann Putnam, Joseph believed he had before him a soul that might be saved. She had sinned almost beyond his capacity to conceive, but he reminded himself that God's forgiveness was unmeasured, Christ's atonement sufficient for all the evil that his chosen ones had done. If Ann Putnam was among them, she could be forgiven if she repented sincerely. His small part was to help her to do that. Kneeling at his chair, he bowed his head and asked his God for enlightenment, that he might show him a way to proceed, and for the strength to open himself to acceptance of all that was asked of him.

When Joseph came downstairs, he sank down onto the hearth bench in the keeping room and looked at his family. His two smallest children, Joseph and Neddie, scrambled over to him as soon as he sat down and he lifted them, placing one on each knee. He held his boys close and lay his cheek against Joseph's silky hair. Watching Nanny, his beloved daughter, laughing at something her brother John said as she helped her mother with the supper preparations, he felt tears well up.

While moving about the room, Betty had been quietly observing her husband, clearly drained and shaken by his afternoon. She felt like holding him close herself. "Can you tell me what Ann Putnam came to discourse with you about?" she asked.

He looked up at her with a little smile. "She wants to join the church," he said.

As surprised and curious as she was, Betty knew there was nothing she could ask him about that. "God be praised," she said. "And God help you."

"Amen," he said.

Chapter 19

1706

When Ann returned on Thursday, Joseph began with a prayer that God might grant them light and guidance as they searched together for Ann's path to forgiveness. As they sat down at Joseph's table, he said a silent prayer of his own that he might find the right way to reach this tormented soul.

"Have you thought about the things we talked of on Tuesday?" he began.

Ann held his gaze, a determined look on her pale little face. "Yes, I have, Mr. Green. I am ready to confess my sins to God."

He nodded. "Let us begin then."

Ann had thought carefully about what she would say, and her words came promptly. "I told lies that led to the execution of Sarah Good and Martha Corey and to the imprisonment of Tituba and the death in prison of Sarah Osborne and Sarah Good's baby. For this I hold myself guilty, and I can only beg forgiveness through the intercession of Jesus Christ my Lord and Redeemer, who has taken atonement for my terrible sins upon himself."

Having relieved herself of the statement she had prepared, Ann relaxed a little and looked at Joseph speculatively. "As for the rest, I need your guidance. If I lied thinking I was doing good because my father told me it was needed in the battle against Satan, was it sinful?"

Joseph straightened himself. "A difficult question to be sure," he said. He pondered it for a few minutes before he answered.

"The simple answer is that a lie is a lie. If you lie, you are breaking one of God's commandments. It is an offense against God and a serious sin. If you try to justify it by the good ends you hope to achieve, you are in danger of endorsing the Jesuitical notion that the end justifies the means. I do believe that if you lie in order to harm someone, you have a heavier burden of guilt than if you lie to ease them. You can tell that by the degree of guilt you feel. But in either case, you must repent for the lie in hope of becoming certain of God's grace and forgiveness. Do you understand this, Ann?"

She nodded. "I understand that the sin itself offends God, but is there a difference between sin that is intended and sin that is unintended?"

Joseph thought for a while. "Leviticus makes a distinction between intentional and unintentional sin," he said. "If you sin without knowing or intending it, you bear less of a burden of guilt than if you sin with a high hand, in defiance of God's law. There are fine points of theology here, Ann, which I confess I cannot parse out myself. The important thing before us is for you to confess all the actions you know to have been sinful and repent for them fully and sincerely. That is all God asks of us to be saved."

Ann nodded. She said earnestly, "I hope you know I do most sincerely repent and beg God's forgiveness for all my lies, and especially those that caused suffering and even death, no matter what brought me to tell them. But if I would be honest, the sin that grieves me most is a lie I told with good intention, having nothing to do with my father, and I want to confess it to you and to God." She looked intently at him. "You know Dorothy Good?"

"Yes," he said quietly, "I think her condition is known to everyone in the village."

The blood rushed to her face. "Her condition is my fault, but I did not will it so," she said. "After Sarah Good was taken into custody, we realized that her child, Dorothy, who was four years old at the time, would be left with her father. Everyone knows that William Good is barely capable of taking care of a dog, let alone a child. My cousin, Mary Walcott, and I thought that we could keep Dorothy with her mother by having her committed to the jail too. So, we called out her name and accused her of sending her specter to bite and pinch and choke us. We even got my sister, Deliverance, to bite us so that our skin would show bite marks with baby teeth.

The judges sent the little girl to the jail, and we thought our plan had succeeded, but then we heard that Dorothy had been sent to the Boston jail while her mother was in Salem, and far from getting a mother's care, she was chained to the wall and fed like a beast." In deep anguish, she continued. "Sarah Good was hanged after four months, but the child was kept in prison for another four months until the court finally released her to her father in December, and by that time she had become the poor creature that you see now, wild and unable to groom or govern herself. I am stricken with guilt anew and humble myself to God whenever I see her, not only for the lies we told, but for the sin of pride in thinking we could direct what happened to her."

"You are right to do so," Joseph said gravely. "What was done to this child is horrifying." He looked down at the table, collecting himself. "Ann," he said, "some small good can come from this terrible evil. You are offered a chance to show your repentance to God. You should do anything you can for this child whenever you have the opportunity." Looking at the haggard little face before him, he said kindly, "This went horribly wrong, but you did not intend it so. Can you tell me of any other times you tried to temper the evil effects of your lies?"

Ann nodded slowly. "There is Rebecca Nurse," she said. "I know this will sound strange to you, given what you probably have heard from the Nurse family these ten years, but I tried to keep from condemning Goody Nurse. I did what my father wanted and called out her name during Martha Corey's examination, but after that, it was my mother and our maid, Mercy Lewis, who accused her of such terrible things."

"What things were they?"

For a moment, Ann looked at him as though she could not imagine that anyone did not know this. Then she explained. "Oh, not just the usual biting and choking and bringing the book to sign, but of beating them with an iron rod and of having killed people. This was very early, at the same time as Martha Corey, before the accusations of murder became common. After my mother had her terrible fit in the meetinghouse, when my father told me I must take all this on myself, I told him I did not think I could accuse Rebecca Nurse of anything more. I had begun to understand the consequences of our actions for the others we had accused, and when I finally put the name and face together, I had recognized her as the woman who had been at our house when my baby sister Sarah died in 1689. I remembered how kind she had been to my mother and to us children.

"I told my father I did not think I could say the things he wanted me to say about her, for she had done us no harm. I had never seen him so full of rage as he was that day when I dared to question his authority. He beat me with a metal chain that was hanging in the keeping room and shouted over and over that I would do as he said and take his enemies, God's enemies, as my enemies or be put out of doors and disowned and never be part of his family again. I was terrified and in a great deal of pain, but I did my best to go about my work as always that day so as not to provoke him more."

She shook her head slightly. "This was another time when Uncle Edward might have intervened if he had been himself. He came to the house that night and saw me. My father even bade me show him the purple marks shaped like the links of a chain on my back and arms and told him that Rebecca Nurse had sent her specter to beat me with it. Of course, I was silent, and Uncle Edward accepted everything my father said. The next day, before the magistrates, I had to exhibit the marks on my back as proof that Rebecca Nurse had hurt me. No one questioned it."

Joseph was silent for a few moments, looking down at Ann's hands as they gripped the arms of her chair. Then he asked, "Why were your parents so hateful to Rebecca Nurse if she had been helpful when your sister died?"

Ann responded quickly. "She was one of the Towne sisters, and my father had a great resentment for that family. It had something to do with our land bordering Ipswich. But this was deeper, more personal than that. Both of my parents thought that Goody Nurse had spread rumors about Sarah's death, that it was not natural, and that they were somehow at fault."

"Did she do that?"

"I do not know. I never heard the rumors. She was kind to us when she visited that day. We children would have been hard put to get through it without her. My mother was devastated and seemed gone from us. To this day, I am horrified by what my family, including myself, inflicted on her, and on John Willard, as well."

"John Willard?"

"Yes, he was another neighbor who was there after Sarah died. He had lived with us when he was younger, working for my father, and we knew him well. He had happened to come to our house that day on some errand, helped my father to dig the grave, then prayed with us and the minister. My parents changed toward him after that day. He had been almost like a son in our household, but after that, my parents kept him at a distance, and we saw him seldom. He was a deputy constable at the beginning of the witchcraft doings, and at first, he helped us and willingly brought in the accused for questioning. But then he became a doubter, and he eventually resigned as deputy constable, 'to keep his hands clean of the business,' he said.

"My father would not forgive him then for what he considered a great betrayal of himself and our family. He told me that John had killed his first wife and that he had whipped our little Sarah to death. That was my order to accuse him in court. For the second and last time, I tried to stand up to my father in the witchcraft trials. John was a friend to our family and did many kindnesses to all of us. He was especially kind to me. I could not call out his name and send him to prison.

"When I was too slow to accuse him, my father beat me and gave me to understand that it was only the beginning if I continued to resist his command. I gave in to him and accused John of these murders. Later, my mother accused him as well. I think he was executed because of our accusations, and for that, I am most deeply aggrieved and sorry. It was, I would say, unpardonable what I did to him, but still I pray to the Lord in his infinite mercy to forgive me."

To Joseph, her unsteady voice and trembling hands and the look of profound grief on her face conveyed the depth of her remorse more than her words did. He felt the necessity of bringing together her contrition and her hope at that moment. "Ann," he said, "I think it is time for us to pray together. Let us call on almighty God to forgive those lies you told, willing and unwilling, that brought untold suffering and death upon those you accused and their families."

They kneeled together, and as he spoke the words of his prayer, she cried. It was not a ladylike weeping, but a storm of sobs, like a child beyond control. It was the most honest sign of penitence Joseph had seen in her yet. He felt that the walls around her closely guarded soul were crumbling.

When the prayer was finished, he excused himself and left the room, giving Ann the chance to sit for a few minutes and compose herself. He went down to the keeping room, where Betty was making preparations for supper with her left hand while crooking her right arm around a nursing Neddie. A look of deep concern crossed her face as she looked up at him. "Is all well, Joe?" she asked.

He looked at her. "I hope to God it is," he said. "I am doing the best that I know how."

"I pray that he guides you. What can I do?"

"Nothing, beloved. Just being here for a moment steadies me. I am giving Ann a few minutes to collect herself." He drew two cups of cider. "I will take this up to refresh her."

When he returned to the room, Joseph set the cider on the table and asked Ann whether she was ready to continue. She nodded. "Let us get on with it, Mr. Green. I feel a great need to tell it all."

Joseph sat down. He looked at her and asked quietly, "Do you know the names of all those you accused?"

She met his look. "You might as well ask whether I know my own name. I have thought of these people every day these fourteen years. I will not forget their names and what I said about them and what happened to them to my dying day."

He inclined his head, acknowledging the truth of this. "Now that you have begged the Lord's forgiveness in a general way, I think it important for you to think of each one individually, of what you did to bring them harm, and what you are sorry for, and to ask God's forgiveness for that one. That can be your endeavor this next week. I know it will bring you great pain to revisit this, but once you are sure of God's forgiveness, I promise that you will feel cleansed and light and free."

A glimmer of hope crossed her face. "If you knew how I yearned for that," she said.

"May it be so," he said quietly. "But now we must turn to the rest of your confession. Have you thought about the other ways you have offended God?" Even to Joseph's own ears, this sounded a little absurd. Was a person who participated in an atrocity such as this to think of little faults and offenses? But still, all sin offended God, and Christ had died to atone for all sins.

"Yes," she said. "My worst fault since childhood has always been lying and deception. I have, I believe, conquered this failing and have not told a lie these seven years since the deaths of my parents. When my father was alive, lying was like breathing to me. I lied often to shield myself and my brothers and sisters from his anger and beatings, and, as I have told you, in order to do his bidding. I also disobeyed him often with, I believe, good intentions, to keep him from hurting us or others." She looked at Joseph as though she had made a decision to trust him completely. "I must confess that I have questioned God's goodness in inflicting us with a father like that, cruel and brutal, who used his wife and children as instruments for his own, I would say evil, desires."

Her voice dropped to almost a whisper. "There is one other thing I would tell you about. I have reason to believe that my father may have caused Sarah's death."

Joseph did his best to appear impassive. "Your baby sister? What happened?"

"I do not know exactly. I woke in the night to hear Sarah screaming. She suffered greatly from the colic and sometimes screamed for hours." She looked up at him. "I believe you have experience with that in your own house, Mr. Green."

He nodded. "Yes, our Joseph suffered dreadfully from the colic when he was an infant."

"Then you know how it can be." She continued, "I came down to see if I could help my mother and saw them all awake—my mother, my father, and Eben and Betty in the trundle bed. My father told me to take the children upstairs and they would deal with the baby. That was the last time I saw her alive. I took the children upstairs, and we fell asleep. Twice when I woke in the night, I heard the baby screaming, and after that it was quiet. I thought she must have gotten better from her terrible fit of colic.

When I came down, she was in the cradle, wrapped in her swaddling clothes, which had become a shroud. At that time, I had never seen my mother in such a state, just staring ahead as if she was not there. That is why I was so grateful to Goody Nurse. When she came, she took care of my mother. Mother finally came to herself and wept in her arms. That frighted us children, but not nearly as much as the way she had been before.

"When we came downstairs, my father was already digging the grave. John Willard came and went out to help him. My father was not happy to see Rebecca and Samuel Nurse there, or to hear that they had sent for Mr. Parris. He got rid of them all as soon as he could, even John, who would normally have stayed to help us. Soon after, my father got it in his head that Goody Nurse and John went about blaming him for the baby's death, and his anger about it was terrible. He hated them. My mother did too. And as far as I could see, it was all imagined.

"Then, soon after the trials started, my father told me that John had killed the baby and I must testify that he had whipped her to death. I resisted as much as I could then. John Willard had been a good friend to us children, especially me. After my father beat me, I did testify as he told me, and my mother did too, although, of course, we both knew it was not true. But it made me think that, if it was in my father's head, perhaps it was what *he* had done. Maybe Sarah's screaming became too much for him to bear and he beat her. He had beaten small children before, though never as young an infant as that."

"Did you talk to your mother about it?"

"No, never. Mother would never speak of Sarah. She resented it even when people expressed their sorrow about her death. That was what she held against Goody Nurse, really, that she would speak of it. And then she made the claim that John had killed Sarah. I know it was my father who made her say that."

"What do you think about it now?"

She looked him in the eye. "I think the worst. I think that my father killed my baby sister and forced my mother to help him hide it. I think I always knew it somehow. I had a deep fear of him that day and ever after. I think in my heart I knew what he had done and was afraid that I or one of the younger children would provoke him into doing it again. It was the real hold he had over me, and my mother, too. The truth is, I hated my father, Mr. Green. I still do, for what he did to me and our family, and for what he made me do and become. I know it is a great sin to hate and to disobey and dishonor your father, and I have prayed about it often, but I cannot see my way out of it."

An image of the tortured face of young Tom Putnam passed through Joseph's mind, and then the image of Thomas Putnam—a bitter, deluded, dying man, suffused with arrogance and self-glory and still trying to get revenge on his enemies.

"I know it is very hard," he said to Ann. "You seem to have been chosen as children, through no fault of your own, to suffer greatly at the hands of your father. The man who should have been your shield against evil and pain was instead the cause of it. This may be very hard to hear at this moment, but we must remember that God hates the sin but still loves the sinner and calls on us to do the same. From what I saw of your father, he seemed to be a deluded man. He did not see the world in the sunlight of truth, but in the dark shadows of his twisted imaginings about his own importance and his constant sense of grievance and his desperation for revenge against any who he thought would oppose his desires. Do you think this is a just description?"

"It is just, Mr. Green," she said.

"It may be that in his mind, the witchcraft outbreak was what he told you it was, a plot of the Devil to attack him personally. With his sense of his own importance, he would naturally see himself as the instrument of God and confuse his own greedy desire for land and money, and above all, for greater importance, with the cause of God. Do you think this could be true?"

"Yes."

"In that sense, he may very well have been a victim of Satan's delusion. Perhaps he did not inflict pain and suffering on his family and cause the suffering and death of so many more because he wanted to hurt you, but because he could not help it. It is possible to see evil working in your father and to hate that as the Devil's work, but to see the man himself as a victim, as you are, worthy of God's forgiveness and Christian charity. The difference is that you are able to see the reality of the evil you have done and to confess it and ask forgiveness for it. He was not. I hope that he did not die unrepentant, but I fear that he did."

"I understand, Mr. Green," she said. "This is a help to me. But I will have to think and pray about it a good deal."

He nodded. "It is a momentous thing you are engaged in here. All of it will take time and devotion and courage."

She looked at him speculatively. "I have another great difficulty that has long troubled me, Mr. Green, but I have never dared express it. I accept Jesus Christ eagerly as my savior and redeemer, but still I struggle to believe in the goodness of a God who would allow such things as we have been speaking of to happen. Why would a God of surpassing goodness bring my baby sister into the world just to suffer and die? Why would he bring me into the world to be nothing but an instrument of the Devil alive in my father?"

Joseph answered honestly from his own experience as well as the doctrine. "Ann, these are the questions that test our faith. If we believe in a God who is all-knowing and all-wise as well as infinitely good and merciful, we must trust his wisdom, unfathomably superior to our own, and have faith in his plan for the world and for each of us puny human beings. It is the sin of pride to think we know better than God. We must trust that our suffering, and the suffering of every apparently innocent one of his creatures, is part of his plan and there for a purpose."

All of his attention was concentrated in his eyes as he spoke. "Ann, you are not and never were 'nothing but an instrument of the Devil.' You may have been that unwillingly, but the wonder of God's infinite mercy is that you can humbly beg his forgiveness for the evil you have done, or helped to do, and become an instrument of good. You can be cleansed of this evil and begin to do good to those you have harmed, and to others too, including those who may have harmed you. That is your path to salvation; not only to refuse evil, but to do good."

She nodded slowly. "I do earnestly hope so, Mr. Green," she said. "I will think and pray about all you have said."

"Well," he said, relaxing a little in his chair, "I think we have come very far this afternoon, and if you are as tired from the journey as I am, perhaps it is time to rest. Let us pray together in thanksgiving for God's wisdom vouchsafed to us this day as well as for forgiveness. This next week, you have much to take to God in secret prayer. Let us meet again on Tuesday and see where we are."

"Yes." Anne did look completely drained, but her tone was emphatic. "Thank you, Mr. Green. I cannot express my gratitude sufficiently. Your discourse truly gives me hope."

They kneeled together in prayer. When they were finished, Ann got up and made her way down the stairs. Joseph could hear her saying goodbye to Betty and the children. He went to the window and watched as she walked slowly out to the road, head bowed, already deep in thought as she began the long, hot trek out to the Putnam farmhouse. "Dear Lord," he prayed, "help me to bring peace to this tortured soul."

When he came downstairs, Betty took in his condition at a glance. "A long afternoon, Joe?" she asked.

"Yes," he said, "long and sometimes very hard, but not without hope. It strengthens my faith in God's wonderworking providence."

Betty smiled. "I am happy for you, Joe, but I also suspect that not every minister would see things in quite that light."

He smiled back. "Perhaps," he said, "but that is my gift."

Chapter 20

1706

When Ann entered Joseph's study on the following Tuesday, he noticed immediately how drawn and exhausted she looked. She dropped into the chair across from him. "I have thought and prayed as you said, Mr. Green," she began. "It has been a very hard time. I thought of each of the victims I caused to suffer and of their families. It is a web of evil that reaches many people I know and many others I know not. Besides those who died or suffered in prison, I think especially of the children deprived of a mother or father and forced to live out their lives knowing how they died. I do not think I could forgive these things if I heard of them in another."

"Remember," said Joseph, "it is not you who are called on to forgive, but God, whose capacity to forgive is boundless. The question is, do you repent for these things?"

A look of utter anguish met his eyes. "Mr. Green," she said, "it shall be the work of my life to repent for these things."

"That is all God asks of you," he said gently. "That you spend your life in repentance and in embracing all that is good from this time out. And let me suggest that the way to start is to do what kindness you can to those you have harmed."

"I mean to, Mr. Green," she said with a look of determination.

"Now," he asked, "are you ready to proceed with your confession?"

Joseph found that the things he usually had to draw slowly and painfully from a suffering soul were nothing for Ann to confess after the last few weeks. She expressed her repentance for all that she had done to offend God, and they prayed together for forgiveness.

Then Joseph said, “It is time to turn to your public confession, Ann. Have you thought on it?”

“I have thought greatly on it, Mr. Green. But I do not know how much to say.”

“That will be as you think right. Some confessions are lengthy, with much that is a prayer to God for forgiveness. Some are brief, a general confession of guilt, a statement of repentance, and a short prayer for forgiveness. With all that you have told me, I do not see the need for a great deal of detail in your public confession, but you need to make a clear and sincere expression of guilt and repentance. Remember that you are not speaking only to God now, but to the congregation you hope to join in loving fellowship. They need to know that you are petitioning them in good faith. Those you have harmed must be assured that you repent for what you have done and that you resolve to live together with them as sisters and brothers in Christ.”

She listened carefully and nodded. “I understand, Mr. Green. Perhaps you can help me to say what is in my heart so they will understand.”

They worked together on the statement for the rest of the afternoon. The result was two pages of writing with many crossings out and insertions. Joseph was satisfied that it said what Ann wanted to say and what he thought would satisfy the Nurses and the other families who had suffered. But it was one thing to write it and another to propound it to the congregation and be subject to their vote. “Ann,” he said, “would you object if I showed this statement to a few church members? It would help to see what their response might be, and it would give us a chance to make more changes if it seems prudent.”

Ann answered quickly. “I would not object at all, Mr. Green. It seems much better to find out now what objections may be raised than to face a meetinghouse full of people without knowing their minds."

"Good. I shall show it to some people in confidence over the Sabbath, and then you can come next week to talk about what is next."

She looked at him, a light in her pale eyes that he was seeing for the first time. "Thank you, Mr. Green, for this and for all you have done. I do not see how I could have made my way through this without your wise guidance."

He smiled. "I am delighted to do my best to help you come to God and to join our congregation," he said, "but whatever wisdom there is comes from the Lord. I confess that much of what you have brought to me takes me out of my depth. I am not nearly as learned a minister as I could be. But I trust in God to lead us both to the light of truth so long as we are sincere."

"Amen," she said. "May it be so."

Joseph made three fair copies of the document they had written. One he put away in his study. The other two he kept out for his regular Friday meeting with his deacons. As he waited for Edward Putnam and Nathaniel Ingersoll, he reflected gratefully that the subject of Ann Putnam would by no means be coming to them unawares. That was one of the facts of village life, often an annoyance, but in this case a blessing. Ann's visits to him would certainly have been remarked upon ever since Deliverance had left her at the ministry house and gone to visit several neighbors in the village. Deliverance had no doubt done this intentionally. She would not have mentioned the substance of Ann's errand, but just the fact that she had visited the minister would quickly have made its way around the village and the neighboring farms. They would also have noticed her returns to the ministry house. There was no doubt a great deal of speculation about it by this time.

Once he and the deacons were seated at his table, Joseph got directly to the point. "We have a matter before us from your niece, Brother Edward," he said. "Ann Putnam asks to be propounded for membership in our church."

Despite being prepared to hear Ann's name, both deacons looked dumbfounded. "She has not spoken of it to me," said Edward, clearly still trying to take it in.

"No," said Joseph. "The only ones she has told besides myself are Tom and Elizabeth and Deliverance. She was tentative about it when we began our discourse, but now she is very firm in her intention. She has made her private confession to me and is ready to make her public confession and be propounded to the congregation."

"God be praised," said Edward, "but I am most surprised. Of course, I would not ask you what she has said to you, but I wonder what has made her decide to do this now."

"I think you may talk with her," said Joseph. "I think she would be happy to talk with you about it now."

He picked up the confession and placed it between the two deacons, who quickly read through it. Ingersoll looked up and said, "I see you have helped her with the phrasing."

"A little, but they are her thoughts. She has struggled a great deal with this, and I believe she is sincere and honest."

Edward was slowly shaking his head. "I had no inkling that she was pondering this. It amazes me somewhat."

Joseph smiled. "I think you will not be alone in our congregation," he said. "That is why I want to hear your thoughts on how best to approach it. I realize it will meet opposition, but I hope there will be enough support to pass it. It may prove to be the final thing that gets us beyond the witchcraft divide once and for all."

"Or it might bring it all back to haunt us," said Ingersoll. "I agree that it feels like a blessing for us. But Edward and I were both on the Putnam side, so to speak. You need to broach this with the others."

"Yes, I plan to speak to Samuel Nurse on the Sabbath. I ask you not to say anything about it yet, but after I speak to him, you could take that copy and show it to others who have influence—Jonathan and Captain John, to begin with. The more people who know about it beforehand, the better. We do not want anyone taken unawares."

"Yes," said Edward. "This will come as a great surprise to many."

"Now," said Joseph, "shall we look at the document carefully and see if changes are in order? I would like to take your advice and give it to Ann when I meet with her next."

Joseph decided not to wait until the Sabbath to talk to Samuel Nurse. He did not want to risk his hearing about this crucial matter from someone else first. His sermons prepared, he decided to ride down the hill to the Nurse farm on Saturday afternoon. All was quiet as he approached the comfortable farmhouse shaded by two big maples. As he rode up to the door, Samuel's wife Mary came out and greeted him. She invited him to come inside and refresh himself with some cider, but he asked if he might go and find Samuel first.

"Yes, of course, Mr. Green," she said. "He is in the meadow there with the boys fixing a breach in the wall." She pointed to some figures just visible at the edge of the meadow downhill from the house. Joseph thanked her and rode out to the group.

After greetings had been exchanged, he asked Samuel if they could have a few quiet words. Samuel nodded and said, "Come into the shade, Mr. Green. We can rest and talk there."

After they had seated themselves side by side under the big oak tree at the edge of the meadow, Joseph got right to the point. He had found that this was generally the best way to approach Samuel Nurse. He told him that Ann Putnam wanted to be propounded for membership in the church and that he thought it important to consult Samuel and John Tarbell about it before anything formal proceeded.

Samuel was clearly surprised, although not as amazed as Edward Putnam had been. "I heard that she was coming to see you," he said. "I thought she must be concerned about her soul, but I never thought she would be looking to join the church."

"She has thought about it for a long time and has at last made the decision that she would petition to join us. She has made her private confession to me, and she is ready to make her public confession to the church."

Samuel turned his head slightly and looked at Joseph. "Did she confess all?" he asked.

"I cannot speak of anything she said to me privately, but I will tell you that she has made a very full and, I believe, sincere confession of her sins. With her permission, I have brought the public confession she intends to make to the church members for you to look at. It means a great deal to her that you would accept it." He handed him the copy of the confession, and Samuel read it through in his slow, deliberate way.

"I see," he said, looking at Joseph. "She does seem to confess it, although she places a lot of it in the Devil's hands rather than her own."

"I think this is what she sincerely believes, Samuel," said Joseph. "Is it something you and your family could see your way to accepting? If you were willing to open your arms and receive her, confessing and repenting, into fellowship, I think it might go a long way to heal the great breach that has divided this village and our church for so long."

Samuel thought of the girl, Ann Putnam, squirming about on the meetinghouse floor, screaming out foul accusations against his mother. He thought of Thomas Putnam, who had filed complaints against even more people than his daughter had accused, and whom he had sat next to in the meetinghouse for one full year without exchanging a single word. He remembered the first time he had noticed Ann Putnam, a skinny little girl, framed in the doorway of her father's house, petrified, and his mother's kindness to her.

Samuel looked at the young minister's face, open and honest and eager. "I know how you think, Mr. Green, and I am as grateful as any for the changes you have wrought here in the village. As you know, it was a very hard thing for me to accept the reseating of the meetinghouse, but now that we have done it these eight years, it seems natural and right that we all sit together in fellowship if we call ourselves brothers and sisters in Christ. But this is something more. This is asking us to welcome one of the loudest voices in condemning our mother to her death to sit among us as a covenanted member of our church."

Joseph responded earnestly. "Believe me, I realize that, Samuel. It seems that I am forever asking you to take the most difficult step toward Christian fellowship when you are the one who has suffered the most. But I firmly believe it is the step that needs to be taken if we are to put this evil behind us and purge the hatred and enmity that lingers from that horrible time. You need not answer now, but you would oblige me very much by thinking about it. I ask you to take the paper and show it to John Tarbell and the others in your family and let me know your feelings about it. As you can see from the confession, Ann Putnam is most concerned to ask your pardon in a way that is satisfactory to you."

"I will think and pray on it, Mr. Green. You can leave this paper with Mary, if you will, and I will show it to John and the others." He got to his feet. "And now I must get back to work. I want to get this breach mended before the Sabbath, so I do not wake up on Monday and find that my sheep have scattered from here to Boxford."

Joseph stood up and said with a smile, "Good fortune, Brother Samuel. I understand about mending breaches and keeping your flock together." He looked into the burly farmer's lined and weathered face. "Thank you," he said. "I believe you are doing God's work here."

"I am not so certain of that," said Samuel, "but I am content to do yours."

At the meetinghouse the next day, Joseph told the deacons that he had spoken to Samuel Nurse, and they should feel free to discuss Ann's petition for membership with other church members. He had prepared his sermons carefully, choosing as his morning text 1 John 3:17, 'But whosoever hath his world's good, and seeth his brother have need, and shutteth up his compassion from him, how dwelleth the love of God in him?' For the afternoon, he followed with the next verse, 'My little children, let us not love in word, neither in tongue only; but in deed and in truth.' He observed his congregation carefully during the time between sermons, seeing the little knots of families and allies in earnest conversation. They were intense conversations, and he was fairly certain they were not just discussing his morning's sermon. No one broached the subject of Ann Putnam to him that day, which did not trouble him. He was content to let the village do its work of spreading the word.

There was an unusually large audience for Joseph's Wednesday lecture that week, and the congregation was abuzz with talk before and after. He approached Samuel Nurse and asked how his family was taking the news.

"This is not a happy prospect for our family," said Samuel. "But most are satisfied with the confession. There are one or two changes that John suggests."

"Thank you, Samuel," he said. "I will speak with John."

Although it was late, John Tarbell was happy to come to the minister's study to talk about the wording of the confession, and after they conferred, Joseph thanked him for his advice. "I know Ann will be grateful as well," he said. "She is sincerely eager to join our church."

"It is not an easy thing to contemplate," said John. "But as you say, we have a duty to extend the hand of fellowship if she is sincere in her confession and repentance."

Joseph felt that the Nurse family had spoken. He set the date for propounding Ann to the congregation for two weeks from then. That would give time for all the responses he was likely to get to come to him, and for him to help Ann make the changes in her confession that would make it as acceptable to the congregation as possible, while still reflecting her belief about what had happened and what she wanted to say.

On July twenty-eighth, Ann Putnam was propounded for membership in the Church of Salem Village. She stood before the full meetinghouse in the clear light streaming from the windows and the cupola, her back straight, her head raised as Joseph read her confession aloud. It began by saying, 'I desire to be humbled before God for that sad and humbling providence that befell my father's family in the year about '92.' She said that she had been 'an instrument for the accusing of several persons of a grievous crime whereby their lives were taken from them' and that she was deceived by 'a great delusion of Satan . . . in that sad time,' through which she had brought upon herself and this land 'the guilt of innocent blood.'

She said that she 'did it not out of any anger, malice or ill-will to any person,' for she had no such thing against any one of them, and she ended her confession with a particular apology to the Nurse family: 'As I was a chief instrument of accusing of Goodwife Nurse and her two sisters, I desire to lie in the dust, and to be humbled for it, in that I was a cause, with others, of so sad a calamity to them and their families, for which cause I desire to lie in the dust, and earnestly beg forgiveness of God, and from all those unto whom I have given just cause of sorrow and offence, whose relations were taken away or accused.'

Joseph knew that, besides himself, the only people in the meetinghouse who understood what she fully meant by saying it was a providence that befell her father's family and that she was an instrument of evil deceived by a delusion of Satan, were perhaps her brothers and sisters. The congregation would simply take it as what was now the standard explanation of what had happened, that the accusers had been deluded by Satan into believing they were bewitched so that he could execute his plan of dividing the people of God's Kingdom in New England against each other. There was reason for someone like Samuel Nurse, and anyone who had witnessed the trials, to be skeptical. But Joseph had learned that the evil and the delusion of 1692 had many forms. What mattered to him was that Ann Putnam, a victim of this atrocity as well as a perpetrator, was deeply sorry for her part in it.

The ministry house was overflowing with church members at the regular monthly church meeting that followed the propounding of Ann Putnam. The congregation had sat on their benches and listened quietly to her confession on Sunday, but on Wednesday, Joseph was obliged to read it aloud twice, and to field a raft of questions. He reminded his congregation that he could not divulge any discourse that had occurred privately in his study, but he did his best to answer questions and address concerns about the public confession. Nearly everyone in the village whose family had suffered by the witchcraft trials felt called upon to say something.

Finally, Samuel Nurse stood up, his burly figure a powerful presence among them. "I think no one here has more cause to be bitter about the things that happened in 1692 than my family," he said, "but we must recognize that we cannot know the mind or the soul of this woman, Ann Putnam. However we may parse the words that are written in her confession, it comes down to this. She asks us to forgive her as God forgives her and to extend the hand of Christian fellowship to accept her into our church. Mr. Green has sat with her and discoursed with her. He tells me he is satisfied that she does truly repent and comes to us in good faith. I have trust in Mr. Green's judgment on this matter." With that, he sat down and placed his hands on his knees.

The simple statement had the effect of quelling the tide of emotion that had been driving the meeting to that point. There seemed to be a general realization that the question did come down to whether the congregation accepted Joseph Green's judgment or not. There were a few more questions about the wording of the confession, but the mood of the meeting had shifted to acceptance. On August twenty-fifth, Ann Putnam was received into full communion in the Church of Salem Village, without objection.

Epilogue

1715

In the spring of 1715, Ann came down with a fever. It was not especially severe, but it lingered, and it weakened her. Finally, her brother Tom went to Beverly for Dr. Hale, who examined her and sent some medicine. For a while, she felt better, but she never felt that she had regained her strength. When the fever returned, more severe this time, the doctor bled her, which seemed only to make her feel weaker still. By early May, she was barely rising from her bed each day. Her sister-in-law continued to nurse her, tempting her with nourishing broths and ale, but she had no appetite. On most days, she lay in bed, something she had never in her life done before, and thought about the things that came into her mind.

Sometimes the events of 1692 forced themselves upon her with unbearable clarity and a familiar burden of guilt and shame. But more often, she thought of the recent past. Ann felt deeply that she had been reborn on the twenty-fifth of August, 1706, when she was received into communion in the Salem Village church. For the first time since her childhood, she had looked into the faces of her neighbors that day and seen not condemnation and hatred, but forgiveness. Tom and Elizabeth had celebrated Ann's joining the church by bringing Thomas, their first child, to be baptized on the same day, a new and joyous beginning for their family.

The next few years had been the happiest of Ann's life. She had lived each day with the consciousness of a new lightness and peace in her soul. The four adults in the household lived together in harmony, all doing the share of the work they were best at. With four of them working, the farm prospered, and they never wanted for anything. Little Thomas provided constant entertainment and reason to celebrate his childhood milestones. Ann took Reverend Green's advice to heart and did what she could to help the families she had harmed. She kept track of those who were sick or in need, and now when Dell went off on an afternoon of visiting, her sister was usually with her, carrying a basket of food or a warm scarf or a pair of stockings she had knitted. With the passing months and years, Ann came to appreciate ever more deeply the wisdom of Mr. Green's advice. The religious concerns were paramount, but he had also been guiding her to see that if she would get her mind off herself and on others, she would find herself much better company.

The charmed life at the Putnam farm came to an end in 1709 when Phinneas, Elizabeth's second baby, died after living just a few months, and the house of joy became a house of grief. Elizabeth's next pregnancy, beginning soon after, had brought hope, and Matthew's birth had given an occasion for renewed happiness. But like his brother, Matthew had lived only a few months, leaving his parents dazed and fearful of having to live through this again. Then, in 1712, the unthinkable happened. Deliverance Putnam, the vital heart of the household, died of a fever. With her loss, the others realized that it was Dell, with her natural kindness and good spirits, her hope for the future, her ability to see through present sorrow to the joy that promised, who had kept them from despair. She was mourned throughout the village, for she had touched most of her neighbors' lives. Her funeral was larger than those of many an important male citizen. But, Ann reflected, no one else could begin to understand how much she missed her.

Ann had done her best to go on helping the neighbors after Dell's loss, but she knew her visits were a pale imitation of what they had been with her sister. Ann could bring food or a pair of stockings, but it was much harder to bring what the people really needed. She talked about this with Mr. Green more than once, and she did her best, but she knew she was no ministering angel.

On a Saturday in May of 1715, when Tom sat down by her bed to drink a mug of cider and talk with her after he had come in from the fields, Ann told him she had been thinking about making a will. His eyes widened as he looked down at his sister. "But surely, Ann, you are not as sick as that," he said. "You are just feeling weak because the fever has gone on so long."

"I do not know how sick I am, Tom," she said, "but it has got me thinking. I should have a will to make it clear that my land must go to you, and how the rest is to be divided. I would not be the cause of division in our family after my death. I have seen that kind of thing too often." She looked intently at him. "This is important, Tom," she said. "Please ask Uncle Edward and Aunt Mary to come here on the way home from the meetinghouse tomorrow. Uncle Edward can write it for me and they can serve as witnesses." Seeing how much it meant to her, Tom agreed.

Edward and Mary Putnam were alarmed when Tom passed on Ann's request.

"Is she as sick as that?" Mary asked. "Has she taken a turn for the worse?"

Tom was quick to assure them that Ann was the same. "She thinks on death a great deal because she has been sick a long time," he said. "She is most concerned to have a will so as not to cause bad feeling when she is gone."

"'Tis a good thing to think about," Edward admitted. "She had that land from her father, and a little money, too. It would be well to be clear about it. We can stop for an hour on our way home today."

Edward was able to write Ann's will quickly. She had thought everything out thoroughly in her mind and he only needed to translate it into legal discourse, something that was quite familiar to him. After commending her soul to God and her body to the Earth to be buried in a Christian and decent manner, Ann turned to the earthly goods that it had pleased God to give her. First, she made clear that her land belonged to her brother Tom already, for he had earned it 'by virtue of a deed of labor from me to him.' Appointing Tom executor, she specified that he should have the largest share of her money after her medical and funeral expenses were paid, two parts to one part apiece for her other three brothers. Her clothing and a few pieces of furniture were to be divided equally among her four sisters. That was all there was to settling the estate of Ann Putnam, Singlewoman.

Ann's illness dragged on through the month of May. She seemed to get neither better nor worse, but she was not able to attend church services or to do her usual visiting in the village. On the nineteenth, Joseph Green rode out to the Putnam farm to see how she was faring. It was a lovely late spring day, temperate and sunny, and the forest was a dappled shade of yellow green as he passed through it. He was reminded of the day he had gone to the farm to visit Ann's father on his deathbed, quite another errand from this. How green he must have been, in truth, a young minister of twenty-four, trying to deal with Thomas Putnam.

Sixteen years later, he had grappled with enough souls in extremity and seen enough of the many faces of evil to recognize it in the poisonous soul of Thomas Putnam. Having spent these years as pastor of his village church, he knew that evil was much less likely to appear in the guise of a Satanic figure than in a very human soul. He had seen little of the battle between Satan and the Kingdom of God, but he often saw the daily battle with the temptations of jealousy, greed, hatred, and the misuse of power over others that every human soul must face. He did his duty in admonishing his flock for fornication, lying and drunkenness, but in his heart, Joseph believed that sin came down mostly to the failure of love. "Now abideth faith, hope, and love, even these three," he said to himself, "but the chiefest of these is love."

Thomas Putnam's had been an enormous failure of love. He had used his own wife and daughter as the instruments of his revenge and self-importance and thirst for power. Joseph thought of his own Anna, now sixteen years old. He could not bear to think of her used in such a way, her innocence sacrificed in such an unholy cause, her soul imperiled. In his nearly ten years as a minister, Joseph had seen a good deal of the darkness that could envelop the human soul, but still, it was almost inconceivable to him that a father could do that to his daughter.

Joseph's wife and children were the most precious gifts that God had given him. He thought of the births of each child, the anxious waiting and then the joy when he first heard the little cries of the baby and the news that Betty had come through all right. He thought of the previous summer when all seven of the children had gotten the measles in the space of a month, and all, by the grace of God, recovered. What a blessing they had felt. And the year before, when Neddie had fallen while running along a stone wall and hit his head. Carrying his limp body to the house, Joseph was terrified that his son was dead, but God heard their prayers and brought him back to them, the greatest blessing of all. The thought that any harm should come to any of his children filled his father's heart with terror. Only a man who was deeply poisoned with evil, bereft of love, could do to his own child what Thomas Putnam had done to Ann.

The other Putnam children had not escaped. Tom and Betty and Eben had all discoursed with him about their father and their desire to bring up their families in a completely different, more loving way than the way they had been raised. And for all her sunny disposition, there had been hidden spaces in Dell Putnam where he knew the terror and darkness of her childhood lurked. She and Ann seemed to have had no interest in marrying. The younger ones were living normal lives after being brought up in loving homes by their adoptive parents, but who knew what they remembered?

When he arrived at the Putnam house, Joseph was greeted at the door by Tom's wife, Elizabeth. After he had said a short prayer with her and blessed the two children, Elizabeth brought him up to see Ann in the little room she used to share with Dell. She seemed even smaller and paler than usual lying there, but she managed a smile when she saw him and thanked him gratefully for coming.

"How are you feeling, Ann?" he asked. "Has the fever abated?"

"It seems neither better nor worse," she said. "What do you think, Elizabeth?"

"I think you grow weaker," said Elizabeth. "Pray, persuade her to eat something, Mr. Green," she said as she went through the doorway. "She will listen to you."

He turned to Ann. "Why do you not eat?" he asked. "Does your stomach pain you?"

"No," she said. "I seem not to have the appetite for it, though Elizabeth does her best to tempt me."

"But you must eat if you can, Ann. You will never mend without nourishment. You must think of yourself as one of the neighbors you care for. You can be an angel of mercy to yourself for once."

She gave a little laugh. "I understand," she said, "but I think I am hardly that. I am not Dell, bringing sunshine and hope to a household when I enter. I bring only some stew, and perhaps some stockings. I hope the people are glad for the stew."

He looked into her eyes. "Think on this, Ann," he said. "It is true you are not Dell. There was but one Dell. But you are Ann. And that means a great deal to your neighbors. They appreciate your generosity and your quiet attentions to them. You are greatly valued here."

She slowly moved her head from side to side. "It is hard for me to think on. I think I shall always be that girl who terrorized them. The tool of Satan. I feel that I creep about forever trying to make it up to them and erase that girl."

"Ann, you know that only Our Lord Jesus Christ can atone for our sins. Goodness is something we must pursue as its own reward and as proof that we are saved. Do you have a feeling of goodness?"

"When I do something for someone that eases them, I feel their comfort, and it takes me out of myself. I feel goodness then. I feel that is what God made me for."

"Bless you, Ann. I think he did. And it is why you must try to get better. There is much for you to do in this world, yet. Salem Village has lost its Dell, but it can still have its Ann."

She smiled. "I will try, Mr. Green."

After they prayed together, Joseph felt that he had done some good that day. On the next Sabbath, Ann's sister-in-law reported that she was eating better, and she improved slowly over the summer, so that she was able to do some work about the house and even to make occasional visits to the neighbors. Joseph was happy to see her again appearing at the meetinghouse, although she was clearly not as healthy as she had been.

One morning in early November, Joseph was working on his sermon for the upcoming Thanksgiving Day when he suddenly felt dizzy. The feeling grew worse when he sat back in his chair, and when he stood up, he almost fell over. He made his way carefully down the stairs and went into the keeping room for something to drink. But as he leaned against the table, the room seemed to be expanding and shrinking and he nearly fell again.

In a moment, Betty was by his side. "What is it, Joe?" she cried, looking into his face and grasping his arm as if to hold him up.

"I do not know," he said. "I feel very strange."

He collapsed into the chair she set for him, and she felt his forehead. "Why, you are burning up," she said. "When did this come about?"

"Just now," he said. "I felt well all the morning until now." Betty went to the door and called the boys in from the barn where they were working. Together, John and Joseph helped their father into bed in the parlor, where he fell into a troubled sleep, his color hectic and his fever, if possible, rising.

After an hour had passed, Betty said, "We must get this fever down, boys." They took their father's shirt off and brought cold water from the well. Dipping a sheet in it, they wrung it out and covered his body with it. This seemed to help for a while, but then Joseph began shivering, as if to rattle his bones. They took away the sheet and dried him off, and then covered him with warm blankets.

"Perhaps we can sweat it out," said Betty. After another hour, the shivering had stopped, but the fever had not abated, and he seemed to be out of his head. Betty kept bathing his forehead, chest, and arms. "John," she said, "you had better go for Dr. Hale. Tell him it is a very high fever and we do not know what to do."

John was gone in a second, and in half an hour, he was back with Dr. Hale. The doctor examined Joseph and talked with Betty about what they had done for him. "It is a very high fever," he said. "I do not see a cause for it, but we can do our best to keep it down." He administered some remedies and gave Betty a mixture of yarrow, elderberry and chamomile, with instructions to get him to drink a tea made from it every few hours. He told them to keep him warm but keep bathing his forehead and arms. He promised to come the next morning.

Joseph spent the night in a fitful sleep, out of his head and saying strange things. At dawn, he fell into a deeper sleep, and when he woke, he seemed to be himself, although drained of energy and still feverish. Betty kept giving him the tea, but he refused any other nourishment. When the doctor came, he again administered remedies and said it was a good sign that the fever had abated somewhat. It would not overtake him with convulsions if they were able to keep it stable. For several days, Joseph lay quiet and seemingly drained of spirit. He drank the tea but would not take anything to eat except for a little broth and gruel. On the fifth day, Dr. Hale decided to let some blood to see if it would release the fever. This did not help the fever and seemed only to leave him weaker.

The next day was the Sabbath. Deacon Putnam had arranged for Reverend Capen from Topsfield to preach, and they both came to the ministry house afterward to visit and pray with Joseph. He was very quiet while they were there but seemed comforted by the prayer. As they rose to go, he looked up at his deacon and said,

"Brother Edward, can you come tomorrow and perhaps bring Mary and Jonathan? I feel the need to make a will."

Edward could not disguise his alarm. "Surely your illness will pass," he said. "You are young and strong and, God willing, you have many years before you."

"May it be so," said Joseph. "My family is young and needs me. But this sickness has made me think on death and consider that we never know when God will call us. I think it is best to be prepared."

"It certainly is best to be prepared," said Edward. "But we pray fervently that the Lord will not take you from us. It is not only your family but your flock and this village who need you."

Joseph's eyes closed. "Thank you, Edward," he murmured. "God's will be done."

Edward came the next day, bringing his wife and his cousin, Jonathan, to pray with him and serve as witnesses for the will. He found that Joseph had indeed prepared well and, being clearly 'of perfect memory and understanding,' he dictated the terms of the will without hesitation.

Joseph's instructions for his temporal estate were simple. Naming Elizabeth executrix, he left ample funds to buy a house when she left the ministry house. He left money to support John's education for the ministry at Harvard and bequests to charity and to his mother, leaving the rest of the estate for Elizabeth to use for the family as she saw fit. It was a simple will but a considerable estate for a man of thirty-nine who had begun life as the eleventh child of a tailor and gone to college on a charity subscription. Edward wrote the will in legal language and signed it along with Mary and Jonathan. He told Joseph that he did not expect him to need it for decades to come.

The will was made on the eighteenth of November. Joseph continued to weaken throughout the days that followed, and although Dr. Hale tried many remedies, his fever did not abate. On the twenty-sixth, he died. Deacon Edward Putnam recorded his death in the church records.

> Then was the choicest flower and greenest olive tree in the garden of our God here, cut down in its prime and flourishing estate at the age of forty years and two days, who had been a faithful ambassador from God to us eighteen years. Then did that bright star set, never more to appear here among us; then did our sun go down, and now what darkness is come upon us!

The loss of Joseph Green was felt not only in the village but throughout New England. He was known as the man who had brought peace to Salem Village, a task that had seemed impossible when he had first come to preach there in 1697, a twenty-two-year-old schoolteacher who aspired to the ministry. His friend, Joseph Capen, preached his funeral sermon, which was published with a preface by Increase Mather, the de facto leader of the New England clergy.

In his sermon, Capen said, "It is not only the work and business of ministers to endeavor the reconciling of God and man, but also to reconcile men to one another. And so your minister hath done well and worthily on this account, as I have heard, and yourselves be witnesses. Matthew 5:9, 'Blessed are the peace-makers, for they shall be called the children of God.'" He urged the congregation to be thankful for "the many good and comfortable days and years you have had together," saying, "surely eighteen years of peace and quietness is worth thanks to Heaven for it. And you that have been instructed, awakened, quickened, comforted, and edified by his ministry, be thankful for it." Knowing Joseph as he did, Capen spoke one final warning to his congregation. "Let me tell you that if it could be imagined that anything in this world could interrupt and disturb the rest and repose of your late minister, his ashes now in the grave, nothing so much as your differing and contending among yourselves would do it."

After Joseph was buried prominently in Salem Village, several poetic tributes were published, most playing on the name of Green and comparing him to the olive tree as a symbol of peace. But Joseph had impressed his contemporaries in other ways as well. One was inspired to write in verse of his devotion to his family and his uncommon bond with Betty.

Our *Joseph was a Fruitful Bough*,
His Virtuous Wife was Fruitful too,
They were a lovely, Loving Pair,
As most that Breathe in Common Air;
As if one Soul had dwelt in these,
What pleased One, it both did please;
They hand in hand did always go,
Both shunning of the Criss-Cross Row.
They were so joined, Heart in Heart
Them Death itself could hardly part.

It was only a few months later that Ann Putnam died, succumbing at last to the illness that had been weakening her for almost a year. Her passing was not marked by any of the public attention or tribute that attended Joseph Green's. She was privately mourned by the neighbors who had benefitted from her kindness in the last ten years. Many of those whose families had endured profound suffering from her actions twenty years before tried hard to remember her repentance and her apology to them and to pray sincerely for her soul's salvation. She was buried quietly by her family next to her parents and her sister Deliverance, the last person to be interred in Thomas Putnam's family burial ground.

The Major Characters

Reverend Joseph Green, Pastor of First Church of Salem Village, 1698–1715; wife Elizabeth (Betty) Gerrish Green; children, Anna (Nanny), John, Joseph, Edward (Neddie), Elizabeth, William, Benjamin, Ruth

Reverend Joseph Gerrish, Pastor of First Church of Wenham; wife Anna

William Brattle, Harvard tutor of Joseph Green, Pastor of First Church of Cambridge

Thomas Brattle, brother of William, Harvard official, scientist, and merchant

Reverend Nehemiah Walter, Pastor of First Church of Roxbury

Ruth Mitchelson Green, mother of Joseph Green; other children John, Nathaniel, Percival (Percy), Ruth (husband Zachariah Hicks), Samuel, Elizabeth, Edward, Thomas, Jonathan, Bethya (husband Joseph Hicks), Benjamin, Mary, Mitchelson

Ann Putnam (Junior); parents Ann (Senior) and Thomas Putnam; siblings, Thomas (Tom), Elizabeth (Betty), Ebenezer (Eben), Deliverance (Dell), Sarah, Timothy, Abigail, Susannah, Experience, Seth

Mary Walcott, niece of Thomas Putnam

Mercy Lewis, servant in Thomas Putnam's house

Deacon Edward Putnam, brother and near neighbor of Thomas Putnam, wife Mary

Deacon Nathaniel Ingersoll, owner of Salem Village tavern

Joseph Putnam, half-brother of Thomas and Edward

Jonathan Putnam, cousin of Thomas Putnam, wife Elizabeth

Abigail Williams, niece of Reverend Samuel Parris, Pastor of First Church of Salem Village, 1689–96; cousin Betty Parris

Samuel Nurse, son of Rebecca; wife Mary
John Tarbell, son-in-law of Rebecca Nurse
Dr. William Griggs; niece Elizabeth Hubbard
Reverend Deodat Lawson, Pastor of First Church of Salem Village, 1684–88
Ezekiel Cheever, near neighbor of Thomas and Edward Putnam
Reverend Increase Mather; son Reverend Cotton Mather, influential Boston ministers, authors, and politicians
Reverend John Hale, Pastor of First Church of Beverly

People Accused of Witchcraft
Martha Corey; husband Giles Corey
Rebecca Nurse; sisters Sarah Cloyce, Mary Esty
Reverend George Burroughs, Pastor of First Church of Salem Village, 1680–83
John Willard
Sarah Good; daughter Dorothy Good
Sarah Osborne
Elizabeth Proctor; husband John Proctor
Bridget Bishop
Tituba, enslaved native of Barbados, servant of Samuel Parris

Judges of the Court of Oyer and Terminer
Chief Justice William Stoughton (also Lieutenant Governor); Samuel Sewall; John Hathorne (also Salem Magistrate); Jonathan Corwin (also Salem Magistrate)

Historical Chronology

1675

Nov 24 – Birth of Joseph Green in Cambridge

1679

Oct 18 – Birth of Ann Putnam Junior in Salem Village

1692

Feb 25 – Abigail Williams, Betty Parris, and Ann Putnam Junior first identify specters who they say have tormented them

Mar 12 – Edward Putnam and Ezekiel Cheever question Ann Putnam Junior about the clothes of Martha Corey's specter

Mar 13 – Ann Putnam Junior identifies Rebecca Nurse as one of her tormentors

Mar 18 – Ann Putnam Senior sees specters for the first time, accuses Rebecca Nurse of tormenting her

Mar 21 – Ann Putnam Junior, Abigail Williams, and other 'afflicted girls' claim to be bitten, jabbed, and choked by Martha Corey's specter during her examination by the Salem magistrates to answer complaints against her for witchcraft

Mar 23 – At examination of Rebecca Nurse, her accusers fall into fits; Ann Putnam Senior appears paralyzed until her husband Thomas carries her from the court

Mar 25 – Ann Putnam Junior shows neighbors bite marks and the imprints of chain links in her flesh, where she says that

Rebecca Nurse's specter has lashed her six times with a chain

Apr 20 – Ann Putnam Junior accuses Rev. George Burroughs of having killed his first two wives

Apr 23 – Ann Putnam Junior claims that John Willard's specter is trying to make her sign his book

Apr 25 – John Willard meets with Ann Putnam Junior at her home

Apr 28 – Ann Putnam Junior testifies that John Willard killed his first wife and whipped Putnam's younger sister to death; says he threatened to kill her if she would not sign his book

May 3 – Ann Putnam Junior says the specters of Rev. George Burroughs's former wives accuse him of killing them and three others

May 17 – Examination of John Willard to answer witchcraft complaints against him

May 27 – Governor William Phips establishes a court of Oyer and Terminer to try those accused of witchcraft

Jun 10 – Bridget Bishop is the first of the accused to be hanged for witchcraft

Jun 15 – The 'Return of Several Ministers' warns against the use of spectral evidence, rejects the use of folk tests in witchcraft trials, and affirms that a demon may appear in the shape of an innocent person

Jun 29 – Rebecca Nurse is found Not Guilty of witchcraft, but the verdict is reversed after the justices send the jury back to deliberate again

Jun 30 – During the trial of Elizabeth How, Rev. Samuel Willard is accused of witchcraft; the judge orders the accuser to leave the court; last appearance in court of Abigail Williams

Jul 3 – By unanimous vote, the First Church of Salem excommunicates Rebecca Nurse; Governor Phips grants her a reprieve; her accusers immediately complain of new torments

Jul 12 – Chief Justice Stoughton signs an order for the execution of Rebecca Nurse

Jul 19 – Rebecca Nurse is executed, along with Sarah Good and three others

Aug 1 – A meeting of the Massachusetts ministers concludes that the Devil can impersonate an innocent person; thus the specters who torment those accusing people of witchcraft may not be controlled by the accused persons

Aug 5 – At the trial of Rev. George Burroughs, who is thought to be the ringleader of the Devil's plot to infiltrate and destroy the church in New England, the 'afflicted children' agree that four specters have accused Burroughs of murdering them

Aug 18 – Hanging of Rev. George Burroughs, John Willard, John Proctor, and two others

Sep 10 – Martha Corey and five others are sentenced to hang

Sep 11 – Martha Corey is excommunicated by the Salem Village church

Sep 22 – Martha Corey and seven others are hanged

Sep 29 – The wife of Governor Phips is accused of witchcraft after she signs a warrant to release one of the accused from prison

Oct 3 – Rev. Increase Mather's essay, *Cases of Conscience Concerning Evil Spirits*, with an Introduction by Rev. Samuel Willard, declares that no folk tests for witchcraft are lawful for Christian use; it is signed by many Massachusetts ministers

Oct 8 – A letter by Thomas Brattle, which makes the legal case for the illegitimacy of the witchcraft trials, is widely circulated

Oct 9 – Many Massachusetts ministers read *Cases of Conscience* to their congregations

Oct 12 – Governor Phips writes a letter to the Privy Council in London, saying that he has halted the witch trials until the Crown should advise a course of action

Oct 15 – Cotton Mather's *Wonders of the Invisible World*, which attempts to explain and support the witchcraft trials, also cautions against accepting spectral evidence and using folk tests

Oct 26 – The Massachusetts General Court passes a bill authorizing the search for a better way to handle witchcraft cases than a court of Oyer and Terminer

Dec 10 – Dorothy Good's bail is paid by Samuel Ray of Salem and she is released from the Salem jail

1693

Jan 12 – Indictments of Phillip and Mary English for witchcraft are dismissed by the Grand Jury for lack of admissible evidence; following this, nearly all witchcraft cases are either dismissed by the Grand Jury, found Not Guilty, or cleared by proclamation

Jan 26 – By command of Queen Mary, The Privy Council approves Governor Phips's course of action in suspending the court of Oyer and Terminer and directs that in future proceedings against those accused of witchcraft, 'the greatest moderation and all due circumspection be used'

Feb 21 – Governor Phips's report to the Earl of Nottingham on the witchcraft trials criticizes Justice Stoughton for accepting spectral evidence and says that he has reprieved all of the eight condemned in the last session of the court

May 10 – Tituba's case is dismissed by the Grand Jury

1696

Jul 7 – Salem Village chooses a search committee to find a new pastor, 'declaring ourselves also now to be at liberty from Mr. Parris.'

Oct 27 – After being turned down by several candidates for their ministry, Salem Village holds a Day of Humiliation to seek divine guidance with the help of neighboring ministers Hale, Noyes, Gerrish and Pierpont

1697

Jan 14 – Salem Village holds a Fast Day to acknowledge the wrongs done during the witchcraft trials; twelve former jurors sign an apology asking pardon for the suffering they have caused, saying 'we would none of us do such things again on such grounds for the whole world.'

Nov 22 – After two more prospective ministers decline, the Salem Village Committee invites Joseph Green to preach

Dec 22 – A general meeting of the Salem Village inhabitants votes to invite Joseph Green to become their pastor

1698

Jan 5 – Joseph Green moves from Roxbury to Salem Village

Jul 31 – Joseph Green is made permanent minister of the Salem Village church

Nov 10 – Joseph Green is ordained

1699

Feb 18 – Joseph Green is married to Elizabeth Gerrish in Wenham

May 24 – Death of Thomas Putnam

Jun 8 – Death of Ann Putnam Senior

1702

Jul 25 – First meeting held in the new Salem Village meetinghouse

Dec 27 – Joseph Green proposes reinstating Martha Corey's membership in the Salem Village church

1703

Feb 14 – A majority of church members vote in favor of reinstating Martha Corey

Jul 8 – The ministers of Essex County, including Joseph Green and Joseph Gerrish, send a petition to the governor, the Governor's Council, and the General Court of the Province of Massachusetts Bay to reconsider the witchcraft cases of 1692 in order to clear the good names of those who have suffered 'upon complaint of some young persons under diabolical molestation'

1706

Jul 28 – Ann Putnam Junior is propounded for membership in the Salem Village church; her public confession is read to the congregation by Rev. Joseph Green

Aug 25 – Ann Putnam Junior is received into full communion by the Salem Village church without objection

1711

Oct 17 – The General Court passes 'An Act to Reverse the Attainders of George Burroughs et al.' including John Willard, Giles and Martha Corey, Rebecca Nurse, John Proctor and Sarah Good

Dec 17 – Acting on the advice and consent of the Governor's Council, Governor Joseph Dudley orders payment of damages to those prosecuted for witchcraft in 1692, including George Burroughs, Giles and Martha Corey, John and Elizabeth Proctor, Rebecca Nurse, John Willard, and Sarah Good

1715

Nov 26 – Death of Reverend Joseph Green

1716

Jun 29 – Death of Ann Putnam Junior

Author's Note

There are a number of historical works that offer interesting explanations for the events that occurred in Salem, Massachusetts in 1692. This is not one of them. This book sprang from my fascination with two figures in the history of the Salem witchcraft episode, Ann Putnam Junior and Reverend Joseph Green. My hope in writing the book was to better understand these two people and the others who were involved in the extraordinary events they experienced through an imagined construction of their story. I am not saying that this is the way it happened. I am suggesting that, given the historical records and events, it could very well have happened this way.

This is a work of fiction that is based on the facts in the historical record. My account of the public events surrounding the witchcraft trials is based on public documents, such as formal complaints, witnesses' affidavits, court records of testimony, church and village records, and official letters, as well as the research of numerous historians to whom I am exceedingly grateful. The characters are based on real people. Public events in their lives are based on documents such as baptism and marriage records, wills and probate records, and church and village records. Joseph Green left behind a daily diary and a spiritual journal which form the basis for his character in the novel.

In general, characterizations are imaginatively constructed based on the written record and the behavior of the historical figures. The "private" events of the story, such as the characters' thoughts and conversations and the events of their personal and family lives, are imagined. Quotations from court testimony, public documents, and published works are from the public record. Biblical quotations are from the Geneva Bible, which was in common use in the New England churches of the period. Spelling and punctuation in all of these sources have been modernized.

Historical Sources and Further Reading

Considering its insignificance as a farming village remote from the seaport of Salem in the Province of Massachusetts Bay, a seven weeks' journey across the Atlantic from the motherland of England, the Salem Village of the 1690s is incredibly well-documented. The colonists were enthusiastic and conscientious record keepers, whether of the family, the church, the village, the courts, or the colonial government. Because of the witchcraft episode of 1692, many of these records have been brought to light by historians so that a wealth of information not only about the events of the trials, but about the everyday lives and deaths of the villagers are accessible to anyone who is interested in them. This is a short account of the historical sources I found most helpful and most interesting in trying to understand the events in Salem Village and the people my characters are based on.

Perhaps the most extraordinary thing about the subject is the easy availability of so many primary documents related to events that happened more than three hundred years ago. The testimony from the trials and many of the related court documents were first collected and transcribed as a project of the Works Progress Administration (WPA) in 1938. In 1977, Paul Boyer and Stephen Nissenbaum made them generally available in a new three-volume edition, *The Salem Witchcraft Papers*. In 2009, Bernard Rosenthal served as general editor for the massive volume *Records of the Salem Witch-Hunt*. Each version has improved on the last, bringing more documents to light and more knowledge to the editing process.

Many records have also been digitized, and more are appearing all the time. One can easily access, for example, Ann Putnam's will, in the hand of Edward Putnam, in the Essex County

Probate Records, through Ancestry.com. A digital version of Joseph Green's daily diary, which is held by the Phillips Essex Museum, is accessible online through New England's Hidden Histories. His commonplace book is available on the website of the Colonial Society of Massachusetts in its *Transactions* for 1938. Ann Putnam's confession, in Joseph Green's hand, can be accessed online through the Congregational Library and Archives website.

Also indispensable for understanding the people and events are the contemporary writings about them, published and unpublished, that have survived for us to see. The published works of the Mathers, Increase and Cotton, are readily available. Collections like Boyer and Nissenbaum's *Salem-Village Witchcraft: A Documentary Record of Local Conflict in Colonial New England* (1972) and David Levin's *What Happened in Salem?* (1960) include many essential documents, like the contemporary accounts of the witchcraft trials by Robert Calef and Thomas Brattle and sermons by Deodat Lawson and Samuel Parris.

Since the nineteenth century, the primary records, public and private, have been greatly enhanced by historical research. Local historian Charles W. Upham's two-volume *Salem Witchcraft* (1867) has an enormous wealth of information that is still being cited today. Marion L. Starkey relied heavily on it for her *The Devil in Massachusetts* (1947), which, along with the WPA transcriptions, served as the historical source for much of Arthur Miller's play *The Crucible* (1953), which in turn sparked a newly awakened interest in the witchcraft episode in the twentieth century. Then a new generation of historians was inspired to apply modern historical methodology to a few years in the life of this little village, beginning with Boyer and Nissenbaum's *Salem Possessed: Reading the Witch Trials of 1692* (1974), as they viewed the witchcraft outbreak through the lenses of village politics, land disputes, power struggles, and familial conflicts.

These classic works have been followed by many contributions that have widened and deepened our understanding by taking diverse approaches to the subject of the Salem witchcraft trials. An awareness of the absence of women in earlier historical explanations of an event that involved mostly women helped to inform studies like Laurel Thatcher Ulrich's *Good Wives: Image and Reality in the Lives of Women in Northern New England 1650–1750* (1980), Carol F. Karlson's *The Devil in the Shape of a Woman: Witchcraft in Colonial New England* (1987), Elizabeth Reis's *Damned Women: Sinners and Witches in Puritan New England* (1997), and Marilynne K. Roach's *Six Women of Salem* (2013).

Mary Beth Norton considered the role of the colonists' wars with the indigenous people of Massachusetts and Maine in informing the cultural consciousness that surrounded the witchcraft outbreak in *In the Devil's Snare* (2002). In 2015, two comprehensive studies appeared. Emerson W. Baker integrated a number of the new points of view to produce a broad perspective on the "perfect storm" of historical and cultural factors that surrounded the witchcraft episode in *A Storm of Witchcraft: The Salem Trials and the American Experience* and Stacy Schiff integrated a mass of the preceding scholarship into a fascinating general history in *The Witches*. A uniquely valuable guide to the whole picture is Marilynne K. Roach's *The Salem Witch Trials: A Day-by-Day Chronicle of a Community Under Siege* (2002), which draws on Roach's encyclopedic knowledge of sources, people, and events.

The preceding summary is just a sample of the myriad of historical resources that are available to anyone who is interested in the Salem witchcraft episode. I have learned by experience that it is easy to go on for years reading about it and to keep finding interesting new points of view and even newly unearthed facts that shift one's own perspective. But however much we learn about the facts of the case, there comes a point when the imagination must take over the quest to understand what could have led these people to do the things they did and what it all meant to them. This is where history ends and fiction begins.

Acknowledgements

This project has been a labor of love and preserver of sanity throughout the COVID-19 pandemic and has accumulated many debts along the way. The first and greatest is to my dear friend and colleague, Gina Barreca, who began by sharing my enthusiasm for the subject and letting me go on and on about Ann Putnam as we sat outside during Connecticut's wintry spring at the Fenton River Grill in 2020. Throughout the long writing process, she read and advised me on the manuscript with the wisdom and smarts of the wonderful writer and teacher she is and the precision of a champion line editor. Her generosity is as extraordinary as her talent. Gina was followed by my sister and historical fiction aficionado, Pat Murphy, who has been an invaluable critic, sounding board, and supporter throughout the writing. Then came Rich, Lamar and Bill Murphy, whose variously informed perspectives on the story and the history helped immensely as I shaped story and history into historical fiction. As editor, Maxine Meyer applied her considerable professional expertise to the text and gave me some crucial advice on the story as well.

I must acknowledge the historians, archives and digital resources I have described in the Note above, and many more, which have made my work on this project both possible and richly rewarding. Quotations from the examination record of Martha Corey, the depositions of Ann and Edward Putnam, Rebecca Nurse's appeal, and Thomas Putnam's letters are from *Records of the Salem Witch-Hunt*, Bernard Rosenthal, gen. ed. (New York: Cambridge University Press, 2009). Some of Thomas Brattle's dialogue is derived from his famous letter and is quoted from David Levin, *What Happened in Salem* (New York: Harcourt, Brace, 1960). Edward Putnam's comments on Joseph Green's death are quoted from Charles Upham, *Salem Witchcraft* II, (1867; rpt. New York: Ungar, 1959). Ann Putnam's confession, the resolution for Martha Corey's reinstatement, and other quotations from "Records of the Salem-Village Church as Kept by the Reverend Joseph Green," *New England Historical and Genealogical Register*, Vol. 11–12 (1857–1858) and "Church Book Belonging to Salem Village" by Samuel Parris, ed. Benjamin C. Ray are from the Salem Witch Trials website at the University of Virginia, based on the original holograph versions which are available through the Congregational Library and Archives website. Quotations from Joseph Green's journals are from "The Commonplace Book of Joseph Green," ed. Samuel E. Morison, *Colonial Society of Massachusetts Transactions*, Vol. 34 (1937–1942) and Joseph Green, Diary (Holograph), New England's Hidden Histories public domain website, based on the original holograph diary in Phillips Library, Peabody Essex Museum. Ann Putnam's and Joseph Green's wills are quoted from the online version of Massachusetts Wills and Probate Records 1635–1991. Joseph Capen's funeral sermon and the verse elegy are quoted from *An Elegy Upon the Much Lamented Death of Reverend Mr. Joseph Green* (Boston: P. Green, 1715). The map image is from W. P. Upham's 1866 map of Salem Village tipped into Charles Upham's *Salem Witchcraft*.

About the Author

Brenda Murphy is the author of more than twenty books, mostly centered on American theater and drama. Her previous fact-based historical fiction includes *After the Voyage: An Irish American Story*, about a family of immigrants making their way in America, and *Becoming Carlotta: A Biographical Novel*, about Carlotta Monterey, a controversial actress at the beginning of the 20th century who was married to an English aristocrat and a famous American artist before her stormy union with the playwright Eugene O'Neill. After teaching at universities in New York and Connecticut, Brenda now lives in Maryland, surrounded by deer and horse farms, where she enjoys writing full time.

Book Club Discussion Questions

1. Is Ann Putnam a sympathetic character? How does she compare with Abby Williams?
2. What do you think of Thomas Putnam? Joseph Green suggests to Ann that she can try to hate the sin but love the sinner when it comes to her father. Is this realistic?
3. What do you think of Samuel Nurse's decisions?
4. How does Joseph Green change in the course of the novel?
5. How are seventeenth-century marriage and family life portrayed in the Putnams and the Greens?
6. Who is your favorite character and why?
7. What do you think is the most effective scene in the novel?
8. The witch trials are primarily legal proceedings. What was your response to the trial scenes?
9. Thomas Brattle is an example of the new scientific way of thinking that was developing at the end of the 17th century. How do older ways of thinking come into the novel?
10. How do Joseph Green's religious views compare with your general sense of what "the Puritans" thought and how they behaved? What seems to be most important to him about Christianity?
11. When does the light break through? Does this happen more than once? Does it make a difference to Salem Village?
12. Were you acquainted with the Salem witch trials before you read this book? Were you surprised by any of its historical information? Did it change your view of the witchcraft episode?
13. Are there conflicts and events in the contemporary world that have similarities to those in the novel? If so, does it suggest a viable approach to them?

Made in United States
Troutdale, OR
10/18/2023